DRAGONS
IN PIECES

First printing, June 2013
Revised edition, December 2014

Dragons In Pieces is a work of fiction. Names, places, and incidents are either products of the author's imagination or used fictitiously.

ISBN: 978-0-9891210-1-9

DRAGONS
IN
PIECES

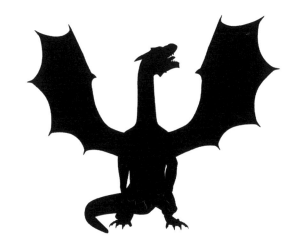

LEE FRENCH

BOOK 1 OF THE MAZE BESET TRILOGY

ACKNOWLEDGMENTS

Special thanks to Erik, Gwen, and Anastasia, without whose encouragement and repeated floggings this would all still be stuck in my brain, trying to eat its way out. Mmmm, brains.

Thanks also to Mom and Dad, and to Bob, David, Linda, Matt, Jenn, Jason, Rex, and Josh. Inspiration, like laughter and stray socks, often comes from unexpected places.

CHAPTER 1

Today called for a cold beer. Sadly, Bobby wasn't old enough to have one. That didn't always stop him, but it did at work. Sitting in the passenger seat of the delivery truck, he idly sipped at his water bottle, wishing Verne would get the damned air conditioning fixed already. That would mean taking the truck out of service for a couple of days, though, and that would mean no deliveries for a couple of days, and that would mean all these poor people would have to wait a couple of extra days to get their damned crap.

"What's next?" Jimbo drove—he was older and that made the insurance cheaper. The truck stopped for a light and he peered over as Bobby picked up the clipboard with the list.

Bobby sighed heavily. "Washer and dryer. I'll take stairs in and out."

"No bet," Jimbo groaned, "not today. They definitely got stairs inside and outside. Probably have to go up three flights or something. Man, why they always gotta get this stuff when it's hotter'n Satan's balls or raining all to heck?"

"Momma always says suffering builds character."

"Yeah, well, I got enough character to last me 'til infinity, then."

Bobby snorted with amusement and shook his head. "Probably don't got a/c, neither. Maybe if it's a hot housewife, we can get some lemonade outta her."

Jimbo smirked. "You ain't old enough to be talking about hot house-wives."

"And you ain't single enough to. Don't mean we can't." Bobby grinned broadly.

"Oh yeah? What about Mandy?"

The grin died, fast and hard, and fell into a mild scowl. Bobby turned to stare out the side window.

When he didn't answer, Jimbo nudged him with an elbow. "What happened? I thought you were crazy about her."

Bobby shrugged and sighed. "She up and left for New York City, like she been talking about for months."

"Damn. How long ago?"

"A week now. That was last Monday."

"Shoulda said something, Bobby. I'd'a gotten you a beer or some-thing, at least."

Shrugging again, he couldn't come up with a good response to that and kept his mouth shut while watching the city go past the window. It hadn't been the worst thing that ever happened to him. Still, he didn't real-ly care for what she said when she dumped him. A guy had to have aspira-tions, apparently. Dreams. Hopes for something better. Plans.

If she'd asked him to go with her, he would have. She made it clear his services as a boyfriend were no longer required or wanted. That first few hours, he walked around in a daze. Then he slept on it, then he spent Tuesday making up dozens of different plans to chase after her. Momma set him straight. She'd been there when Mandy dumped him. It still sucked to be told he had no worth.

"I guess this explains why you been a little quiet lately. All a'sudden not getting laid anymore'll do that to a guy."

Yeah, he missed that part. Didn't so much miss having to do the stupid chick crap to get some. He thought they were fine, then she up and says he's a lazy good-for-nothing Momma's boy and she wants to be a star up in lights. He'd only hold her back and slow her down. So long and thanks for the sex.

"Aw, come on, boy. She weren't special, right? Just a good lay. You can get that anywhere."

Bobby grunted. "I just need to burn up a little steam is all."

"That's what I'm saying." Jimbo gave him a manly shove on the arm and nodded his satisfaction. Another few minutes later, they reached a nice house in the nice subdivision. They carried out the old washer and dryer, then brought in and hooked up new ones. It had steps up to the front door, but at least the laundry room had been put on the main floor. For once, the house had air conditioning, and they lingered for a few minutes under the guise of double-checking the connections and tweaking the feet to make them level. If only the Hispanic maid had been young and hot, they would have had a reason to dawdle even more.

Two more deliveries later, they returned the used appliances to the shop. In there, Kenny would either fix them up to sell used, or scavenge parts, sell what they could for scrap, and trash the rest. With that kind of back end money, delivery came for free with everything. Bobby liked the job. He put on muscle, had Jimbo around to talk to, and got a decent pay-check with benefits.

After eight hours of deliveries, rearranging the showroom, and shifting store stock around, he walked home from his bus stop with his hands in the pockets of his loose denim shorts, too worn out from working all day in this heat to pay much attention to anything. When he got home, all he wanted to do was collapse in a chair and stare at nothing.

He gazed longingly at the two wicker chairs on the porch, but went inside anyway. "I'm home, Momma," he called as he stepped out of his shoes just inside the front door. They didn't have air conditioning, but they did have a bunch of fans, and right now, the ceiling fan in the living room could be his best friend.

"Haul your butt into the kitchen and you can have cold lemonade, boy."

Pausing at the couch, just about to flop onto it, he sighed and shuffled to the other room where Momma worked on dinner. He got a glass and the pitcher and poured himself a cup. "What're we having?"

"Sandwiches with a salad and popcorn. That sound alright?" She stood shorter than him by about half a foot, but he wasn't tall, only about five foot ten. She had dirty blonde hair and light green eyes nothing like his own icy blue ones. In her fifties now, she showed some wear even though her job—bookkeeper—wasn't too hard on her. Bobby, on the other hand, had been hard on her. Her husband, too, for being away all the time and getting himself killed almost eight years back. Still, he thought she was pretty: just a little plump without being fat, took care of herself, didn't let life get her down much.

"I s'pose. Ain't really hungry, though."

"Gotta eat anyway, boy." She set two plates and a bowl down on the table and he got salad dressing out while putting the lemonade pitcher away. They both sat down. "Lord, we're grateful for everything we've got and can live without everything we don't."

Bobby bowed his head while Momma said her version of Grace over the meal. "Amen." None of the food was exciting or wonderful, but he appreciated that she made it for him when she didn't have to. "How's things at work?"

"Oh, same old, same old." She shrugged a little. "Mr. Peterson is getting a little pushy again, but it's nothing to worry about."

A grunt of disapproval escaped Bobby. "I oughta beat the crap outta him," he grumbled.

Momma looked at him sternly over her sandwich. "You'll do no such thing. He's just a man, acting like a man. And he's my boss. Won't do us no good for you to lose me my job."

Simmering, he crunched a handful of popcorn. Mr. Peterson had a wife and a family. Not only that, and more importantly, Momma didn't like him that way. "He oughtn't be doing that is all. Ain't right."

She reached over and patted his hand with her own. "You're a good boy, but I can handle myself. You leave him alone. I'm gonna have words with his wife if he doesn't stop soon."

More wordless grumbles pushed their way out of him, but he stopped talking about it. If she didn't want to get into it, he wouldn't keep needling. Man needed to be dealt with, though. This had been going on for a few months now, so far as he knew, and no one else would stand up for her. Grandpa passed a few years ago, and she had no brothers. Dad's family didn't have much to do with them; Bobby wasn't his son and they never did get along with Momma.

"How was your day?"

The question pulled him out of brooding and he looked up with a shrug. "Hotter'n heck. There's a new dryer in, might be cheap if'n Kenny can fix it up."

She shook her head and waved the suggestion off. "I don't mind using the line. So long as there's enough hours in the day to get done what I need to, I don't want a machine doing it for me."

She'd said this before, so Bobby nodded and picked up a handful of popcorn. "Probably going out with Jimbo sometime soon." The popcorn had no butter and a shake of salt, the way he liked it best.

"You finally tell him about Mandy, then?"

"Yeah, it done came up."

"You tell him I don't want you coming home drunk. You drink that much, you can sleep on his couch or something."

"Yes, ma'am."

Reaching over, she cuffed him upside the head with a smirk. "Don't sass me, boy."

He grinned, like he always did. "Sorry, Momma."

"I just ain't cleaning up after you like that, hear?"

"Yes, Momma." It happened once. He threw up all over the place. Since then, he kept it down to a drink here and there, mostly to help with the heat. That scolding, combined with things he later discovered he'd done while drunk, put the fear of God in him about alcohol.

She nodded her satisfaction and picked up dishes. If he didn't interfere, she'd clean everything up herself. Sometimes he stopped her and sometimes he didn't. It depended on how much of a pain he thought he'd been in her behind that day. Right now, he figured it reached the level of 'enough', so he shooed her off and took care of the dishes himself. After he stacked the last clean dish in the drying rack, he grabbed a beer out of the fridge and walked out to find her sitting on the couch, relaxed and content with the TV on.

Not wanting to disturb her and uninterested in the show, he went to his room and sat down on the bed, popping open the beer and taking a long drink. His head needed to settle before he'd get to sleep tonight, though it didn't matter. Tomorrow was his day off. People didn't need new appliances so much on Tuesdays for some reason he'd never know. Thursdays, too, and he also got that day off.

That Peterson, he needed to stop bugging Momma. It'd be one thing if she liked it, though that'd be wrong to bust up his family. If she liked it, though, he wouldn't care because it wouldn't be any of his business. She didn't. The more he thought about that man, with his foofy hair and fake smile, his smarmy handshake and suits with 'funny' ties, the more he wanted to punch the guy in the face. In fact, he wanted to go do that right this damned minute. Bastard needed to know he did something wrong. Dog craps on the rug, you smack it on the nose.

He looked over at his clock: only 6:30 yet. The fire of determination got him off the bed. Empty beer bottle in hand, he stalked out. "'M going out," he tossed towards the living room. Without waiting for a reply, he headed out the door and walked to the bus stop. Time like this made him wish he had a car or motorcycle, but he didn't, and getting bothered about it wouldn't help anything. It was really Peterson's fault they didn't have one. He could cut Momma a deal on one, so they could have it for emergencies. Not Mr. Peterson. Employees got paid already. So he said.

As he walked the two blocks to the bus stop in the evening sunshine, he imagined that jerk grabbing Momma. Peterson's face had an oily smirk and Momma shied away. She needed someone to make him stop, because she had too much fear for her job to do it herself. He flung the beer bottle at the sidewalk, the smash of the glass feeding his anger rather than venting it.

The bus came along shortly after he reached the stop, not giving him time to think more before getting on and swiping his pass. Only a few other people rode it, normal for this neighborhood at this time of day. Even though it had plenty of empty seats, he felt too fidgety and cranky to take one. Instead, he grabbed a pole and stood glowering out the window, watching the scenery go by and thinking more about Momma putting up with Peterson's sloppy advances. Bastard.

Not long after it trundled out of his neighborhood, the bus reached the dealership, and he boiled off—a dark cloud looking for someone to storm all over. Peterson could take those hands and shove them where the sun doesn't shine, and that's exactly what he would to help the man do. No, Peterson didn't deserve the word 'man'.

Once he reached the lot, it only took him a minute to find that prick, showing some unsuspecting couple around. His navy suit had him sweating up a storm in this flat heat while he tried to get them to pick the expensive car over that cheaper one they seemed more interested in. That his hand touched the woman's shoulder made Bobby's blood boil.

The husband caught sight of him first. The guy put his hands protectively on his young wife, the woman with the rounded belly. It must have been obvious who Bobby headed for, because the guy pulled his wife a few steps out of the way without doing anything else. That movement alerted Peterson. He looked around, then put up a hand in a placating gesture. Bobby ignored it and clocked him across the jaw.

Back in school, Bobby got into scrapes all the time. Everybody liked to pick on the small kid, even when he bounced up and fought back. He'd thrown plenty of punches in his time, and knew how to do it. Peterson went down. He hit the ground with his ass and stayed there.

"Who the Hell do you think you are," Bobby spat at him. "You touch my Momma again, and I'll come back here and kill you, hear?"

"Hi, Bobby," Peterson said with a grimace. Touching his lip, his hand came away with a smear of blood.

Bobby stood there, ready to kick the prick if he didn't say something more useful. "She ain't interested. And if you fire her, you and me are gonna have more words for that, too."

Peterson nodded and pulled out a handkerchief to press it against his mouth. "I didn't—" He stopped when Bobby's eyes narrowed and his foot twitched. With a gulp, he scrabbled back a few inches. "I hear you. She's off limits, I got it."

It seemed clear he'd say or do anything to not get walloped again. Bobby decided to take the words at face value anyway. "This ain't the kinda thing that expires, neither." Now he'd gotten that punch out of his system, he lost his taste for it. Guy gave his word and acted helpless. He didn't beat guys when they were already down. It reminded him too much of some of his own beatings. He needed another beer.

"Yeah, yeah, I get you." Peterson wobbled to his feet and flashed an apologetic smile at the young couple. "Sorry, folks. Little personal squabble, that's all."

Bobby shut his mouth and glared at Peterson another few seconds, then turned and stalked away. Nowhere would serve him alcohol except home, and he didn't want Momma to see him all frothed up like this. He stuffed his hands in his pockets and let his feet carry him. Peterson got what he deserved, and things would be better for Momma from here. Now what? No idea. If he still had Mandy, he'd go to her place.

But he didn't. Since last Monday night when she dumped him, he'd been ignoring that. She was just gone for a week or two, he told himself, and things would be alright. He didn't have to tell Momma—she overheard them arguing and Mandy told her straight up about it. Momma had been nice to her, that's what she said. She deserved to know the truth, instead of whatever he'd tell her. Because, obviously, he would lie.

Now that Jimbo knew, it hit home and couldn't be ignored anymore. They dated for seven months, and in that time, she never told him he was dumb, no matter what he said. They went to the park sometimes and stared up at the stars and she'd talk his ear off for an hour, her voice a soothing drone that erased whatever worries he fretted over. The sex had been great, too.

Without that sex, she said last Monday, their relationship wouldn't be one. Her whole litany of reasons replayed in his head. When she called him a stupid hick, she meant it. Why did he even start dating her in the first place? When he met her, he'd been working for about six months already, had a little muscle on him finally. Lots of girls took notice, eyeing him up and doing that whispering, giggling thing when he went by.

She walked up and said something. He remembered it as clearly as yesterday. One warm summer day thirteen months ago, he sat out back at the store on his lunch break. This girl went past with two friends and smiled at him. Sunlight glinted off her long blonde hair. Short shorts showed off bronzed legs with the right amount of meat for his tastes. He smiled back to be polite. They went on their way, then she returned five minutes later by herself. Her red shirt had the top three buttons undone, enough to give him an eyeful.

Before that day, he'd dated four girls. None of those lasted more than three dates. All of them picked him out of pity for the little guy with the bloody nose or black eye. Mandy never saw that. She saw the guy with a regular job, who could pick her up and would sit through dumb romance movies. He did whatever she wanted, believing he could never hope to find another girl half as pretty who'd let him anywhere near her. It helped that she pushed her breasts in his face that day, and gave him her real phone number.

Having walked a fair distance, he climbed up out of his reverie to see where he'd gotten to and didn't recognize the area. He saw a gas station ahead, at least. Inside, he asked the guy working the register where he could find the nearest bus stop and got himself a Coke since he couldn't buy a beer. He waited a good ten minutes for the bus to show up, and went straight to bed when he got home a half hour later.

Chapter 2

Bobby sat on the covered porch, too hot to care about anything more than how he probably ought to be wearing shorts instead of jeans. His glass of lemonade had only been sitting there with him for maybe ten minutes, but it was already tepid, the ice gone so fast he almost missed it being there by blinking. What he would give right now for someone to walk up and douse him with a supersoaker full of ice. He spent his day off mostly feeling sorry for himself, with a little light housework thrown in. A few things needed fixing, so he fixed them, the best he could do to take his mind off things.

Momma went to work and came back already, and now puttered inside. Peterson must not have mentioned Bobby's visit, because she didn't say anything. Actually, she seemed in a really good mood, so probably she had her needlework keeping her company. Doing it reminded her of Dad some, and best to do that sort of thing when she wouldn't dwell on the bad stuff.

An Atlanta police cruiser pulled up in front of the house and stopped there. Two uniformed officers got out and started up the walk. Bobby couldn't think of anything he'd done recently to warrant that kind of attention, other than maybe decking Peterson, so he frowned at them without getting up. It was too damned hot to run anyway, so if they wanted him in that air conditioned car to take to the air conditioned station, he didn't have a lot of incentive to resist. "Can I help you officers?"

"Robert Mitchell?" The first one had his hand on his weapon, the second one stayed far enough behind him to be in a good position in case Bobby decided to take off.

"Yes, sir." He did have to admire the two cops for being dressed in dark blue uniforms in this heat and not looking like they would rather be back in their cruiser. "What's it to ya?"

"Son, you're under arrest for vandalism at Bailey's Package Store."

Bobby blinked and still didn't get up. "Huh?" In fairness to these fine officers of the law, he had committed a few minor acts of what they might call vandalism over the years, but nothing since he started dating Mandy, and he hadn't felt the urge since she left. The name of the store didn't ring any bells, either. "I got no idea what you're talking about. Why're you picking me up for it? I got no reason to even go to a package store, I'm underage."

"Funny." The first cop took his hand off his gun to grab his handcuffs. "C'mon, son, don't make this hard on us. It's too hot to wrangle or chase you down."

Heaving out a sigh, Bobby lifted his hands for the restraints, acquiescing to being arrested. "My Momma's inside, can we at least tell her before you haul me off for something I didn't do?"

"I'll handle it," the second cop said, and he hustled up the steps and inside. He knocked as he walked in, calling out, "Mrs. Mitchell?".

Bobby cooperated with being stuffed into the back seat of the cop car. His mother came out of the house with the second cop, staying on the porch and watching while he got in the cruiser. Bobby watched her cover her mouth in shock and stand there, stunned. Though he felt confident he'd be home in time for dinner, he watched until he couldn't see her anymore. Something inexplicable about the situation made him unable to tear his eyes from her.

For the rest of the ride, he ignored the two cops and watched the scenery go by. He'd been taken down for questioning before, but never arrested. This time, he had no idea why it went to an arrest from the start. They couldn't possibly have any actual evidence he'd done something. He had no idea where this Bailey's place might even be.

Nothing for it but to wait and see what happened. The cops hauled him through the station with a hand balled up in the back of his shirt, then tossed him into a dingy little closet with a table and two chairs. One kicked the back of his knee while the other shoved him down into a chair. The rough treatment surprised him, since he had no record. Then again, if they mixed him up with one of his 'buddies', it made sense they'd treat him like some kind of hard core asshole. Further reinforcing the mistaken identity theory, they left his handcuffs on.

"I ain't never been to that store that I know of," he told them, now getting truly worried. "I been clean for more'n half a year, on account of a girl."

"Don't care." The two cops left the room and shut the door. About five minutes of solitary silence passed before a plain clothes cop walked in. This surprised him more, since he didn't think they usually did this kind of interrogation for something like vandalism. Then again, all he really knew about that came from watching TV, and that usually involved homicides.

"Robert, I'm Detective Cornell." He laid a file folder on the table, currently shut. At a guess it had ten or fifteen pages inside it.

"Nice to meet you, aside from the how." So far as Bobby could see, there wasn't any harm in being polite. "Everybody calls me 'Bobby'."

"Bobby, then. Right now, I have a witness statement putting you at the scene of a crime, some vandalism at a liquor store. There's also a spray can with your prints on it, so I can get you for that. Truth of the matter, though, is I don't give a rat's ass about that, it's kiddie stuff. What I do care about is I got two witnesses that saw you have an altercation with one Jerry Peterson."

Bobby sighed heavily. "Come on, really? That sonofabitch pressed charges? He's the one harassing Momma."

"No." Cornell opened his folder, and the top page had a glossy color image of Mr. Peterson, badly beaten and covered in blood. "He's dead. According to two witnesses, you said you would kill him if he didn't back off your mother."

"Whoa." Bobby blanched and gulped. "I didn't mean it like that." He'd never seen a real dead person before, not even in pictures. The sight made him queasy. Worse, they thought he did it.

"They said you were pretty angry."

"Well yeah, heck yeah I was angry. Bastard's been schmoozing on Momma for months! Touching her and saying things and stuff. But I didn't kill him. Jesus, I hit him once, then I left."

"Right. From there you walked to a gas station." Cornell pulled out another picture, this one from a security camera. It showed him walking up to the front door, looking perturbed, and had a time stamp in the corner. "The attendant said you were agitated and unhappy, asked for directions to the nearest bus stop, bought a Coke, and left. Jerry Peterson's body was found behind that gas station, with the garbage, time of death about the time you left." He slapped another picture down, from the same security camera, showing him leaving and heading around back.

"I didn't kill nobody. I just hit him once, I swear, at the dealership."

Panicking, he showed his knuckles with their light bruising. "The bus stop was that way, and I didn't see nothing or nobody back there when I went past."

Cornell snorted at him. "Fine, stick to your story. A jury sees this and they'll lock you up and throw away the key." A knock on the door made him turn. It opened as he stood. The man barging in held a badge in a wallet, but Bobby wasn't looking. He had no idea what to think or do, and his head filled with images of the awful things everyone knows happen in prison.

"FBI Special Agent Steve Privek. I'm taking custody of your prisoner. You don't have a choice. He's on the Terrorist Watch List." The Fed walked right in, grabbed Bobby by the arm and hauled him to his feet.

Cornell took a moment to digest that, then he reached over and grabbed Bobby's other arm. "You can't just take my murder suspect."

"Yes, actually, I can." Privek yanked Bobby forward, smacked Cornell's hand, and produced some papers Bobby didn't get to see. "If we're ever done with him, we'll return him to the state of Georgia."

"Wait, what?" Bewildered even more than before, Bobby stumbled after Privek, still handcuffed. Privek and another guy in the same suit bodily hauled him off, and he realized that as soon as he got into their car, he was basically dead to the world. Terrorist? Heck, they'd throw him in a deep, dark hole and not give a crap about guilty or innocent. He threw himself into suit and lurched to run for it, but they had a good grip. Still, he wouldn't go quietly, not for this.

Privek punched him in the face, hard enough to draw blood. It knocked him for a loop, and his wits didn't regroup until he'd already been stuffed into their black SUV. Somewhere in there, the Feds replaced his handcuffs with zip ties and tossed the cuffs back at the cops.

Reaching up to rub at his face, he discovered a sore spot and some blood on his lip. "You pack a heckuva wallop."

"You wouldn't calm down." Bobby couldn't really tell one Fed from the other and didn't bother trying.

"I ain't no terrorist, and I didn't kill nobody."

The Fed looked unamused, unimpressed, and unrepentant. "What did you do to get on the Watch List?"

"You're asking me?" Bobby snorted. "Heck if I know. Sure didn't blow anything up, or whatever else qualifies these days. Unless sneaking a beer counts. This has gotta be some kind of crazy misunderstanding."

"Nobody winds up on that list by accident, kid. Nobody."

"Always a first time for everything," Bobby muttered. He glared at the smirk Privek gave him. When the agent said nothing else, Bobby set himself on the task of not freaking out. Someone made a mistake, and they'd realize it before he got waterboarded or whatever other crazy stuff they did to suspected terrorists these days.

They drove through the streets of Atlanta, past places Bobby rarely saw. He lived on the outer edges of the city, and had no reason to go in deeper. They pulled into a parking garage and hustled him into an office building. In the basement, they forced him to strip down and put on an itchy orange jumpsuit and too loose white socks with shoes he didn't think he'd like to be caught dead in. His new threads kept him company while he waited in a holding cell by himself.

Sitting there, he thought his bizarre journey would continue with more interrogation. Why else would they bring him here, instead of a jail? For an hour he stewed, imagining Momma hearing about this. She'd be horrified at her son. He hoped she'd deny it and protest his innocence. Then again, they might not tell her anything. It could be kept quiet. Her son would never come home, and she'd never know why. He had no idea which would be worse.

When they came back, he cooperated, unable to see an upside to resisting, or a way to get free. They hustled him into a van where he was chained down in the back like a... Rabid dogs got treated better than this, he thought. At least he hadn't been crammed into a cage? The two agents gave him nothing, nor did they stop for anything. They drove for long enough that it got dark out, and Bobby, bored out of his mind, fell asleep. A boot to his middle parts woke him up to see harsh lights in a parking garage. They shuffled him through a door that put them in an elevator. Privek removed his handcuffs and tossed him into a new cell.

It had to be the weirdest cell he'd ever seen. It stunk of bleach and other cleaning chemicals, enough that he had to cover his nose to breathe. In the back, it had a blank wall, white painted cinder blocks or something like it. The two side walls were some kind of thick glass or plastic, completely see-through. The front wall was made of shiny silver metal bars. A three foot wide space separated his bars from the bars of another cell. This area had a total of five on each side, so ten cells. Bobby's was the second from one end. In the one closest to the wall on that side, another guy sat on the floor, arms crossed, scowling in his own orange jumpsuit. He had a kind of a Native American look to him, and was in good shape, like he lifted weights all the time. Across from Bobby was a girl, Asian of some sort, and pretty, though the orange didn't do much for her. The cell across from the other guy had another Asian girl.

"Hey, any of you know what's going on?" Bobby moved to the bars and grabbed them with both hands, finding the cold somehow comforting. The were solid and real and so far, the only thing out of all this that made sense and did what he expected.

"No." The guy grunted out the word, sounding tired and cranky. Not that Bobby blamed him for it. "They told me I'm a terrorist," he growled. The queer thing about the guy, though, was his eyes.

Bobby knew he had unusual eyes. They had an almond shape, which he'd seen on other people, but with an extra bit of tilt and uptick at the outer corners. He remembered seeing some posters for some online game or something with elves, and his eyes looked a lot more like theirs than any Arabic or Asian person. So far as he knew, nothing else marked him as strange.

This guy had the same eyes with the same icy blue color. On Bobby, a light brown haired white kid, the blue didn't look off, and most people barely noticed. On this other guy, with his darker skin and hair, they looked downright weird. Now that he took a peek, the two girls had the same funky blue eyes, too. It made them look weird, too.

"Yeah," the closer, thinner one said with a nod. "We all have the same freaky eyes. We noticed that, too." She didn't have an Asian accent, which surprised him. Most of the Asian folks Bobby had heard talk before were on TV and in movies, and they always had an accent. He never met any in his neighborhood, except for the one family that ran the Chinese place. She also didn't have a Southern accent of any kind.

"And they think we're all terrorists? Any of you ever do anything at all like that? I been a little rough around the edges sometimes, but never nothing that hurt nobody."

"I'm a straight A student at Stanford, pre-med." That came from the shorter, heavier girl. She wasn't chunky, just meaty where the other one was slight and waifish. That one had no Asian or Southern accent, too. "I have better things to do than get into trouble."

"How'd you get arrested, then? I'm Bobby, by the way."

"Alice. My car had a brake light out, and some bored cop pulled me over for it. Asshole. When he came back with my license, he arrested me, said I was wanted on a federal warrant."

"I'm Ai. I was getting on a plane with my parents to go visit relatives in Japan. I got stopped in security and pulled off to the side because I was on the Watch List."

The guy sat there, nodding. "Name's Jayce. I was getting on a plane, too."

"Huh. So they ain't actively looking for us, just when we showed up in the system someplace where they check stuff like that, they grabbed us up. Weird."

"What's weirder," Alice said dryly, "is that all four of us are wanted for terrorism when we aren't terrorists and have the same eyes."

Ai nodded. "And we all happened to get picked up now. Why didn't I get flagged when I got my passport? I just got it about three months ago."

The door at the other end of the cells banged open, cutting Bobby off from agreeing with them. Three men in Army uniforms walked up the aisle between the cells. Two had rifles in hand, the other had a pack he carried to Bobby's cell. "Stand back," he ordered. His name patch read 'Carver', and he seemed older, with salt and pepper hair. To emphasize his demand, the other two lifted their weapons and pointed them at Bobby.

Suddenly faced with the prospect of being shot, multiple times, Bobby let go of the bars, put his hands up, and stepped back. "What's going on?"

"You're going to do exactly what I tell you to, or they're going to hurt you. We clear?"

Bobby gulped. "Um, yessir."

Voice full of indignant outrage, Alice snarled at them. "You can't just do whatever you want to us, we're American citizens. We have rights."

Instead of responding, Carver snapped a latex glove on and pulled a needle out of his pack. Bobby backed up until he hit the rear wall, and then flattened himself against it.

"Stand still, Mitchell." He opened the cell door and grabbed Bobby's arm with a steely grip, his two goons right behind him with their weapons pointed.

Bobby gulped. "What're you gonna do?"

Carver pushed Bobby's sleeve aside and stuck the needle into his arm. Blood splashed into the little tube attached to it, which filled him with relief. Taking his blood gave him much less cause to worry than an unknown injection. Confusion followed swiftly on its heels. What did they want his blood for? When the tube filled, he pulled the needle out and stuck a small bandage on the site, then directed Bobby to fold his arm to stop any bleeding. "Do you normally have trouble sleeping?"

"Uh, no?"

"Are you asking me or telling me?" Carver demanded.

"Go to Hell," Alice growled.

Carver let the question go and pulled out a swab. "Open up."

Bobby gulped. They wanted his DNA, too? Couldn't they get that from the blood? "This ain't gonna include a cavity search, is it?"

"Not unless you give me a hard time."

Bobby opened his mouth and let the guy use the swab on his cheek. Carver gave no further orders and left the cell, taking his two goons with him. The door clanged shut and Bobby slid to the floor, wondering what the heck was going on. Stuck in a daze as these men did the same thing to the other three prisoners, he rested his chin on his knees and stared. Ai cooperated, and so did Jayce, but Alice had to be held down and got a smack across the face for her struggles.

Up to the moment he'd been forced to give up bodily fluids, Bobby still held onto a shred of hope that this would turn out to all be some giant misunderstanding. Suddenly, it was very serious and not going to go away. Alice cried softly in a corner. Ai paced. Jayce stood against the wall, flexing his fists. Bobby laid himself down on the blank concrete floor and stared at the ceiling, hoping someone would come along and at least explain something about this nightmare.

Time crawled past, and he had no way to measure it. If they meant to break the four of them with boredom, he thought it might work. Between threads of panic, he had the thought to start conversation with the others a thousand times. His mouth opened, then he closed it again, not knowing what to say. He could talk about himself, or Momma, maybe his job. None of them had any reason to care, and if one of them started to do the same, he'd tune it out, too.

His thoughts went fuzzy after a while. A weird thump from Jayce's cell interrupted it. He spent several seconds blinking, trying to understand through the haze of dozing. Sitting up, he looked over to see the large man had fallen down and lay in a crumpled heap. "Hey, Jayce, you okay?" Fresh panic surged through him and he sprang to his hands and knees. Crawling to the glass, called it out again, louder, but got no response. He pounded on the glass and still got nothing.

"Is he dead?" Ai breathed, the words laced with terror.

"Shoot, I don't know." Bobby shook his head, suddenly dizzy. Maybe Jayce keeled over from the fumes of whatever they sprayed this place down with. Why a beefy guy like that would drop before a scrawny guy like himself or a thin little girl like Ai, he had no idea. "Alice, you okay still?"

"Yeah, but I feel like crap." Her voice cracked, but that might have been from the crying.

"Hey!" Bobby turned and called out, hoping some FBI agent had the crappy job of listening to them. "He needs help! Something's wrong with him!" No one came running. Either they weren't being monitored, or... Bobby shuddered as it occurred to him that maybe this happened on purpose. It looked like his blood had been drawn. What if Carver injected something at the same time? He didn't get his blood drawn very often, and didn't know for sure what the doodlydad was supposed to look like.

"Nobody—" Alice dropped over in the middle of saying something. Bobby saw her eyes roll up and her body go limp. It was the creepiest thing he'd ever witnessed.

"Oh, God. We're all going to die," Ai wailed.

Too panicked in his own right to reassure her, Bobby shut his eyes and curled up in a little ball. Within a minute, Ai went quiet.

CHAPTER 3

Bobby's skin felt cold and clammy. His heart raced like he'd had the worst nightmare ever, but he had no such memory. Nothing happened between panicking in that cell and waking up now. An annoying beeping noise matched his racing heart beat and slowed as he woke up. He tried to move his hand to rub his eyes, but it wouldn't do what he wanted.

It took trying to sit up and forcing his eyes to flutter open to realize he'd been strapped down. There was a strap across his chest, another one at each wrist, one over his waist, one over his thighs, and two more at his ankles. His right arm had an IV in it, and several wires snaked down into various places on his body. He could see them all by lifting his head because he'd been left naked. They didn't even give him the modesty of a sheet over his privates.

"Hey! What's going on?" Eyes darting around, he saw machines, white curtains, a fluorescent light surrounded by industrial ceiling tiles, and tray table with silver tools on it. He'd been strapped to something hard enough to qualify more for the word 'board' than 'bed'. What kind of hospital did they take him to? One that used dentists instead of doctors?

"Where am I?" Ai's groggy voice came from the left.

"I dunno, I just done woke up."

"Oh God, are you strapped down, too?"

"Yeah." He struggled against the bindings, trying to pull one or the other hand loose. "Good and stuck."

"Calm down, you're quite secure." Bobby didn't recognize this man's voice. A figure stepped through a break in the curtain and scared the heck out of Bobby. Surgical blue covered him from head to toe, with a mask hiding his face, work glasses covering his eyes, a hat, a gown, and gloves. "The more you thrash about, the more chance you have of hurting yourself. Just relax."

"Relax? The heck? You crazy or something? I ain't gonna relax when I'm strapped naked to a bed 'gainst my will!" Panic hitting him full force, Bobby bucked and strained to get free.

The covered man sighed and brandished a needle, then stuck it into the IV draining into Bobby's arm. Within seconds, Bobby felt a soft, fuzzy malaise stealing over him. His eyelids got heavier with each passing moment. "You'll cooperate, Mitchell, one way or another."

The last thing he heard this time was Ai making little mewling noises of panic. He woke briefly with agonizing pain in his left foot and a light shining in his eyes. Another time, he seemed to be floating as if he'd been submerged in water. A third time, he couldn't open his eyes and heard a woman screaming in pain and terror. The fourth time, he felt like he might really be awake; he saw the curtains and machines and ceiling with nothing weird. Without waiting to see what might happen, he launched into full-throttle struggling. If he could just get free before They came back, he'd be able to make a run for it. Or something.

Quite unexpectedly, his body exploded. Sort of. His body separated into hundreds of tiny pieces, and each one was him, while they were also not him. Something else had a kind of control over his individual parts, yet he still could direct each one. All the parts, each the size of a quarter, made a swarming cloud of tiny silver creatures that all were him, yet also not. His mind, the part that he identified as himself, floated in the middle of it all, detached. Trying to explain this to someone else would be a major challenge.

Figuring this out could wait. He was free! The straps and wires and needles couldn't hold him down as a swarm of tiny pieces. The cloud responded to his desires, floating off the bed and flowing under the curtain. He/they found Ai, strapped naked to a board just like he'd been. Needles had been jammed into her in six different places, a tube ran under her nose. Her eyes darted around under her eyelids, making her appear to be dreaming. Could he free her like this, or would he need thumbs? He sure couldn't carry her like this. Instinctively, he knew the little parts couldn't handle any more weight than he could all together, and it would be harder for them to carry something. They weren't good at that. They were good at doing lots of small things at once.

He sent his little parts to work undoing her straps and pulling out needles and wires and things. Quick and clever, they dated about, using tiny front claws to manipulate the objects in small groups. When she didn't wake up right away, he directed the swarm to find and free anyone else who might be here. Leaving Jayce or Alice behind... He had no intention of allowing anyone else to go through any of this if he could prevent or stop it.

As they surged under the next curtain, he noticed the lights had been dimmed. It might be night, with no one around, so there might be a good chance of escaping. He found Jayce next and the swarm freed him, though the little pieces noted his skin had turned a funny color, an odd shade of brown with black streaks.

They found Alice last, and her skin had a weirder color: blue. Not a bright blue, but rather the purplish blue of a dead body. Did they kill her and not get around to disposing of the body yet? No, her bare chest rose and fell with even breaths, and the monitors still showed her heart beating slowly and steadily. He floated the swarm in closer and parts touched down to do their job. The first jumped off the moment it touched, finding her flesh ice cold. Another found the same thing and they all backed away.

This job needed thumbs, maybe. How did he get back into his body? Could he get back into his body? Maybe he was stuck like this forever. He heard Jayce's groggy voice say, "What now?"

Bobby desperately wanted to answer him. All the tiny mouths opened and made tiny chirps, trills and shrieks. Admittedly, a lot of tiny little mouths made all that noise at once, ensuring he'd been heard. Understood, on the other hand... He needed to be able to talk. Without a body, he couldn't take a deep breath, clench his jaws together, or make fists. Instead, he thought about how doing each of those things felt, wanting to make them all reality and wanting to be Bobby again. The little pieces somehow understood, and he could somehow tell.

It made no sense. At the same time, it made perfect sense. Despite being separate pieces, they all made up Bobby. The swarm flew together and melted into each other, forming his body. As the pieces came together, he lost the feeling of being detached, then he stood as himself again, staring at his hand.

"I got free," he hissed, resolving to wonder about what happened to him later. "Come help me with Alice. Something's funky about her."

"Her? What about me? I'm...I don't know what I am." Jayce stumbled into the curtain and thrashed to get through it. As soon as he did, there stood Jayce, the same brown as the board he'd been strapped to, complete with grain lines on his skin. His hair was the same, his lips, everything

—really everything—but his eyes. The eyes stayed that same icy blue. "What did they do to us?"

"I got no clue. Look at Alice, though. And she's freezing." Bobby grasped a frozen needle and tugged. It refused to budge. He let go and rubbed his fingers to warm them. "The heck?"

Jayce unbuckled the straps, finding them cold and stiff. "This is insane."

"Don't I know it." Bobby tried wiggling one needle, then finally yanked as hard as he could. It came away with a jagged chunk of ice attached to it, the crystals appearing to be skin and blood. "Damn. She's made outta ice now?"

Jayce pulled at a wire sensor pad and found it to be stuck, too. "I think it's frozen to her." He patted her face. "Alice, wake up."

"Can I pull the tube off the needle, or will that make stuff worse?"

"I'm a security guard, I've got no idea. Try it and see what happens."

Bobby nodded and pulled out tubes. For good measure, he yanked the power cords of the machines out of the outlets in the floor. "Ai, you awake yet?"

Ai groaned. "Am I dead?"

"Don't think so. If you are, so am I, and this is the weirdest afterlife I could imagine. You're free, see if you can walk and come this way."

"I'm naked."

Jayce rolled his eyes. "That's what she's worried about right now," he muttered. Reaching over, he yanked a curtain down and ripped it apart, then another one. His effort produced four pieces of white cloth suitable for covering themselves up.

Bobby took one to Ai, who blushed when she saw him and wrapped it around herself immediately. She didn't look any different, but her hand shook so fast it almost seemed blurry as she used it to avert her eyes from his own nakedness. "Sorry," he mumbled, taking his own section of curtain and wrapping it around his waist like a towel.

Alice sucked in a breath, and Bobby turned to go back to her side. Ai took a step in that direction, then Bobby felt a breeze blow past him. The remaining curtains ruffled in the breeze and Ai disappeared.

"What was that?" Now with his own curtain fastened around his waist, Jayce pushed the still hanging curtain between them aside. "Where's Ai?"

Another breeze blew past them and Ai reappeared. "Oh my God, oh my God, oh my God, oh my—"

Bobby grabbed her hands and held them firmly. "Calm down. What happened?"

Ai squeezed her eyes shut and shook her head. "I went so fast I couldn't— It was crazy."

"This is all crazy," Bobby pointed out. "Tell me something here that ain't crazy."

Alice groaned, getting everyone's attention. "Who turned the heat up? Hey, we're free." She looked down at her hands and her eyes went wide. "I... I'm..."

"Icy," Bobby supplied helpfully. "Look, this is all freaky, but we gotta get while the getting is good, yeah?"

"Seconded," Jayce nodded. "Can you pull the needles and things off?"

Alice focused on the simple question and tugged at one. For her, the needle slid right out. "Yeah." She quickly yanked it all out and off and hopped to her feet. Where they touched the floor, ice formed. She gulped. "My hands are itchy, like..." Putting one out, she grimaced with confused effort and a spray of ice shards shot from them. Her mouth opened and shut wordlessly.

"We're superheroes," Ai breathed. "Bobby, what can you do? How did you get free?"

"Later." He waved off the question and started moving. Someone had to. Otherwise, they'd all stand around, freaked out by themselves and each other, until someone came back and drugged them again. "There's gotta be a door here someplace."

"Oh! This way." Leading by pointing, Ai walked with Bobby across a room full of computers and equipment that put him in mind of a modern torture chamber. Vague, dream-like snatches of memories made him think they'd used at least a few of these things on him.

"Where are we?" Alice looked around in horrified wonder. "The island of Dr. Moreau?"

"Don't know what that means, but we gotta be careful getting out or else they'll put us all down before we get anyplace." Bobby went to the door and put his ear against it. He heard nothing. It might have been too thick to hear through. "Anybody got any bright ideas?"

"We don't know enough about the facility to make a plan." Jayce reached out and checked the knob. "It's not locked, we should at least open it and take a look. If anybody sees a weapon, I've got experience handling them."

"I've fired a rifle a time or two," Bobby nodded, "but it's been a while."

Alice gulped. "I...guess...I can shoot ice at people."

"Don't worry, the goal here is to get out of this place, whatever it is, not to kill nobody or nothing."

"Anybody."

"What?" Bobby blinked at Alice, confused.

"Not to kill anybody." She hugged herself and rocked on her heels, giving the impression she thought most of her sanity had already leaked out and she had to clutch at what remained. "You said 'nobody'."

Jayce rolled his eyes. "I'm opening the door." He grabbed the knob again and turned it slowly. The silver color of the knob infected his hand, then sped up his arm. Bobby imagined an invisible man with spray paint cans assaulting him. When it reached his shoulder, it spread across him until his entire body took on that color. He tapped a thumb and forefinger together and it made a metallic tinging sound. "Huh."

Deciding not to get sidetracked by that, Bobby took over and pushed the door open. From there, they crept through a labyrinth of epic proportions, though it had all been laid out in grids, like any other building. Ai sped ahead by accident several times. Alice left icy footprints. Jayce avoided touching things, as the weird change seemed to only happen through his hands. Nothing happened to Bobby. He decided those little parts must have been a fluke, or his imagination.

They trudged up three flights of stairs, checking each floor as they went, before finally finding a dark window. This place reminded Bobby of horror movies in sanitariums. Every door they passed made him wonder if a lunatic with rubber gloves and an axe or a chainsaw would lunge out. As they went, most sections, including the stairwell, had been left in darkness. Those few with lights had little of it, dim bulbs straining against the inky blackness of dank underground passages.

Jayce checked the first window they found for an alarm trigger and found one. "Okay," he whispered. The room they'd slipped into had a narrow path circling around stacked filing cabinets. "We can't go out the window without raising an alarm for whoever is monitoring the place. I could try breaking the glass, but I'm not sure what kind of alarm it is. I can just tell there is one."

Bobby peered out the window into the night, able to make out three cars in the reflected light. "It don't look like there's anything to really stop us once we're out of the building. The parking lot ain't very big, and I don't see no fence."

"I'd rather get out without them noticing, if we can." Jayce also peered out, frowning. "They'll find we're missing soon enough, but not as soon as if we set off the alarm. A few hours' head start could make a very big difference."

While they spoke, Ai poked through filing cabinets. Her newfound speed didn't manifest during this activity, and she picked random folders to open and leaf through. "Hey," she pulled a page out, "this one has my name on it. And here, Robert Mitchell, right? Yours is on here, too."

Footsteps went by the door, the sounds of someone patrolling the hallway outside. They all froze, except Ai, who shoved the one page down the front of her makeshift dress. It must have made enough noise to catch the sentry's attention, because the footsteps stopped, then approached the door. The doorknob turned and the door opened, a flashlight clicked on and shined in. By that time, all four of them had hidden among the cabinets, but the one drawer hung open. "Somebody in here?" The man's voice was deep and, to Bobby, sounded dangerous, though that might have been his imagination.

Despite their silence, the sentry walked in to investigate. So much for getting out without a fuss. Bobby didn't want to hurt the guy, but maybe if he got walloped without realizing what happened, they could still get away more or less clean. The guard paced to the filing cabinet and looked it over, then pushed it shut.

A whoosh of air announced that Ai took her chance and ran out the door. The guard turned to look, shining the light. Jayce and Bobby both surged at the guard, the bigger man reaching him first and shoving him against a file cabinet. He staggered into Bobby, who followed up with a slug to the gut.

This guy had to be in good shape, because he failed to fall to the floor. Instead, he doubled over and waved the flashlight around. "Hey," he shouted, "help!" Jayce socked him in the face, which shut him up and dropped him to the floor. Bobby grabbed what he could from the man's pockets and belt: keys, baton, radio. Alice picked up the flashlight where the guard had dropped it.

"Come on," Jayce hissed. "Let's get out of here." The three of them found themselves face to face with another guard, already holding his baton ready.

This new guard stared, blinked, then pointed. "Hey, who are you? What arc you doing here?"

"Leaving," Jayce snarled as he charged forward. The guard's eyes popped wide as he took in the sight. The metal man plowed into the poor guy, sending him flying backwards into the wall. He made a dent and fell to the floor in a heap. "Move it," he called back. "There could be more."

They rounded the next corner and found a gate of iron bars between them and the solid white front door. Ai stood at the gate, holding the bars and shaking them so fast she blurred. Bobby ran for the security booth where the second guard must have been and slid into the seat. He checked the camera feeds and looked over the buttons and knobs and things. In a stroke of good luck, everything had a label.

"Should we try to erase camera footage?"

"Is there an obvious way to do that?" Alice followed him in and peered around. Jayce stopped a step behind Ai, trying to calm her down.

"Um...well, it's a computer. You're a college student, right? You got any ideas?"

"Sure, medical students are all about hacking."

"Hey, I barely scraped through high school, like I know what people do in college."

"Argue later," Jayce called in. "Just open the damned door."

Bobby nodded and hit the button for the gate. They'd just have to hope that whatever got caught on tape wasn't especially useful in tracking them down. Jayce held the gate open while they all filed out and through the front door. "Maybe we should steal a car," Ai suggested, pointing at the three vehicles parked near the door. "We have that one guy's keys, right?"

Bobby held the ring of keys up and flipped through them. "These are all just building keys, ain't no car keys here." Since they weren't useful, he tossed them into the landscaping, leaving him with a baton and radio. The radio didn't seem useful, either, but he held onto it. Might be worth something in trade to someone for something. No question the baton could be useful.

The four of them ran for it. Ai either couldn't spark her super speed or managed not to so she could stay with the group. They crossed the parking lot and hustled across some grass with scattered trees that led to a patch of woods, then found a street and crossed it and kept going. Alice couldn't keep up the pace for very long, so they slowed to a walk and looked around as they went.

Perhaps two hours later, when dawn gave the eastern sky a rosy glow, Bobby said, "Where in heckbiscuits are we?"

"'Heckbiscuits'?"

Bobby shrugged and gave Alice a sheepish grin. "It's something my Momma says."

Alice rolled her eyes. "Who knows." They walked down the side of a tree-lined road with no signs so far, other than a white one with nothing but a number. Grasses and shrubs grew all the way to the edge, and the asphalt had cracks with scraggly weeds growing in them.

"We should have gone a different direction," Jayce grumbled.

Ai whined. "My feet hurt."

Bobby frowned and looked around more. "Anybody see a house or something? Can't just be nothing. There's a road. Roads don't get put where there's nothing."

Alice groaned, plodding along in front of him, her head hanging with exhaustion. "What are we going to do? Knock on the door and ask to borrow some sugar?"

"Hey, it's not like I ever broke outta a secret experimental facility before. How'm I supposed to know what to do?"

"I see a house." Jayce pointed at a building in the distance, one they wouldn't have to cross the road to reach. "Alice has a point, though. We should decide what to say."

Ai pouted. "Maybe just one of us should walk up and ask how far to the next town?"

Alice stopped. "Okay, look, we need to make some decisions. Just going without a plan isn't going to work."

Everyone else stopped too, and Bobby sighed. "Fair point." He looked at his three fellow escapees and took in the sight of them. "Okay, imagine you're a regular person and somebody walks up to you wearing a ripped down curtain, chewed up and spit out, and says they need directions." The three of them mirrored his thoughts with their disapproval and disappointment. "Yeah, we need a plan. In the movies, folks always steal clothes and then pretend they're normal."

"I don't want to steal," Alice declared. "I have a bank account. For that matter, I have a family. We should just find a phone and call home."

Jayce scratched at his chin, a week's worth of beard growth making the metal-on-metal sound raspy. "We were picked up by FBI agents. That means this is the government trying to experiment on us. They'll want us back."

"We gotta stay off grid," Bobby nodded. Alice and Ai both looked unhappy about that, but neither disputed him. "What do we really need?"

Ai pulled the list she grabbed out of her curtain-dress and scanned it. "There's more to it than that. There's a Jayce Westbrook on here, and an Alice Fielding. Is that you two?" Both nodded. "Okay, there are...thirty-five names on this list. What about all the rest? Once they find we're gone, will they just go and try picking up four more? Or eight more? Or all the rest? Shouldn't we do something about that?"

"What all is on that page? Just our names?" Bobby stepped closer to peer over the top.

"This is my Social Security number, and the city I live in, and my birthdate."

"Dang."

Jayce nodded for everyone to follow him a short distance farther, where the wild forest dropped away from the side of the road in favor of grass and a farmer's field. He sat himself down with a clank. "I wouldn't wish what happened to us on anyone. They should at least be warned. We're not really in any position to mount a rescue, though. Come with us, we have nothing and nowhere to go, but we're hiding, too! No, it's a crappy sell. I'd slam the door in my face."

The other three followed and sat down with Jayce. "We need some clothes," Bobby suggested, "some money, and a place to go. Transportation and phones would be good, too."

"Can't we go talk to the press?" Alice picked at the spot where Bobby ripped out a little piece of her flesh. It had scabbed over when she reverted back from being blue during the walk.

"I don't know I want people knowing about what I can do." Ai shivered. "You've heard of the X-Men, right? Regular people hate them because they have superpowers."

"How do they have a list with all that on it," Bobby mused. "I mean, what're the odds that all four of us, with these eyes, just wind up on the same list with that much information about us?"

"They knew we were different," Alice nodded. "They knew there was a reason to have us on a list."

"We must have something else in common then. I know my daddy wasn't my daddy," Bobby offered. "My Momma met him when I was three."

"My father died when I was young, but I've seen pictures of him, and he didn't have these eyes." Jayce tapped his temple.

Alice sighed lightly. "I was adopted, my parents are white."

They all looked at Ai, and she shrugged. "If my parents aren't my parents, they never told me, but yeah, neither of them has these eyes."

Alice pursed her lips. "I'm only *pre*-med, but I do know the odds of us having the same highly unusual eyes and not being related somehow are pretty small."

"That means the folks on that list are our family. Even if it's the decent thing to do to warn 'em, that makes it the right thing to do, too." Bobby shrugged. "I don't know if we should be public about ourselves or not, but I feel like that's a decision we ought to make as a whole group, not just four of us taking it 'pon ourselves to bat our baby blues at the camera."

"That's a good point," Jayce nodded. "We should be careful not to elect ourselves leaders of the whole group."

Bobby looked to the girls to make sure they didn't disagree, and found them nodding. "M'kay, well, we all got pretty obvious superpowers —"

Alice interrupted by poking him in the arm. "Except you. You said later, it's later."

Bobby pursed his lips, but he nodded. He knew what they could do, it was only fair they know what he could do. Even if he still hoped it hadn't been real. One deep breath followed another, then he came apart. Some of the swarm had to break free of his modesty curtain, but once it did, the little critters romped about in the grass and the air. The other three reacted with sharp intakes of breath. Ai held out her hand, so he directed one to land there, and it walked on her palm.

"They're cute! How cool is it to be made of tiny little silver dragons?" The one on her palm reared up on its hind legs and splayed its wings out.

"You win the prize for weirdest superpower." Alice shrank away, so he directed them to leave her alone.

Jayce held up a finger, and when one landed there, he brought it close to his face. "They look like they're robotic, even. Do they need to eat separate from you? Actually, Bobby, can you talk through them?"

Bobby made the effort to re-form, doing his best to put himself together under the curtain scrap. He adjusted it as soon as his hands were whole. "No, least I can't figure how. They can make a little noise, though. Dunno if they need to eat. Guess I'll find out at some point. I think I might be able to do just part of me at a time, but I'm not sure how to control it like that yet. Probably take practice. Anyway, I was trying to make a point. Which is that if any of the others ain't got their superpower yet, or it takes something they injected into us, we all got visible powers that we can use to show 'em we're not just crazy."

Alice pointed her hand away from the group and made a shower of ice shards skitter across the road. On the heated blacktop, then melted into puddles. "Yeah. Not crazy. We need clothes and money, then. We're back to that problem. If we *have* to steal, can we at least try to keep it to stealing from people who can afford it?"

"Sounds fair."

CHAPTER 4

They skipped the house and kept going in hopes of something better. Like Alice, the act of walking a long distance eventually let Jayce lose his silver sheen in favor of his normal cinnamon skin. About an hour after dawn, a beat-up old pickup truck drove by. It stopped less than a hundred feet in front of them. When Bobby, who wound up in the lead, saw an older man in jeans and a t-shirt with a concerned look on his face getting out, he perked up. Either they'd have to beat the crap out of him to take his keys, or they could get a ride someplace.

"You kids need some help?" He had a mild Southern accent, which made Bobby guess Virginia, Tennessee, or a nearby state.

Bobby threw down some good old Southern 'aw shucks'. Momma called him a punk when he did it, then she'd tousle his hair and tell him to go fix something. "We're totally lost, sir, and real embarrassed. Car broke down, so we thought we'd have a little romp in the woods, ya know? Make the best of it while we wait for a tow.

"Bad storm hit while we was, er, *busy*, and all our clothes got blown away. When we got back to where we left the car, it was gone, only we got no clue where to. This is the best we could do to avoid walking around naked." Ai reached him first, so he slid his arm around her waist and she tried not to be surprised by this. Behind him, Jayce stopped with Alice and set his hands on her, suggesting a claim on her.

The older man raised bushy eyebrows, and then cracked a grin and chuckled. "That's a streak of bad luck. Hop in, I'll give you a lift to the next town."

The truck had a bench seat, offering only enough space for three across. Ai perched on Bobby's lap and he placed his hands carefully on her waist. "This is mighty kind of you, sir. Most folks'd just drive on by. What's the next town?"

"Purcellville. Where were you headed to?"

The town name was unfamiliar, giving Bobby nothing to work with. "Oh, we come up from the Atlanta area and we're just kinda taking a road trip to nowhere in particular. I guess we found it, huh?"

While the old man chuckled, Jayce asked, "You from this area?"

"Born and raised, Virginia's in my blood, through and through. You kids come up through Gainesville?"

"No, sir, we've been driving up the country roads, mostly." Northern Virginia, then. Bobby didn't know Virginia too well, but he knew where Gainesville was. "Last big city was Charlottesville. Nice place."

"Sure is." The man filled the truck with chatter for the next half hour, telling them about family he had in Charlottesville. Bobby had no interest in his four granddaughters and two grandsons, all of whom apparently had won awards, science fairs, beauty pageants, or talent contests. Ai had the presence of mind to make appropriate noises, keeping him talking and not asking about them.

Purcellville didn't have much, but it did have a gas station, which was good enough. Jayce politely wished the man well when they climbed out, and he went on his way. The teenager manning the gas station stared at them all, and Jayce went over to talk to the guy while Bobby took the girls around back. He saw a garbage dumpster and decided he might as well take a look. Worn, dirty shoes would be better than barefoot.

He hopped up and climbed inside, finding it to be free of anything terribly disgusting. It looked like most of what got dumped back here was packaging from this and that, and it must have been emptied within the past few days. "There's cardboard in here, we could use that for shelter if we gotta."

"I live in an apartment." Alice whined. "I have money. Not a lot, but enough to afford an apartment. This is not fair."

"You're talking like fair matters," Ai said. "Fair left the building the second we were arrested."

Finding nothing other than cardboard and clear plastic, Bobby levered himself back out again and hopped to the ground. "Sorry, ladies, no designer dresses inside."

Alice glared at him. Ai snorted. Jayce found them, carrying a paper cup. "Best I could do was some clean water to drink." He offered the cup to Ai, who took a few sips before passing it on. "I asked what's in this town. He said there's a diner, a doughnut shop, a bar, and a few small stores. Most people drive someplace else to do their major shopping. There are two churches, so we could maybe try them for a little charity, but the more we ask for, the more risk we run of being remembered or recognized.

"I ain't going to a church with the story I fed that old guy." Bobby smirked and handed the cup to Alice to finish off.

Jayce chuckled. "No, probably not the best choice for that. Any other excuse I can come up with, though, is something we should go to the cops for."

"Even that excuse, we ought to be going to the cops for, to find the car. Hate to say it, but stealing's probably our only real option. We kinda need a city, I think, but I got the impression we ain't exactly near one."

"No, we're not. There's a map up inside. We're in the north part of the state. Washington, DC is relatively close, but outside walking distance. The border with West Virginia is only a mile or two straight north. We're not quite in the Appalachians here."

"That kinda makes sense, I guess. If'n you were gonna set up a secret government lab for human experimentation, you'd put it in the middle of nowhere, but not far from someplace like DeeCee or a military base or something."

Jayce nodded. "One of the shops might be willing to trade for that radio, but one of us really needs to be wearing clothes."

"This isn't really that bad." Ai futzed with her makeshift dress. "With some kind of cord for my waist, maybe a little effort with folding, it could pass for a dress. I still don't have any shoes, though."

"I know we don't want to take from folks if we can help it, but you can go so fast..." Bobby shrugged uncomfortably. "You could probably swipe something without being seen."

Ai opened her mouth to say something, then shut it.

"These people are probably not in a great situation, economically speaking." Alice tossed the empty cup up into the dumpster behind her. "Small towns is where recessions hit the hardest, usually."

"Yeah, well, we got nothing." Bobby turned to Ai. "Just grab some sandals, maybe a shirt. I can go airborne, I guess, and have a look around, maybe even find out how fast I can go like that. If I get the chance, maybe I can grab something, too."

Jayce looked around. "We'll stay back here. It's out of sight."

"Okay." Ai took a deep breath and squinted off into the distance. "Here goes nothing." She shot off faster than the eye could track, leaving a small whoosh of wind in her wake.

"Yeah, me too." Bobby handed over the radio and baton, then exploded out into dragons and went up. Focused like this, and with nothing in the way, they actually moved pretty fast. To avoid being seen, he had the swarm spread out. He got images from all the different eyes, and his mind somehow—he chose not to think about it—put them together without making his head explode. Wherever that might be. As a result, he had a birds' eye view of the town and the sky for miles around.

As an experiment, he picked five dragons and sent them off to investigate specific spots, on a mission to find food. Right now, he'd be willing to grab anything edible. The rest of the swarm kept spreading out until he covered a sizable area. Instead of seeing through all the dragons, he saw through the majority of them in the large swarm. If he was whole and had a skull with a brain inside it, he'd say there were five little tickles in the back of his head to let him know five dragons had gone elsewhere.

By focusing on one in particular, he saw what it saw and heard what it heard. A queer sensation, to be sure, since he got the distinct impression the tiny dragon had something of a mind of its own. Not an advanced intellect, but instincts and a kind of intelligence. It could solve simple puzzles, probably, without his input. He had to wonder at that, but not for long, because this one found a dumpster with food in it. Another of the 'tickles' got excited, so as he started the swarm moving towards the first scout, he focused on the second. It had found a rusty old car with the hood stuck open.

Why, exactly, that would make the dragon excited when he sent it for food, he had no idea. Until it dove in, grabbed a small gear, and devoured it. Oh. The dragons needed to eat, and they ate metal things. Great. If the dragons ate, would that fill him up, too? How about the other way around? Only one way to find out. Since he wasn't sure exactly what the dragons needed, he went for the people food. Re-forming at that dumpster, he found himself naked again, this time in an otherwise empty alley.

This dragon had found stale baked goods, fruit past its prime, and floppy vegetables. Starving, he ate without caring about the mushy, moldy spot on the apple or the bites out of a mushy grilled cheese sandwich. He started with the stuff that looked the least appetizing and went from there. For the moment, he had to know if filling himself up also filled up the dragons, or he'd have another problem. The others could wait.

Once he'd taken the edge of his hunger off, he looked down at himself. He had four other dragons still out there, and that ought to equate to four bits of him missing. With a brief inspection, he discovered each foot had the two smallest toes missing. Apparently, each dragon didn't correspond to a specific part of his body, which struck him as both interesting and disturbing.

He sated his belly enough to trust it would last a few hours, then blew out into dragons again. Except for that one, all of them gurgled with hunger to his mind. Damn. At least it seemed they could go for a while yet. From listening to them, he got a small child vibe, reminding him of the grandkids of some of Momma's friends.

When he touched down and re-formed, Ai had already returned, now in a red shirt and sandals with her curtain serving as a skirt. Alice had a pair of the same sandals on, without the shirt. Jayce handed Bobby his curtain piece without a word.

"Looks like you did alright. The dumpster behind the diner has some food that's decent and free. I went ahead and filled myself up because I got a new issue. Apparently, my dragons need to eat separate from me."

Alice gave him a flat look. "That makes no sense."

"Tell me how you spitting ice from your hands makes sense." Bobby shrugged, because the amount of logic his life operated on now didn't much matter to him. "Anyway, I'mma go off and see if I can find something for them while you all do what you gotta do." Before any of them could object, he blew out into the swarm again. Somehow, he'd have to figure out a way to bring clothes along with him. It wasn't the best possible way ever to travel if he couldn't manage that, but it did still beat walking around barefoot.

He saw the other three head off in the direction of the diner and trusted they could take care of themselves. With four scouts already out, he sent ten more, looking for whatever they wanted to eat. The one that found its meal rejoined the swarm, carrying another gear it found. It could barely manage the weight and other dragons helped by converging and devouring it. By the time it was truly back with the swarm, he had fifteen happy dragons and no gear. At that rate, these things would be a plague of locusts for metal. He was made up of hundreds of the things, maybe even thousands. Hopefully, they didn't need to eat very often.

Twenty minutes later, he noticed his three fellow escapees leaving the alley behind the diner. Jayce licked his fingers. The girls had no such issues. Few of his scouts had managed to find anything he considered acceptable to take. Functioning machinery needed to be left alone, and people needed to be avoided. Aside from a handful of old cars with a few gears and cogs, they had nothing to eat. Most of the swarm remained cranky, so he dove down to the alley and re-formed there.

"Just get cash if you can, but if you see something that would help us a lot, try to swap for as much as you can." Jayce handed the radio over to Ai. He tossed Bobby's curtain at him without looking.

Ai and Alice both nodded. Ai took a deep breath and grabbed Alice's hand, tugging her across the street and into the general store a few buildings up.

Bobby sighed lightly as he watched them. "I didn't find nothing worth going for."

"At least the girls have shoes now." Jayce leaned his bare back against the wall of the building behind him. "What do you really think about hunting down the people on that list?"

The question made Bobby raise his brow and blink a few times. "I said what I meant. It'd be crappy if anybody else had to go through this. Even worse if they decided their superpowers made 'em above the law in a big way. Imagine if Alice decided she just wanted stuff and took it."

Jayce crossed his arms over his chest, looming over him. "Ai already did that. You encouraged her to, even."

"Just for survival, though." Bobby had been intimidated and beaten up by badder guys than Jayce. He shrugged. "I wouldn't tell her to go get a 'spensive handbag or something if she wanted it. I think we really just need to get clothes, then start finding the others. They won't have the same problems getting their own money as we do. They'll be able to pack a bag, even."

"True. If we did want to wreak some havoc, though, we could do quite a bit."

"Oh, sure. I can see that. Ai could rob a place blind. You can probably kill a person with your fist. Alice, she's pretty deadly, or plenty of chaos. Me, I can be a horde of gremlins and the ultimate big brother, both at once. We're real dangerous, and we need to keep everybody else from realizing that. 'Cause the second they do, we're not walking free anymore, we're either in a cage or hiding."

"I'm glad you see that." Jayce gave him a small smile. "Alice and Ai, I'm not so sure they really do. Alice seems more in denial than anything else. Ai... The small theft she did do seemed like it left her more excited than I feel comfortable with. As far as our continued survival is concerned, anyway. I really don't care if she steals a Gucci handbag, I just care whether her stealing it leads to someone deciding I need to be in a hole in the ground."

The girls backed out of the store with the radio still in hand and hurried to the alley, cutting off Bobby's reponse. He frowned and gestured for Jayce to duck farther into the alley with him. The obvious question was obvious, so he didn't bother voicing it, and neither did the bigger man.

"They had a TV on inside," Ai whispered. "It had a breaking news report. They called us federal fugitives, extremely dangerous. I don't think the guy working there saw us before we backed out."

"They had pictures of us." Alice wrung her hands together. "Why are they saying we're dangerous?"

Bobby looked past them, reflexively wanting to see the TV somehow, and recognized the front end of a cop cruiser. "Come on, we need to move." He noticed Jayce saw it, too, and they both herded the girls away from the mouth of the alley. "I guess it's safe to say they noticed we were missing by now."

Alice snorted. "Ya think?"

"Maybe we should split up." Ai peered out the other end of the alley, checking both ways before waving to indicate the way was clear. "I can get pretty far in a short time."

Jayce shook his head. "I don't think that's a good idea. We'll be better off if we stick together."

"Even if we aren't, at least if one of us gets nabbed, the others'll know. And shoot, facing all this alone is kinda crappy." Bobby checked behind them and saw another cop car driving past the alley. He wasn't sure if the cops inside saw them, but how could they not? Likewise, before they had to cross that last street, the cops—he amended himself to use the word 'deputies', because this car had 'Loudoun County Sheriff' plastered on the side—in that other car had to have seen them, also. "Why ain't they getting out and pointing guns at us?"

"Are you upset about that?"

"No, it just..." Bobby stopped. "Hold up a sec." He could see they considered that a dumb idea, and he held up a hand to ask for a minute's grace. "Just listen for a minute. S'posing the deputies," he pitched a thumb over his shoulder to where the car went past, "are here in this podunkville because that old guy heard about us on the radio and called it in. Now, we walked here from that lab, right? So we ain't real far from it. If I was the bad guys here, I'd have a van or something, full of guys with big guns, just waiting to scream out to wherever we got sighted."

Jayce narrowed his eyes as he stared at the mouth of the alley. "You think they're herding us."

Bobby nodded. "It makes sense, and explains why these deputies ain't all trying to be heroes by taking down the known terrorists."

Ai rubbed her face and mewled. Alice's eyes watered and she hugged herself.

Jayce, on the other hand, kept staring, his eyes gone hard. "If we engage them here, they'll get a good handle on what we can do."

"How can we avoid it?" Ai shook her head. "Scratch that. How can you all avoid it? I can just run right by."

"And I can fly away." Bobby frowned and tried hard to think. "We gotta go backwards, or do something unexpected. Come on." The quartet hurried back the way they'd come for one block. Instead of sticking to the alley, they turned down the next street and ducked into the first open door they came across. It was somebody's house, and a voice came from farther inside almost immediately.

"Rich, is that you," a woman's voice called out. "Did you forget something?" They heard the babbling of a young child, too. While this place might be better for a few minutes than running up the street, it sucked as a hidey-hole. Before any of them did more than make a face to express unhappiness at this turn of events, the owner of the voice turned the corner and stopped, her expression comically surprised. She turned out to be a pretty, petite, and very pregnant brunette.

"Ma'am, we don't mean you no harm at all, and we ain't here to rob you or nothing." Bobby put up his hands in the universal sign of 'I'm harmless'. Thank goodness Jayce hid the baton and radio behind his back. Thinking fast, he searched for words to make this better instead of worse. "We had a bit of trouble, and are really just lost and confused and stuff. I gotta admit, we were hoping to get a drink of clean water and maybe use the phone, and if you weren't here, we mighta took some clothes, but that's all, I swear on my daddy's grave."

The woman stood there, blinking in stupid shock. "We don't have a lot, but, um, if all you want is a drink of water, I...um, suppose that's...not a problem."

He hurried down the hallway to her, mostly to make sure she didn't slip in a phone call to 911, while doing his best to keep looking harmless. "Hi there," he said cheerfully to the little girl in the high chair, her hand stuck in a bowl of dry cereal. He waved to her, she waved back. "She about eighteen months?" Glancing back, he met Ai's eyes and jerked his chin for her to join him. She struck him as the most harmless looking of the group.

"Um, nineteen, yes," the woman said with a nod, her wide eyes darting between them. She edged towards the little girl.

"I swear we will not harm you, or her, or the one yet to come." He gestured to her belly. "We're just really having a rough time right now. It ain't your fault, and we ain't gonna put it on you." He could see Alice and Jayce having a whispered conversation out of the corner of his eye, probably around the topic of what to do now, and ignored it.

Moving slowly and keeping her hands in plain sight, Ai got herself a cup from a cabinet that hung open already and filled it with tap water. She gulped the water down and gave a satisfied sigh as she refilled it. "This is a really nice house. And you have good water. The water at my parents' house is really crappy. We have to use a filter."

"Thanks." The woman put her rather substantial girth between Bobby and the little girl, her hands reaching behind her to grip the tray of the high chair. "What do you want from us?"

"Not much." Bobby looked around the kitchen and imagined Momma in it. She'd be tickled pink to have this much space. When his eyes fell back on her, he realized that made him appear to be casing the place. He threw on his 'aw shucks' smile. "Not calling the cops would be real nice."

"Why are the police after you?"

Bobby felt Ai watching him and thought for a moment how to answer the question. "We ain't rightly sure. It seems like a mistake to all of us, but they sure do seem to want us."

For the first time, the woman's eyes traveled down his body. He hoped that meant he'd managed to get her to relax enough to not scream the second they left. Even better, she appreciated what she saw. His job did, after all, having him doing manual labor five days a week. She tore her eyes away from his bare chest and cleared her throat. "How did you lose your clothes?"

"We all woke up naked in a lab and broke out." In reaction to this, Ai goggled at him. She turned away to avoid letting the woman see it. He scratched at the back of his neck to keep Ai from distracting both of them. As he'd hoped, the woman found his flexing bicep more interesting than Ai's sudden movement. "Don't rightly know what they were doing to us, don't rightly much want to know, we just wanted to be outta there."

"Oh my goodness, that's horrible. Who would do that?" The woman let go of the high chair and held her hands out in a kind of low-key invitation. "Are you hungry? You know, my husband, he's not that much bigger than you. Some of his clothes might fit you reasonably well. Sweatpants, maybe." She pointed and tried to lead them out of the kitchen.

Bobby put up a hand to stop her. "You should stay with your daughter, ma'am. If you don't mind us just taking something to wear, we appreciate that, and we won't take nothing else." Out of the corner of his eye, he saw Jayce head off in the direction he saw some stairs. "I swear I'm being honest."

Ai huffed in exasperation. "Why are you explaining this stuff?"

"I don't know." He sighed and shook his head. "I guess I figured if I told somebody, it would make more sense or something."

"I've never seen an Oriental person with blue eyes before." The woman decided to sit down beside her daughter, her hand on her belly. The little girl ignored everyone in the room and stuffed more cereal in her mouth.

"Japanese." Ai filled the glass back up and handed it to Bobby. "Nobody in my family has blue eyes but me. We don't know how it happened."

"There's...well, you know. A...usual sort of way for— For that to happen." The woman shifted as she spoke, and dropped her eyes to their feet.

Bobby chuckled, hoping to disarm her more. "Yes, ma'am, there sure is. Right now, our eyes seems like the main reason why they want to experiment on us, though."

Brow furrowed, the woman lifted her head again and cocked her head to one side. "Isn't that the kind of thing the Nazis did? Experimenting on people because of their genetics. Twins and all."

"I didn't do all that great in school, but that sounds about like what I heard of 'em."

One corner of Ai's mouth curled into a scowl. "Our government has done plenty of that kind of thing, too."

Bobby heard Jayce making his way back and turned in time to catch the pair of boxer shorts thrown at his face. "We really do appreciate your kindness," Jayce said politely. "We'll get out of your home shortly."

"Yeah. Do you mind if we use your bathroom before we go?"

CHAPTER 5

It was good to have underwear, Bobby thought as they hurried through backyards to avoid being seen on the streets. He hoped that saint of a woman got the long, happy life she deserved. Maybe someday, he'd come back here and do something nice for her and her family. All because he now had boxers, shorts, and a t-shirt—a significant improvement over the curtain kilt. Without shoes, he still had to watch where he walked, but at least he didn't have to worry about flashing anyone anymore.

Jayce now had flip-flops, putting extra bounce in his step. The sweat-pants and plain shirt fit tighter on the bigger guy, making his buff physique somehow more obvious than it had been without. The girls got underwear, too, which made both of them instantly less cranky. For whatever reason. Bobby didn't really understand women that much.

"Do you think she'll call?" Alice took Jayce's help to get over a low fence the rest of them had no trouble hopping.

"'Course she'll call."

She frowned. "Why all the talking, then? We could have just backed out again and tried another house or something."

Bobby opened his mouth to give her the same reason he had given Ai. Someplace between his brain and his mouth, he realized there had been more to it. "It ain't never killed no one to be polite. 'Sides, she's gonna wait a few minutes, I'd wager."

Jayce grunted in agreement. "She'll give us a head start, maybe ten minutes or so."

"What makes you so sure?" Ai peered around, but they hadn't yet seen any sort of official vehicles tracking them, or even trolling along looking for them.

"She didn't feel threatened," Jayce said.

Bobby grinned and let the unspoken compliment sustain him for a minute or two. They dashed across a street and plunged through more backyards, skirting around a house surrounded by hedges. "I say, next time we see cops, we go towards 'em."

Alice panted, having trouble keeping up as they kept moving without a break. "Are you crazy? They have guns."

"We got superpowers." He wagged his eyebrows at her, feeling clever. "I been thinking, you know, those lab guys must have some clue what we can do already. They maybe don't know the limits, but they must know what kinda things we got up our sleeves."

"If that's true," Jayce nodded as he hopped over a kid's bicycle, "we won't lose much by using them."

"'Specially on regular cops what ain't going to believe what they saw anyway." Bobby spent so much time paying attention to everything else, he jogged into a tree. His body exploded into tiny dragons and his clothes fell to the ground.

Jayce stopped and scooped the clothes up. "You need to figure out a way to take these with you, Bobby," he groused. "Might as well stay that way for now." His eyes rested on a metal swing set in the backyard they stood in. "Actually, I might as well be something else, too." He gripped one of the legs, sending white painted aluminum spreading down and across his body.

Ai stopped and leaned against a shed near it, and Alice dropped to the ground to take a break. Apparently, she spent all her time with books and none of it with exercise.

Rising up into the sky, the swarm spread out. Bobby watched Jayce give Alice a hand up, then he flew along with them as they hurried through yards again. He saw the cruiser half a second before everyone else did, and they all followed the plan to converge on it.

Ai disappeared, a handful of leaves blown around by her passage. The cruiser bucked like a bronco and the front dented like a rock fell on it. Bobby's best guess had her jumping on the hood.

The two Sheriff's deputies scrambled out of the car, both reaching for their weapons. Jayce put his head down and charged them, plowing into one and throwing him to the ground. Something smacked into the other deputy, knocking him on his ass and sending his gun spinning away across the asphalt. Alice ran up to the car, screwed her eyes shut and grimaced, then flung ice shards at it, ripping two of the tires apart.

It looked to Bobby like the three of them had the situation under control. He sent the dragons in to swarm the deputies anyway, so Ai could grab the gun if she wanted to. The dragons behaved like a big pile of flies on rotting garbage, provoking a lot of swatting and cringing from one. The other seemed to be down for the count, so he left the poor guy alone.

"Damn," Jayce said as he stooped to check for a pulse, "I hit hard. He's still alive, though." The metal man hurried around to the other side of the car, where Bobby had the other deputy distracted. Bobby pulled the swarm away and Jayce punched him in the jaw. The dragons caught the deputy as he fell, and set his limp body on the ground.

Bobby re-formed and grabbed the boxers from Jayce. "We should see what they got."

Ai picked up the gun, holding it gingerly and away from her body. She cringed and asked, "Do we want these?"

"I'll take it." Jayce traded her the baton for the gun.

"I... I could kill someone," Alice whimpered, staring at her hands.

Bobby climbed into the car and checked for anything useful. Catching sight of the radio, he did as much damage to it as he could. He found some spare clips of ammunition in the glove box, and guessed there might be something worth taking in the trunk. He popped the release and went to take a look. "I think we could all kill people pretty easy if we put our minds to it." Inside the trunk, he found flares, vests, jumper cables, all kinds of things. A red canvas bag caught his eye. "Whatever we want, we got something to carry it in." He grabbed it and tossed it to Alice.

She watched the bag hit her arm and fall to the ground. "This is wrong. Really, really wrong."

Bobby pursed his lips and looked her over. The girl's eyes seemed stuck on the nearest unconscious deputy, wide and horrified. Taking a step closer, he poked her with a finger. "Do I gotta slap ya?"

She gulped and shook her head, then bent and picked up the bag. "No."

"Good. My Momma says only assholes hit girls."

Jayce helped him pull out everything that seemed useful. As the strongest, he'd carry it, so his opinion of the weight mattered the most. "We should check their wallets and take whatever cash they've got."

Ai zipped away while they did all this, checking all the closest streets. She breezed through several times, crossing back and forth.

"We can't do that," Alice whined. "We can't steal from the *police*."

Bobby rolled his eyes and knelt beside one deputy, yanking his wallet out of his pocket. "This one's got thirty-three bucks." He left the guy with three ones. "I left him with snack money, you happy?"

Alice flared her nostrils and scowled hard enough to be sulking. "No."

"We don't have time for this argument right now," Jayce said.

"Ain't that the truth." Bobby took both the deputy's spare clips for his gun, then moved to the other one. He had another two spare clips, and two twenties in his wallet. In a show for Alice's benefit, he left the five and two ones. "We got fifty bucks now. That ain't much, but it's something." All of it, he handed over to Jayce. "Which way ya think?"

Alice paced back and forth between the cruiser and the sidewalk, wringing her hands and muttering. He thought she said something about medical school. Treating her as a distraction, he gave Jayce his full attention.

"Depends." Jayce hefted the bag over his shoulder and looked around. "We could head for a city, or we could go into the wilderness. So long as we don't go east, we'll hit The Appalachian Trail at some point. We could get lost there for a while and probably survive one way or another. That would mean abandoning the others like us, though."

"I don't see that as an option. City, then. We ain't really that far from DeeCee." Bobby shrugged back into the shorts and shirt as he spoke. "You got the list, or Ai still have it? If there's one in DeeCee, we maybe got a serious destination."

Jayce pulled the crumpled page from his pocket and ran his finger down it. "Jasmine Milani is in Washington."

"Sounds like a plan, then. That's east." Looking up at the sky through the trees, he pointed. "More or less that way." He looked back at the beat up cruiser. "Shame about that."

"Alice is going to have a heart attack, but we should steal a car."

Bobby pursed his lips and checked up and down the street. He saw a beat up old Nova on the street, even pointing in the right direction. Must be fate. *"You smash the window, I'll hot wire it."*

"You've boosted a car?" Jayce raised his brow and smirked.

"Nah," Bobby shrugged. *"Girlfriend broke the key off in her ignition once, couldn't afford to get it fixed."*

Chuckling, Jayce led the way. He rammed an elbow through the passenger side window and unlocked it. After tossing the loot into the back seat, he leaned against the car and watched Alice with a sigh.

Bobby slid into the driver's seat and grinned. "Suck it up, I got work to do."

"Yeah, yeah." Jayce patted the car and jogged away.

Five minutes later, Alice sat clenched up in the backseat with Ai hunkered down on the floor beside her. Jayce leaned back in the passenger seat with the brim of a Nationals ball cap they found in the car lowered over his face. No one should look at three kids in a car with the windows down on a warm summer day and think anything of it.

Bobby drove them towards the nation's capital. For the first time since they broke out of that lab, they finally managed to be accomplishing something and getting somewhere. They had a goal and plan, of sorts. He spared a thought to wonder and how many more cops they were going to have to beat up to get it all done. Cities should be relatively safe, he thought. They could blend in around the homeless, and probably find folks willing to trade for what they had now.

Construction on the other side of the highway made him think of roadblocks. He kept the car going near the speed limit, and paid attention to the other cars. After a half hour of this hypervigilance, he decided they hadn't yet realized the car had been stolen. They'd keep the search focused around that town until someone noticed, he guessed.

"I'm thinking we should ditch the car pretty quick. Soon as somebody notices it's missing, they'll have plates to look for."

"Good plan," Jayce nodded.

Alice grunted. "This is all screwed up."

"Ayup." She reminded Bobby of this girl he knew back home: prim and proper, and wouldn't date him to save her life because he occasionally strayed from the straight and narrow. That would ruin her reputation, of course. He glanced in the rearview mirror and saw she stared out the window and had let her arms relax enough to no longer have them crossed over her chest.

"I'm going to Stanford."

"Yeah, you told us that," Ai snapped, "like, fifty times already. I'm sure that makes you five hundred times better than the rest of us."

"I worked my ass off to get into that school!"

"And now you're a superhero who can make ice instead of just being made of it," Ai sneered. "Grow up, seriously. Like this is only happening to you or something. We're all sooooo sorry your carefully planned and manicured life is all messed up. News flash, ours are, too."

Alice scowled and huffed and glared out the window. Bobby and Jayce both chose not to get involved. The exchange and the silence that followed it made the car awkward and uncomfortable, so Bobby switched on the radio to find it tuned to a station with a male announcer talking.

"...considered extremely dangerous. The four fugitives are ages nineteen to twenty-one, two males and two females. The two females are of Asian descent, one male is white with light brown hair, the other is of Native American descent. All four have blue eyes with a shape being described as 'somewhat unusual'. We've got pictures on our website—"

Jayce clicked the radio back off. "We could split up to deal with contacting the rest of the people on the list. We might have enough money to get some cheap pre-paid cellphones to keep in touch with."

"I think we'll need more than we got for that."

"Oh, great," Alice growled, "we can just go steal some more. What a brilliant plan. I guess we've already done grand theft auto, so why not a little more assault and battery?"

"Alice, if'n you wanna get outta the car and let them pick you back up so they can stick you with needles again, that's fine. Just say the word, I can pull over anytime. If'n you got a better idea, we're listening. 'Til then, we're kinda stuck. None of us even has ID, and even if we did, using it would just lead 'em to us."

"Be part of the solution or get out of the way," Ai said.

Alice glared at the window in silence.

CHAPTER 6

The bridge over the Potomac had a toll. Bobby took an exit in Arlington and found a place to park. They piled out and left it behind, the bag slung over Jayce's shoulder. Walking across the bridge slowed them down, but a toll would take cash they couldn't afford to spend on something avoidable. Time cost nothing.

As Bobby hoped, the area had endless city, and he felt confident a body could get lost and never found here. This helped them and complicated their mission. With only fifty bucks and no phone, computer, or transportation, they had to find one particular person. The best option seemed to be hitting an internet cafe and using the time there to look up addresses for everyone on the list.

Alice took the ball cap from Jayce and went to go pay for internet access by herself, in the hope that one of them alone might not get noticed. Bobby went for a flight, leaving his clothes behind with Jayce, who sat on a park bench as a point for them all to return to. Ai ran off to find food.

From above, Bobby could feel the dragons getting impatient about eating. The vast horde dwarfed the tiny group of satisfied dragons. He sent scouts again, looking for them to find enough food for the whole swarm. For a while, he drifted around, watching cars and people moving around.

One scout hit the jackpot, finding a junkyard. Eager to reach it, the little things flew at a good clip, faster than they had before. Motivation put a fire under their tails. The swarm slipped into the back of the junkyard and slipped through. Dragons stopped and settled as the mass wormed its way through, delighted at finding pieces to devour.

He noticed they ignored most of the large metal pieces, choosing mainly gears and cogs and other small, shaped parts. It seemed to be certain kinds of metal, and the thickness mattered. They might be less picky in a pinch. This particular junkyard, though, offered more than enough of their preferred 'food'. Each one gorged itself and streaked up when it could eat nothing more. When the last dragon, happy and sated, rejoined the swarm, he directed it back to the park.

"I scored for the dragons," he told the other three when he'd re-formed behind the bench.

Jayce held up his clothes, and he shrugged into them before a cop could notice and get annoying about his nakedness. "There's a sandwich for you, and some carrots and juice."

"I managed to get addresses for all the names, but I have no idea if they're all the right people, or current. In cases where there were multiple choices, I wrote them all down. I also made copies, so we all have one." Alice handed Bobby his copy as he hopped over the bench to claim his lunch and sit down with them.

"Not sure how I'm gonna carry it with me." He stuffed his face with sandwich and his pocket with the paper.

"Just don't lose it." Jayce patted the red bag beside him. "We should go together to try to trade the stuff, I think. Stick to the sketchy parts of the city and we should be okay."

"I think we should split up," Ai said. "I'll go find Jasmine."

"I'll go with you," Bobby told Jayce. He crunched a carrot stick, then looked to Alice. "You should come with us, too. Let Ai go zippity and you get to have a say in what we get for what we got."

Alice pursed her lips and furrowed her brow. "I guess."

Bobby wanted to say something friendly, something that would make her feel more welcome, maybe. He scratched his head and tried to think of what might be taken well right now and came up empty. Chewing his bite of sandwich, he decided to be grateful she'd left some of her attitude behind in the car and leave it at that.

Jayce, who'd been looking at a city map for a while now, suggested a place they could meet back up that he felt confident had to be a lousy part of town. Ai took off before Bobby finished eating, and the trio set off with his hands and mouth full of food and juice. When he finished what he had, he knew he could pack more away without feeling full. The next time they sent Ai to swipe food, he'd ask her to grab extra for him.

An hour later, they still had twenty bucks, and Jayce and Bobby had jeans and t-shirts, combat boots, and trenchcoats with pockets. Alice had pants and a shirt and a sports bra, along with regular, cheap shoes. They got the same for Ai. They also had four super-cheap pre-paid cellphones. The bag had been replaced with a gray backpack, and now held a set of basic tools, the extra clips for the gun Jayce hid in his trenchcoat, the baton, and a battery-free wind-up flashlight.

The meeting place turned out to be a gathering point for homeless people, and Bobby looked around with interest at their tactical approaches to life without stuff. Actually, a lot of them had plenty of stuff, in shopping carts and shabby wheeled packs. With nothing better to do while waiting, he sat down next to a guy in an old Army jacket and asked about the weather. Nearby, Jayce leaned against a streetlight and watched everything happening around him.

Alice hugged herself and took excessive care to not touch anyone or anything. She gave the impression of a fish out of water—one with disdain for its new surroundings. Bobby noticed a woman deliberately bump into Alice, then stop and growl at her, too low to be overheard.

Brushing her arm off, Alice stepped away and shook her head. She used both hands to ward the woman off and kept taking small steps towards Bobby. Jayce's head shimmered to the same mottled gray as the lamppost and he stood away from it.

A man stepped up, blocking Bobby's view, and pushed Alice hard enough to make her stumble a step. "Why you come down here, girlie, if you don't want to see any of this?"

"You come down here for a school project, Princess?"

"No, wait, I know, court ordered community service!"

"Some new church come to save our souls?" Several different people bumped Alice around, all unhappy to see her here.

"Stop touching me!" She covered her head and repeated the plaintive wail over and over.

Jayce pushed one man aside without using his full strength, his low voice murmuring something soothing. His action had no effect, and the group pushed Alice around until she screamed. With the scream, which Bobby recognized from having heard it before in the lab, the air temperature dropped like a rock. Ice shot out of her in jagged shards and covering everything with frost.

The ice smashed into Jayce, his body protecting everyone behind himself. It tore through the four people directly harassing her, ripping them to shreds in seconds. Those farther away suffered less deadly cuts and scrapes, and several slipped and fell.

"Alice," Bobby cried out, far enough away to be safe, "Stop it, you're killing them!" He rushed in to check on the woman nearest to him while Jayce dropped down to check for a pulse on the other one next to him. "You killed them."

Shaking all over, Alice's eyes had gone wide and wild and her flesh had turned deathly blue. Her mouth hung open, panting breaths coming out in frozen puffs of cloudy vapor. She slowly stood from a crouch and turned around on the spot, surveying the disaster. "They wouldn't stop," she whispered. "They wouldn't stop."

Ai showed up out of nowhere and slipped on the frost covering everything. She fell on her ass, letting out a squawk of surprise. A dead body stopped her slide, leaking blood all over the ground. The moment she noticed, she scrabbled away from it, through the pool of blood. Despite her mouth moving, no sound came out.

"Let's go, we gotta go now." Bobby nodded for Jayce to take control of Alice while he hauled Ai to her feet and hustled her away. "Where's Jasmine," he asked as they kept moving. When she didn't answer, he squeezed her arms a little. "Do I gotta slap ya?" It worked before.

Shaking her head, Ai took a deep breath. "She invited us to dinner. When I got there, I was a little confused about what to say, so it kind of came out all wrong. I should have gone over what to say with you first. What happened back there?"

"Alice freaked out and blew up."

"She killed those people."

"Yeah. As if things weren't screwed up enough before. Which way to Jasmine's place?"

Ai pointed and they walked. Jayce herded Alice along in silence. She had nothing to say all the way to Jasmine's apartment complex. It was a big place with lots of shade trees around three tall buildings. Bobby would call the neighborhood nice, though he suspected Alice needed more to be impressed. Rather, she would if she wasn't so busy being numb. Little Miss Follows The Rules had to be exploding inside from what she just did, and when it came out, the mess wouldn't to be pretty.

"Is she nice?"

"She's sweet," Ai nodded, "really nice, yeah."

"Let's go in, then."

Jasmine answered the buzzer with a voice so cheerful it felt weird. She also let Ai in without question. In the middle of a middle floor, the door had a sticker of a squirrel with a word bubble over its head, the word 'hi' printed in large block letters inside.

The woman who answered the door had a squirrel in her hands, and stood aside so the four of them could come in. She smiled and greeted each of them, delighted to see them all for no apparent reason. Jayce steered Alice to the couch and forced her to sit, then sat himself down on the floor, away from her. Jasmine hugged Ai enthusiastically. "I didn't expect you back so soon! Is everything okay?"

Her olive complexion hinted at Mediterranean ancestry, and she had long brown hair in a perky ponytail that hung to halfway down her back with the ends forming loose curls. Bright and pleasant, her open face welcomed them as much as her words did, and Bobby found himself smiling at the pretty lady in the ruffled floral blouse despite what they'd just dealt with.

"This is Jasmine," Ai explained. "Jayce, Bobby, and Alice."

"Hi." Jasmine gave them all a really cheerful wave instead of shaking hands with any of them. "What she said sounds pretty serious." She bobbed her head and seemed disturbed by the idea anything could actually *be* serious.

"Have you had an episode recently where you woke up cold but sweating all over, without remembering having had a nightmare?" Jayce spoke up first, a fact Bobby appreciated. They needed to discuss how to have this conversation.

"Oh!" Jasmine rubbed her cheek on the squirrel still in her hands. It seemed content there, not struggling or squirming. "Yes! About a week ago, I scared Will half to death, he said I passed out and he thought I was dead for a minute."

"Who's Will?"

"My boyfriend. We live together. He's a veterinarian." Jasmine pronounced the last word very carefully, like she'd had to practice saying it a lot, or had to say it that way to get it right.

Bobby scratched his forehead. "That kinda complicates things."

Jayce waved Bobby off. "And has something unusual happened to you since then? Like, I can do this." He touched a finger to a button of his trenchcoat and the pattern flowed up his hand. After a short delay, during which it must have spread to the rest of him, it covered his face. Then it dropped away and he looked normal again.

Jasmine nodded earnestly and set the squirrel on the counter, where it sat gazing up at her. She scrunched her eyes shut and made fists. In the space of about two seconds, her body shrank in on itself until a normal squirrel stood there instead of Jasmine. All four of them blinked down at her, then she sprang back up into herself. "Will says I'm a very healthy squirrel." She leaned in and used a loud whisper to say, "He said I shouldn't tell anyone, but if you all have superpowers, too, it's probably okay."

Bobby recovered first, downright jealous—she got to keep her clothes when she did that. "Dang, that's pretty cool. I don't suppose we could meet Will?"

She picked her squirrel up again and cheerfully rubbed noses with it. "He's at work, but he'll be home for dinner."

Out of thirty-one names, the first one they picked happened to be a really sweet, trusting girl who already knew she was special and could do something so unbelievable and obviously real, she didn't reject any of it. Not to mention the understanding boyfriend in a medical field. Bobby had to stop himself from staring in awe of this happy accident. It took no effort to smile, though. "That sounds great. I'd really like to meet him. Maybe he can have a look at my dragons and help me out."

"I love having guests for dinner!" Jasmine clapped around her squirrel and danced into the postage stamp kitchen. "Will is very smart. If anybody can help with dragons, it's my Will." She gently hugged the squirrel in her hands, then rushed over again to show it to Bobby. "This is Walnut. I rescued him when he was just a baby." Fortunately, she set him on the floor, and he scampered over to a cardboard box full of shredded paper, jumped in, and scratched around. If he'd been expected to touch it or something, Bobby wasn't sure what he would've done. Where he came from, squirrels were for shooting.

"He's cute," Bobby said, trying to be nice. "So, I guess Ai said we're kinda all in danger from the government?"

Jasmine nodded earnestly. "She said the government is going around arresting people for having eyes like us."

Ai ducked her head. "I didn't really know what to say."

"Uh-huh." Bobby smirked. "It seems all of us are on a list." Pulling his copy out of his pocket, he laid it out on the counter for Jasmine to see. "That there's me, that's Alice, Jayce, and Ai."

"Oh, and there's me!"

This news, in Bobby's mind, didn't seem right for excitement. He plodded on, hoping he could make her understand the gravity of the situation. "The government is using laws meant to deal with terrorists to pick us all up offa this list. We four got arrested like that a few days back. They took us to some kind of creepy horror movie lab and stuck us with needles and stuff. It was really bad. We escaped in the middle of the night, found this list on the way out, and figured the best thing to do was see about not letting those guys get their hands on anybody else, especially not anybody as nice are you."

"Oh my gosh, that's terrible." She covered her mouth. "You think they'll want to do that to me?" Bobby wanted to pat her on the head and hug her and tell her everything would turn out alright. Whoever this Will guy was, if he turned out to be a jerk, Bobby would deck him, hard and repeatedly.

"Pretty sure, yeah."

Jasmine sucked in a breath and her eyes popped wide. "What do I do?"

"We aren't rightly sure what you should do, Jasmine. So far, we're kinda on the run. Our faces got put up on the TV. They're out there, looking for us. You, though, we don't know when they'll come for you. We're just sure they're gonna."

Her eyes bounced from one somber face to another, and she gulped. A moment later, she smacked the counter and nodded with firm determination. "Will will know what to do." With that, she turned to the kitchen, the matter apparently settled and out of her mind already. Bobby watched her open the fridge, worries and cares slipping off her shoulders like rain off an umbrella. Inside the fridge, he saw pink and yellow post-it notes on several things, including the door itself. "Do any of you eat tofu, or should I make it just vegetables?"

She moved on to other things, so Bobby got out of her way. "Whatever's fine." He could follow simple directions, and knew nothing else about cooking. Scanning the room, he decided somebody needed to do something about Alice, and since Ai bustled into the kitchen to help Jasmine and Jayce seemed to be meditating or otherwise ignoring the problem, that left him.

He sat down next to Alice and rested his forearms on his knees. Momma called it his 'thoughtful pose', since he always sank into it when he had to think a lot. "You wanna talk about it?"

Curled up in a tight ball, Alice shook her head.

"It looked kinda intense," he offered. "All of 'em pushing and stuff. Jayce tried to wade in, but they were kinda being difficult about it." He paused and rubbed his chin, the stubble there feeling strange even though he noticed it hours ago. They saw a newspaper, so they knew they'd missed five days. Wrapping his head around that took some effort. "I imagine it's hard to control something like what you got under a circumstance like that."

"Cut it out," Alice snapped. "I said I don't want to talk about it."

For a few seconds, only the sounds of Jasmine and Ai banging around in the kitchen filled the air. Jayce sighed and raked a hand through his dark hair. "They know we're here now, or will shortly. How long before they figure out why?"

"Hopefully, a while. They don't know we got that list. Even if they do, they probably don't expect us to start using it right away. Not while we're still trying to get basic things. 'Sides, that spot is pretty far from here. They'll find the car soon enough and know we're on foot again."

"If they do know we have that list, they might come here to look for us, just on the off chance."

Bobby looked over at Jasmine, happily cutting up some kind of vegetable. "They'll swipe her if they come here."

"We won't let them," Alice growled. Her jaw set with determination and she glowered and the floor.

A beat passed while both men stared at her in surprise. Bobby lifted his hand to reach out and pat her on the shoulder or knee. Before it got there, he thought better of it and settled for thumping his own knee. "No, we sure won't. A fight here would be a bit less than ideal, though."

"They might leave her alone with Will here," Jayce said. "Dealing with him when she clearly hasn't done anything wrong could be more trouble than they want to get into."

"You think we ought to hide if'n they show up."

Jayce nodded. "In such a way that if they decide to grab her, we can resist on her behalf."

"Sounds like a plan. Means we need to decide where to hide out now, instead of later." What they really needed right now, Bobby thought, were scouts. But if he was dragons, he couldn't actually be here or relay a warning. Before, he managed to re-form with four missing. Could he just send a few off without having to blow up into a whole swarm? That would certainly be handy. It would mean that even if he got caught, he could have a dragon on the outside. It would mean he could get into all kinds of things without having to be a swarm.

"Easy enough for you," Jayce snorted. "You just explode into dragons and fly out the window. I can probably do low level camouflage, the kind that wouldn't stand up to close scrutiny, but will do fine with just a glance. Ai can run out when they open the door. That just leaves Alice." Again, the two men looked at her.

"I can hide in the bathroom," she grumped.

Bobby nodded his satisfaction and held up his finger and stared at it. He thought about getting just one dragon to separate. For a good five minutes, he concentrated on the idea of one of them going off on its own. Nothing changed, and he couldn't fell their little minds or bodies at all.

He needed a different approach. If he wanted to use a fork or a pencil, he also needed a different hand. Switching to his left hand, he held up a finger and thought about what would entice him to come out and play. As soon as he considered it that way in his head, he watched in horrified amazement as the tip of his thumb turned into a tiny silver dragon and climbed onto his index finger. Its tiny claws tickled.

"That...it's...I mean—" Alice stared with a grimace, shying away from him.

"Yeah, I know. And it's me doing it."

Jayce blinked once, then shrugged, sighed, and returned to meditation.

"They are cute little guys, thought, ain't they?" It trilled at him, a tiny little noise to say 'hi' to its master.

"You do know that 'ain't' isn't actually a word, right?"

Bobby rolled his eyes and ignored her. He took a deep breath and got four more to separate, each taking its own fingertip with it. "Okay, little guys, I need y'all to watch for cops and stuff. You think you can do that for us? It's really important." With the words, he thought about what he wanted them to be alert for. The tiny dragons all trilled their acceptance of the mission and flew out the open window.

Jayce raised an eyebrow. "You gave them more instructions than just that, right?"

"Ayup." Bobby reached up to tap his forehead. With his finger missing the part past the last knuckle, the gesture felt awkward. "I think at 'em," he added.

"Good to know."

Alice took his hand and examined the smooth nubs on the ends of his fingers. "Where does your brain go?"

"Heck if I know. It's like a hive mind thing going on, but I'm still aware and in control. Mostly. They got little minds of their own."

"I didn't mean to kill those people."

"'Course not."

"They wouldn't leave me alone."

"I saw."

"I was outnumbered."

"Ayup."

Alice went quiet for a beat, then threw his hand back at him and snarled. "Why aren't you outraged?" Her shouting made Ai and Jasmine turned to look. "I just killed four people, and you're acting like it's nothing worse than running a stop sign, for fuck's sake! They're dead because I'm a twink-eyed freak!"

She took a breath to rant more. Bobby started talking in the hopes she'd stop and think instead. "They're dead because they were poking a tiger with a stick and didn't know it. And I don't mind you calling me a 'twink-eyed freak', but you should make sure everybody in the room don't mind before you start tossing that around. Jasmine is a real nice person, and I ain't gonna sit here silent-like while you say something like that about her. Also, I don't think you ought to be cussing like that in her house. My Momma says you don't do that when you're a guest in somebody's house, less you know it's okay already. It's rude."

Alice goggled at him for a second, then she got up and went to use the bathroom. Ai whispered to Jasmine and they turned back to their cooking. Jayce chuckled. "I don't think she was expecting calm."

Bobby shrugged. "I got a lot to say about Alice, but not much of it is nice, and Momma was pretty clear on that sorta thing, too."

"Mmhmm. My mom said things like that, too, but I didn't always listen."

"I got a selective memory, just like anybody else." Bobby smirked. "We gotta learn to deal with each other, though, 'cause we're stuck together, like it or not. Can't see how letting her get all riled up is helping that. 'Course, it's a thing, killing somebody. I never done it, got no idea what it does to ya. She's gotta figure that out for herself. Preferably without yelling at any of us."

"No argument here." Jayce moved to the couch. "You know, now that we're superheroes, maybe we should have superhero names."

"What, you mean like Batman and Superman?"

Jayce snorted. "Yeah, only original."

"I s'pose." Bobby shrugged. "ZippityGirl, Dragon, MetalMan, and Frosty The Snowgirl. And Squirrel."

Jayce grinned. "Frosty the Snowgirl, I like that one. I'll come up with my own, though, thanks."

"Don't rightly matter much, since they already know who we are."

The front door opened, cutting Jayce off. Bobby recognized the man who walked in from pictures around the apartment. Everything about him, from his short, neat blond hair to his slacks and polo shirt screamed out 'respectable professional'. His hazel eyes caught Ai in the kitchen, then swept into the living room to notice Bobby and Jayce, and Alice as she emerged from the bathroom.

Jasmine squealed with delight and jumped on him. Apparently expecting this, he had an arm out and ready, and he caught and squeezed her close. "Hey sweetheart, are we having guests for dinner tonight?"

"Yes!" She planted a kiss on his lips and introduced everyone. "This is Will," she told the room with a delighted smile while bouncing from foot to foot.

Bobby stood and shook his hand. "I'm sure this is a surprise, and we don't meant to be an inconvenience. We're here, though—"

"Because of the eyes? Are you...?"

"Heh, yeah, we are. Different, but yeah." Bobby held up his hand with the missing fingertips and let another dragon pop out, taking another knuckle with it. "You wanna sit down with us, we can tell you what's going on, as much as we know, while the girls finish up dinner."

Will stared at the dragon, watching it climb on Bobby's hand, then re-form back onto his finger. "Yes, I believe I'd like to hear what you have to say." He sat down with Bobby and Jayce, and he listened carefully while they told him everything that happened since they were arrested, the things they knew and the things they guessed. Bobby showed him the list they had, and Jayce shared their suspicions. When they finished, the girls stood in the kitchen with drinks, chatting while waiting for the food to be done.

Sitting back in the chair, Will frowned. "You're kind of asking me to leave my practice. I understand that's not really what you're saying, but I can't send Jasmine off to who knows where and just go on with my life without her. If I knew it would only be a week or two, then sure, yeah, hide her away and bring her back. But indefinitely, no, I can't do that." Where Jasmine wouldn't see it, he pulled out a little ring box and showed Bobby and Jayce, then tucked it back into his pocket. "I just haven't found the right time yet," he murmured.

"Part of our problem," Jayce said, "is that we're not sure what to do with ourselves. Constantly being on the run isn't going to work, but if we stand still, they'll find us, and we aren't completely sure we can avoid capture, or escape again if necessary."

Will nodded. "If you're going to ask people who haven't been through what you have to leave their lives for their own safety, you really need someplace for them to actually go. What about taking over an abandoned property somewhere, until you can figure out how to buy it without revealing yourselves?"

Bobby scratched his cheek and considered the problems that immediately leaped to mind: water, electricity, food, defense. On the other hand, a solid destination would change the ball game. "It's worth giving some thought."

"I agree," Jayce nodded.

"Were you going to ask any of us?" Ai reminded Bobby of Momma right then, when she found out he did something stupid.

"Sure," he said with an easy smile. "You want to think about it, too? Plenty of—" He blinked and had to focus on one of his dragons. What he saw through its eyes made him sit up straight. "They're here, pretty sure. It's two guys in suits and six more in tac gear. So much for hoping they wouldn't bother.

"Will, if they try to grab Jasmine, you gotta trust us to deal with them. We don't want you getting hurt or took yourself." With that, he poofed out into full dragon swarm, leaving his clothes behind. He heard Jayce ask Will to give him a hand collecting those up, then he dove out the window.

From his new vantage point, saw eight men heading for the building and going inside. The two suits went in front. It occurred to him that if he wanted to help rescue Jasmine, he needed to know whether rescue became necessary. He sent one dragon back inside, and had another zoom off to follow the men in. That would give him two different angles to see and hear the episode. For the moment, he focused on the one following the men in. They all trooped into the elevator and one of the suits punched the button for Jasmine's floor.

"This is the signal to storm in," Suit Number One said as he made a hand gesture of two fingers together, pointing forward. Not terribly subtle as signals went, but knowing it would give him an advantage. Somehow. If he could figure out how to use it. "Miss Milani is not a target at this time, so don't treat her like a suspect without a reason to."

"How far back do you want us to stand until there's a signal?" one of the SWAT guys asked.

"Stay out of sight if you can, as close as possible. We're hoping you're not needed at all, but if you are, we want you close. These people are capable of causing serious damage."

"Yes, sir." The SWAT guys looked unconcerned and ready for anything. His dad had been like that: always ready for the unexpected and never showing fear. It had probably been what got Marine Sergeant Edward Mitchell killed in Afhganistan.

The elevator doors opened and the SWAT guys poured out around the two suits, lined up half on each side of the apartment door. When they were ready, they nodded to the suits, and one of them knocked on the door. About two seconds passed before Will answered it.

"Can I help you?" He had a properly confused and suspicious look, Bobby thought. One that said 'who the heck are you and why are you knocking on my door?'

One of the suits said, "We'd like to speak with Miss Jasmine Milani."

"And you are?"

Suit Number One pulled a badge wallet out and held it up. When he tried to whisk it away, Will snatched it out of his hand.

Will's brow furrowed as he examined the badge. "Do you have a war-rant?"

"We don't need a warrant to speak with someone."

"You do if you want to come inside to do it," Will told them with a frown. "I know my rights, and hers, too."

Suit Number Two made a face. "Can you ask her to come to the door, then, please? We'd just like a few words."

"What's this about?" Bobby had to admire Will for being obnoxious about all this. He knew they had men with them even though he couldn't see them. Would he be this paranoid about the whole thing if they hadn't been here to warn him?

"We just want to ask her a few questions. Who are you, exactly?"

"Her boyfriend." Will handed the badge back. "I'll talk to her. Just a minute." He shut the door and locked it. Bobby heard the deadbolt clack home.

"Are we going in?" a SWAT guy hissed to the suits.

"Not yet."

After several long seconds, Jasmine cracked the door open enough to see out without letting them see in. "What do you want?" she breathed, her voice small and scared. Bobby had a feeling it might not be an act.

"Miss Milani, have you been contacted by any of these people?" Suit Number Two held up a piece of paper Bobby couldn't see. He assumed it had pictures of the four of them.

Taking the paper, Jasmine ran her fingertips over it. "They have eyes like mine."

Both suits blinked at her. "Ah, yes, Miss Milani, we noticed that, too. Have you seen any of them?"

"That would be so neat! I've never met anyone with eyes like mine before. They're like Persians'. Mom has eyes a little like this, but not blue and less," she lifted a hand and made a funny little motion to suggest the unusual tilt her eyes had.

"Miss Milani, can you focus please? This is important." Suit Number Two tapped the paper again. "These people are dangerous, and we want to help you stay safe. Have you seen any of them?"

"What kind of dangerous? Do they have guns or bombs or something?"

"They may have one or more guns, yes. More importantly, they may come here to try to harm you specifically." Suit Number One fished a business card out of his pocket. He paused in the act of handing it to her when someone inside sneezed. It sounded too high pitched to be Will. "You have company, Miss Milani?"

"No, I'm a waitress." Her answer came from so far out of nowhere that Bobby couldn't help but wonder if she was kinda dumb or kinda brilliant. It made no sense in such a remarkable way that he thought a person would have to stand and stare and forget about everything else until they understood.

"What?" Suit Number One, apparently not as entranced or impressed as Bobby, gave the hand signal.

Bobby did what he could: the little dragon in the hall trilled a warning. At that noise, someone yanked Jasmine out of the door and slammed it shut. The deadbolt locked while the SWAT guys moved. Bobby sent the swarm back into the window. If they needed him in there, he'd be in there.

The SWAT guys looked around for the source of the noise. One aimed his weapon at the doorknob and fired three times. Two shoved the door open. Bobby recognized the signs of Ai's passage in the form of men shoved off balance for no apparent reason. The door slammed shut.

As the lead SWAT guy kicked the door in again and pointed his rifle straight at Jayce's chest, Suit Number One staggered back into the shut elevator doors. His phone disappeared from his hand. Suit Number Two dropped to the floor with a grunt of surprise for no apparent reason.

"I wouldn't," Jayce said to the SWAT guy, his flesh silvery. He grabbed the barrel of the gun and squeezed it, crunching the metal with an unpleasant creaking, shrieking noise. The SWAT guy pulled the weapon back and tried to kick Jayce in the privates, but he hit solid metal. Jayce grabbed his foot and shoved him back. "We don't want any Girl Scout cookies, gentlemen," he told the hallway. "No means no."

The swarm flowed around Jayce and into the hallway. It must have looked to the SWAT guys like the tiny dragons came from him, somehow. He split the swarm into two halves and surrounded the Suit Twins, focused on their heads and hands so they couldn't accomplish anything at all. They swiped at the dragons , and it was so ineffectual Bobby wanted to laugh. The dragons made little chirps and trills and growls of amusement in his stead, filling the hallway with a cacophony.

Stepping into the hallway, Jayce paused while a SWAT guy punched him. The guy pulled his hand back with a yelp of pain, while Jayce failed to react. Another fired his weapon. The bullet bounced right off Jayce, though it put a hole in his shirt. With that, the SWAT guys backed away, in both directions.

The one on the floor put up a hand to ward him off and scrabbled backwards. "Stand down," he shouted at the rest, "stand down and back off!"

"Gentlemen." Jayce held his fists ready, yet made no move to charge anyone down and use them. "You're doing the bidding of men who want to perform experiments on us. We have no quarrel with you, or even with them, we just aren't excited to be treated like lab animals. All of us are patriots; we love this country and have no intention of doing anything against it. So long as it decides not to do anything against us."

Figuring the fight had, more or less, ended, Bobby let the two suits go and re-formed there in the hallway. Much to his surprise, he still wore the boxer shorts this time. Maybe he just needed time with clothes he felt comfortable in to have them defy physics with him. The boxers fit well enough and had been with him for several hours now.

Movement to the side made him look to see Suit Number One backing away. Suit Number Two, sitting on the floor next to him, jammed something into his thigh. His fingers worked frantically to push the plunger of a needle down.

Jayce stepped in and shoved the suit away while Bobby stumbled back. His fingers managed to grip the needle and pulled it out, then tripped and fell to the floor. He met Jayce's eyes and they shared a look, a nod, then he blinked a lot. One blink, he heard the sounds of fighting. Two blinks, Jayce growled angrily. Three blinks, he felt a strong breeze. Four blinks, Ai patted his cheek.

"C'mon, Bobby, we have to go. It's a mess and we have to get out of here. Jasmine and Will are packing their stuff up, Jayce and Alice are helping."

"Whu'uppen?" Everything felt heavy, and his mouth refused to do what he wanted.

"One of them stuck you with something. In your leg. It knocked you out, but not completely." She held up the syringe, half-full of clear liquid. "Jayce smashed that guy's head into the wall, the cops tried to take him down, they retreated. I saw them outside, they're hanging around by their van. Will and Jasmine have a car, were going to try to get to it with their stuff. Jayce and I will go out first and clear the way, to keep them from stopping any of us."

"Alice?" Bobby remembered not seeing her in the apartment when stuff started going down. He caught a whiff of an unpleasant, pungent smell, one his brain couldn't put its finger on.

Ai sighed. "She's curled up in a ball in the bathtub. We're kind of ignoring her until we're ready to go."

Bobby put his hands out and tried to lever himself up and get to his feet. "Wha's in tha' thing?" He sounded drunk. He felt drunk, too, the kind that came from five too many beers.

"No idea." Ai shrugged. "I'm an accountant, Jim, not a chemist."

Bobby frowned. "Who's Jim?"

"Forget it. It's a joke. Maybe some water will help." She happened to have a glass and handed it to him.

He chugged down half the glass. His vision continued to clear along with his head. The smell got stronger, too. To the side, he noticed a a small pile and associated spray of vomit next to the body with its skull smashed and brains splattered across the wall and floor. Oh, that must be the smell.

"Who threw up?"

Ai coughed as she draped his arm over her shoulders and helped him stand. Between her and the wall, it worked. "That was me. I saw him do it." She averted her eyes from the whole sight and helped him lurch into the apartment.

"Damn." Just inside the door, he realized he still had two scouts out. He stopped and leaned against the wall, waving Ai off. Each scout had a different view of the parking lot. Picking one, he focused on it. "They're talking to someone on their radios."

Ai nodded. "Jayce thinks if we go charge them now, they'll bring a nuke next time."

"Jayce also thinks we're about ready to go, except for Alice." The man himself stood there with a large bag full of stuff slung over his shoulder. "They're leaving a lot behind. Jasmine will go squirrel in the car to save space, and we're hoping you can handle following along as your swarm. Nice job keeping the boxers, by the way."

"Thanks." Bobby grinned, now tired more than woozy. "I'll see if'n I can talk Alice out. And yeah, I can go as dragons."

"I'm going to try running alongside the car," Ai said.

"Good deal." Bobby lurched toward the bathroom. Ai left him there with an encouraging smile. "Alice," he called in, "we gotta go or they're gonna take us down." When she gave no answer, he opened the door and leaned against the frame. He saw here curled up in the bathtub, as promised. "Whatever they stuck me with, it's a doozy, and they'll be able to stick you with it, too."

"I can't do this," Alice whispered. Her voice cracked in the middle.

"You got two choices, Alice, you know that, you just don't wanna deal with it. Choice one, you let 'em take you. They do whatever they want and you're just a guinea pig. Choice two, you run for it. We're running, you can come with us if you want. At some point, we'll stop running and make a stand and take what rights we're owed, but we gotta find someplace and the rest of our kind and do it all together.

"One of us on our own is gonna get took. Five of us working together can run. Thirty-five of us, shoot, we can do a lot more'n that. But we gotta get up and get going now if we're gonna have that chance. Your choice." He waited, feeling himself recovering with every second that passed. Thank goodness he didn't get the full dose. "I know you're shook up. I ain't gonna let you curl up and die on account of it. We're in this together, and don't nobody hate you or nothing."

She sniffled while he stood there, waiting. He checked on the two scouts, making sure they had no lingering effects from the drug. It seemed they hadn't been affected at all, which he figured could only be a good thing.

Jayce tapped him on the shoulder and gave him a significant look, then nodded towards the front door. Bobby nodded and held up two fingers. In return, Jayce shook his head and held up one. They needed to get going now, not ten minutes from now. He nodded again.

"Look, Alice, there's guys out there that'll be happy to shoot you. They'll either kill you or knock you down, just 'cause there's so many of 'em. If they just take you down, then you'll wind up hogtied and poked and prodded again. Guaranteed. The rest of us, we're not looking for that. We're gonna go ahead and resist. In order to do that, we gotta leave now, before anyone else comes to back these guys up."

Standing away from the wall, Bobby found he still needed it to brace himself. He took three steps before Alice croaked out, "Wait. I don't want to die."

"Then get your ass up, hon, 'cause we're getting while the getting's not too bad." He put one foot in front of the other, heaving with the effort.

Behind him, she scrabbled out of the tub and hurried to slip under his arm. "Lean on me," she murmured. "I'll get you out."

"Thanks." He considered saying something like 'welcome back'. Walking took too much energy to waste it on something stupid like that, especially when she had to still be raw on the inside. In her position, being the one ripped up about all this, he felt confident it'd piss him off something fierce.

Out in the hallway, they had two full size suitcases and a carry-on stacked up and ready to go, all with wheels. That would make getting them to the car doable, given how that had to happen. "If nobody minds, I'm gonna give my dragons as much time to recover as I can before I make 'em work. I got two outside, watching for us, they seem fine, but I ain't keen on finding out the hard way that dragons on this fly drunk."

Still silver and carrying the one bag again, Jayce nodded. "Works for me. The plan is I go out first and make it clear we're not surrendering. If any fighting needs to happen, Ai will assist. When we're clear enough, everyone else goes for the car, it gets loaded up, then we drive away. Ai and Bobby stay there as deterrents until the car is on the road."

"Sounds good." Bobby nodded his approval. He noticed Alice kept quiet, not asking about her role in all this. This time, they'd all let it slide. Next time, he had no intention of cutting her any slack. He suspected the others felt the same. At least she took the small carry-on to drag it behind her. Will and Jasmine wheeling the other two along.

No one stood guard at the elevator on the ground floor, and Jayce left his bag outside the front door. Will picked it up and handed the other suitcase off to Alice, who left Bobby to sit for another minute or two. He took a deep breath. This moment seemed important to him. They'd tangled with cops for the first time, and Jayce killed someone in a fight. After this, anyone they tangled with would leave the kid gloves at home.

He focused on a scout dragon, watching while Jayce walked up to the group of SWAT guys and smiled at them. "We're leaving. You can assault the apartment as much as you want, but none of us are staying behind there, so you won't find much. You can try to stop us, even follow us if you want, but I think you already know we're not going without a fight, and we will kill to stop you from taking us."

The lead SWAT guy, the one whose weapon got crunched, nodded. "Message received, loud and clear. Westbrook, right?" At Jayce's nod, the man continued. "We have orders to bring you and the others in and are authorized to use lethal force if necessary to protect ourselves. Just so you understand the position we're in."

"Officer, nothing would make me happier than knowing you get to go home to your family tonight, something none of us will be able to do. With that in mind, I strongly recommend you don't follow us and suggest to your superiors that we're not worth the effort. I'm not completely certain what I can withstand or not, but I'm willing to bet you'll need a nuke to take me down, and even that might not work. The others are going to be pretty hard to take down, too. Something to keep in mind."

"Sir, I don't think we have much choice here."

Jayce nodded. "You should listen to him."

The leader thought about it for a second or two, then nodded. "We won't follow you, but I can't guarantee anything else."

"Just pass on the warning." Jayce turned and went for the car.

Bobby huffed in relief. At the questioning looks around him, he said, "They're backing off, at least for now. Let's git."

CHAPTER 7

For three hours, Bobby followed the car from above. They drove on the main highways to Philadelphia, where they could find the next closest person on the list. The little car pulled into a parking lot for a small apartment complex and he dropped down to re-form. His belly growled so hard it hurt, and Jasmine bounced out of the car to shove a granola bar into his mouth. She did the same when Ai stopped in front of the car and slumped against it.

Everyone else piled out of the car and produced what remained of the food they'd been eating along the way: pita chips with hummus, vegetable curry, bananas, apples, and a salad. The pile seemed impressive, yet it had been picked over already. Bobby let Ai eat her fill, knowing he could eat nearly anything and not grouse about it. What she left barely took the edge off his hunger for now. He'd find more as soon as he knew what kind of plan they'd cooked up.

"It seems to us," Alice said, surprising him by speaking up, "that odds are good they'll ignore us now and go for trying to take the others by surprise."

Nodding, Bobby stepped into his clothes. "We need to find a base location and split up to get to as many of them as possible, as fast as possible."

"Yes, exactly," Jayce agreed. "Another of ours lives in that building." The small complex had two floors and a fence around it. "We're hoping that not only do we not have another run-in here, but that we might be able to crash here for the night. If you can keep things in a pocket on you come morning, we can split up more."

"I'm good with that. My guess is I gotta feel like it's mine for it to stay with me, or something like that. Hoping, anyway. Who's gonna do the intro?" They all looked at him. Of course he should do it, since he hadn't been around to veto the idea. He sighed and nodded, too tired to resist. "Yeah, fine, okay. Jasmine, you're harmless looking, you come with me." He scraped himself up off the asphalt and trudged that way.

Jasmine squealed with delight, like she'd been chosen first for dodgeball. The fence had been designed to keep out casual riffraff. Bobby had no trouble with it. He'd hopped fences worse than this when he was fourteen and could handle this one with a hand tied behind his back. Being ready to conk out for the night barely slowed him down.

Taking the easier route, Jasmine went squirrel and walked through the bars. "What do you want me to do?"

He sighed and hoped he'd be able to keep his clothes while swarming soon. "Stand there being yourself. Say something if it seems right. Turn into a squirrel when I ask you to."

She nodded earnestly and smiled. "I hope she's nice."

"Me too. That'll make this all tons easier." He checked numbers and found the right one on the ground floor. A pretty girl answered the door, showing them polite interest. "Hannah Parson, my name is Bobby, this is Jasmine, we'd like to talk to you for a minute, if you don't mind." Damn if he wasn't getting surrounded by gorgeous women.

Hannah had that girl-next-door kind of look. Her straight, blonde

hair had been put up in a casual ponytail and her pink tee and shorts suggested she had no plans to go out tonight. Her eyes, of course, were the
same blue as theirs, and she noticed that sameness right away. "Are you selling something?"

"Not in the way I'm pretty sure you mean." Bobby reached up and
tapped beside his eye. "The two of us and a few others, we all have the same
eyes, just like you." He pulled his now crumpled list from his pocket and
offered it to her. "All of us are on this list, and some part of the government
is hunting us down because of it. They'll come for you, sooner or later, and
we'd like to help you avoid becoming a lab rat for some kind of crazy experimentation."

She smoothed the list out and used her finger to scan it. When she
reached her own name, she tapped it. "You're nuts."

"Yes, ma'am," he agreed. "Don't mean I ain't right."

With one eyebrow quirked, she smirked at him. "So, because we
have funky eyes, the government wants us."

"Not exactly. Jasmine, this is the time." Since he'd already seen the
show, he watched Hannah to see her reaction. Her smirk disappeared and
she said something his Momma would smack him for. He picked the squirrel up gently and offered her to Hannah for a closer look. Adding to the
experience, he popped a dragon off his thumb and it buzzed around them
once, then returned to him. "Can we come in?"

"Whoa. Um, yeah, okay. Sure." Five minutes later, the entire group
sat at her table, on her couch, and on her floor. Jasmine chose to remain a
squirrel, and attacked a can of mixed nuts Hannah happened to have. Like
they'd done for Will, Bobby and Jayce told the story, now with what happened at Jasmine and Will's apartment added on.

She listened without interrupting and showed no signs of denial or rejection. "That waking up thing happened to me yesterday, actually. In the middle of the night. I woke up cold and sweaty, except I was trapped and couldn't move. One panicked freakout later, it stopped and I could move. Now..."

Lifting her hands, she flicked them out, the same way Bobby did to spritz Momma while washing the dishes. A near-transparent blue edged disk about four feet in diameter popped into existence with a brief hum to announce itself. "It's a force field. Blocks everything in both directions. So far, that's all I can do with it, but it's only been a day. I think when I woke up, I was encased in it, so I'm guessing I can shape it if I try hard enough."

"That would make an excellent shield to hide behind if we get shot at again." Jayce reached out and poked it. His finger shimmered blue, then stopped. "Nope, can't take that on. Such a shame."

Hannah shrugged. "I haven't thought much about how to use it yet." She grabbed her laptop from the nearby counter and opened it. "I'll see what I can find for properties we might be able to use."

Bobby raised his eyebrows. "You don't want to think about pulling up your stakes and trucking off with us?"

"After everything you just told me? Are you nuts? I'd have to be six kinds of stupid to stay here and wait for them to come grab me. Even if they didn't want to experiment on me, can you imagine the military getting their hands on us? No, thanks. If I'm going to serve my country, it'll be willingly, and after I figure out how to use this power, not with them constantly pushing me with what they think I might be able to do. The second I realized what I'm capable of last night, I started thinking about running for it, I just didn't have a clue where to go. Now, I have a clue."

"This was easier'n I expected it to be."

Hannah laughed. "Maybe we could make a video and send it to

everyone, so they all know they aren't crazy as soon as possible and can make their own way to wherever this base winds up being."

Will said, "That's not a bad idea, actually. Getting it into the right hands and not the wrong ones is the biggest problem."

"Not in the wrong ones is the problem," Jayce agreed. "We could just put it up on the internet and get it to everybody it needs to, but our would-be captors will see it, then."

"I was joking, but if you all want to try to figure something out, I have a laptop." Hannah gestured to the machine in question for emphasis. "First things first, though. You can all crash wherever, but my bed is my bed. It's not really big enough for anyone else, either. Besides that, where do you want to put this base?"

"Someplace in the middle of nowhere," Alice said.

Ai added, "Not too far from a city, though. We'll still need to get supplies and stuff."

"Middle of the country somewhere," Bobby suggested. "It'll need to be big, too. Lotsa space so we got a buffer 'tween us and the neighbors. Ten acres ought to be enough, I expect."

"At least ten acres, within...we'll say 75 miles of a big city, in the middle of the country. Okay, I can work with that."

Bobby shifted so he could see the screen. "What is it you do for a living?"

She smirked. "I'm a secretary for a real estate agency."

Grinning, he huffed a quiet laugh and noticed everyone staking out their spot for sleeping. Will and Jasmine settled together on the couch, Jayce grabbed some floorspace off to the side, Ai commandeered the easy chair, Alice curled up on the other end of the couch. Bobby figured he'd wind up doing what Jayce did, and probably soon.

Hannah paused in her churning through web pages and leaned over. "If you promise not to do anything," she muttered, "you can share the bed with me. One hand starts wandering, though, and I'll shove you on the floor. I would have offered to one of the others, but you seem like the nicest of the lot, aside from Jasmine, and she's doing fine."

"Thanks, that's nice of ya. Don't want to make you uncomfortable, though. I'll just take a pillow."

With a shrug, she returned to flipping through property listings. "It's really okay if you change your mind."

"Good to know." He pointed to the picture of a derelict farmhouse she clicked onto. "What's that one?"

She peered at the screen and scrolled down the page. "Thirty miles from Fort Morgan, Colorado. Fifty acres, they want half a million for it."

"Dollars?" He goggled at the picture.

"Yeah." She chuckled. "That's a lot of land, and it's not so far out of the way as to be the total boonies. Let me see if I can find out who 'they' is."

Bobby kept watching the screen as she clicked and typed and typed and clicked. Within fifteen minutes, his head nodded and eyes drooped enough that he noticed. He saw Jayce lying on the floor probably already asleep. It looked inviting, compared to the chair he sat in. His eyes drifted to Hannah and her offer popped back into his head. Thanks to her generosity, he could sleep on a soft bed tonight. It sounded like heaven after the past week. "I'm gonna take you up on that offer after all," he told Hannah softly.

She nodded and checked the time. "I should get some sleep myself." After shutting her laptop and setting it aside, she led him to her bedroom. Five steps in, she paused and looked him over. Her hands moved toward her hips, then shifted in mid-motion and she crossed her arms.

The last time Bobby felt this awkward in a girl's bedroom, the night had gone less than stellar. She never spoke to him again. He had no intention of doing anything like that here. As much as he found her attractive overall, he needed sleep too much to think about her as anything other than a nice host. To put an end to the uncomfortable moment, he turned his back on her and looked down at himself to decide how much to strip down. The more he kept on overnight, the more likely he thought the dragons would let him keep it.

After half a minute of deliberation, he pulled off the boots and trenchcoat. He could sleep in jeans and a shirt, and this would be the last time she slept in this bed anyway. It occurred to him that he might have a harder time getting his clothes washed if the swarm rejected something afterwards. That problem could wait, though. He sat on the edge of the bed and sighed with pleasure at the softness.

A beautiful woman climbed into the bed next to him, and he had to resist the urge to touch her. It had nothing to do with sex and everything to do with wanting to check this all was real. The creepy doctors could be playing tricks on his brain, or he could have passed out on the side of the road, or something else. How touching her would prove that, he couldn't say, but it made sense in his head. The urge to start a conversation bubbled up next. To kill it, he shut his eyes and thought about dragons. It surprised him when Hannah shook his shoulder a few seconds later.

"Breakfast is ready. I didn't have the heart to wake you sooner. You seemed really peaceful."

Bobby rubbed his face. "I'm thankful for that. I did plenty yesterday, and today promises to be more."

"Thanks for not grabbing my ass." She left the room before he opened his eyes again.

He sat up and took a deep breath of cinnamon and coffee. For that reason alone, today started better than yesterday. His belly growled and his bladder pressed, which helped him to get up and get moving. A few minutes later, he grabbed a bowl of oatmeal and some fruit. The chair he'd used last night remained empty, and he took it.

"So," Hannah said as she turned her screen to show him, "this property is owed by the state of Colorado. I didn't find the whole story, but the main gist is that it was seized by eminent domain for some energy project that failed due to budget cuts. The owners were already reimbursed and moved on, so the state just held onto it in case the project went forward.

"At some point, I expect everyone forgot about it. Now it's just sitting there, growing wild. We'll have to do a lot of work to make it livable, and there won't be any electricity, possibly no running water unless we can figure out how to set ourselves up with that. Odds are really good, though, that by the time anyone notices we're using it, we can defend it from anyone who wants to evict us."

Alice groaned. Ai shrugged. Jasmine bounced in her seat with a delighted smile. Will sighed, nodding his acquiescence. Jayce sighed. "If that's the best we can do, then it's the best we can do."

"We should split up here, I think." Bobby looked around the room. "I can fly on my own, Ai can run. Hannah, you have a vehicle?"

"I have a van, yeah."

"That's two cars. Y'all can split up however you want. Ai and I can go west and see who else we can convince. The rest of you go up and down the coast and stuff, hit as many people as you can as quick as you can. We keep in touch by phone, so everybody knows who's been visited and no one wastes any time.

"Tell folks to get money and as much of their stuff as they can, point out what the conditions'll be like. No sense in springing that on 'em. Maybe we get lucky and someone can do something about power and water. We all got pretty obvious powers, so we can all demonstrate. If'n anybody else is willing to go around and find more of us what's also got an obvious power, get 'em to do it. Otherwise, send 'em there."

No one objected.

"Will you all stay and help me pack my stuff?" Hannah asked the room. "I have a van because I've moved a bunch of times in the past few years, and it's just cheaper this way. I can go from living here to being packed in the van in a day, but it'll go a lot faster with help."

Jayce nodded. "Bobby, you and Ai go ahead. I'll help pack and go with Hannah in the van."

The group spent the next ten minutes discussing how to explain this to others. After that, Bobby, Alice, and Ai sat down and divided the names into four lists based on location while everyone else helped Hannah pack. Bobby would take a southern track to the west coast, starting in Baton Rouge. Ai would take a northern one, starting in Chicago. He'd be the one who got to go out to Honolulu, and she'd go up to Juneau. Jayce and Hannah would go north from here, Will and Jasmine would go south. Alice decided to ride with Will and Jasmine, for safety. And because Jayce failed to fully smother a frown at the idea of her coming with him.

"That's that, then," Bobby said around a mouthful of reheated Chinese takeout. Breakfast had already worn thin, and he took a few minutes to stuff his face with food Hannah would otherwise have to throw out. Dumping the empty box into the garbage, he blew out into dragons to see what stayed and what came along. Much to his surprise, nothing fell under the swarm. He had no idea how it worked and had no intention of questioning it; somehow, all his clothing and everything in his pockets got gobbled up by the dragons. He re-formed with a grin, stuffed more things into his pockets, and saluted the others before going swarm again and setting off.

Bobby knew he had about three thousand miles to cross, plus however much father for Hawaii. He'd have to sleep, and eat, and had no idea how far he could push himself before he'd have to stop or fall on his face. Faces. Wings, maybe? Whatever. Without knowing his speed for sure, he could only guess how long it would take. Besides, he had to go down and around, and stop to talk to the others on top of sleeping and eating. His best guess put him at their new base in two weeks.

He went up. The dragons had no problem with heights, so he kept going until the highway he needed to follow became a tiny ribbon cut across the land. Nothing should see him up here, other than maybe people in an airplane. The hardest part, he figured, would be turning at the right points. Without a map in hand to keep track of his path, he'd need to stop often to check his progress and stay on course. At first, he put the ocean at his back. That approach only worked for a while, then he had to rely on his limited knowledge of the region.

Flying felt different up here. Going at full speed with nothing to stop them, he reveled in the freedom. His dragons flew with their mouths open, letting the air stream out the back somehow, gears on the inside using it to propel them faster. That made no sense to him, considering the fact they ate metal. Where did it go? Resolving not to think about it, he let his mind go blank and enjoyed the simple sensations.

Eventually, he noticed the sun had climbed high enough to guess it must be around noon. He ought to be hungry. Without a belly, maybe he couldn't feel that. Despite being made from his body, the dragons had no connection to it. Suddenly concerned about starving to death by accident, he sent the swarm diving into the nearest city. In a run-down part, he flooded into an alley and re-formed himself. His stomach hurt so much from emptiness, he groaned and had to double over.

One of the things he'd pocketed at Hannah's happened to be an apple, which he grabbed and devoured. He ate everything but the seeds and stem, spitting those out onto the ground. It took the pain away without curbing his hunger, and he went looking for more. He also looked for something to tell him where he was, a map or signs. At the mouth of the alley, he found a newspaper dispenser for the Charlotte Observer next to one for the Charlotte Post.

When he looked at the map on Hannah's laptop, he hadn't noticed his route might take him right over his own house. In a direct-line path, Atlanta sat squarely on the way from here to Baton Rouge. He could stop in, tell Momma everything was okay, grab a few things, and be on his way. Maybe empty his bank account. What would the cops have told her? Would he be better off sneaking in and out and not seeing her? What if she believed this garbage about him being a terrorist?

Questions circled around his mind, refusing to answer themselves and give him peace, so he walked. Normal people passed him on the street, doing normal things with their normal friends and families. He wanted to stop someone and shake them, to tell them what their government had done to him. What would any of them do about it? Nothing. Their lives, as he could plainly see, weren't affected by any of it. If someone else asked him for help with this, he liked to think he'd try, but knew well enough he wouldn't.

He happened across a park with a group offering free meals and joined the line. When he reached the table, he encountered kids his own age spooning up pasta and salad and some kind of casserole. They all had that hippie college look, with hair in dreadlocks and weird piercings all over their faces and bold patches on their clothes. The hand drawn sign proclaimed them to be 'Food Not Bombs' in large blocky letters. A week ago, he knew he would have passed these people by with a sneer. Not because they fed the homeless; because they looked like hippie college students.

"Is that enough?" The girl with the ladle smiled at him.

He glanced back at the line and saw plenty of people still waiting. "I reckon it'll do, yeah. Thanks." His belly growled loudly enough to be heard a few feet away.

She picked up an extra plate and covered it with food. "Here, let me help you." Carrying the plate, she led him to a nearby bench and sat down beside him, offering the plate. Another person stepped in and took her place.

"This is real kind, but why're you sitting with me?" His stomach refused to be ignored, so he started feeding it.

"Most of these people," she waved at those eating and waiting, "are regulars. We come here every week and see the same faces. I've never seen you before, and you haven't had it rough for very long, I think. At the same time, you look awful, like someone killed your puppy or best friend." She patted his knee, and it managed to not seem condescending. "I thought maybe you might want to talk to someone. You know, instead of finding a bottle or a needle to climb inside of."

He sat and ate, and she sat and waited. When he emptied his plate, she traded with him. "It's kinda complicated."

"Everybody's life is kinda complicated." She shrugged. "It's okay if you don't want to talk to me. But you should really talk to someone. Soon."

"Yeah." He sighed. "I lost everything, I guess, and there was cops involved, and I'm not sure about going home to my Momma. She's gonna be real disappointed."

The girl gave him an encouraging smile. "She's your mom. Just tell her you love her and, if you think you need to, ask her to forgive you."

Bobby took a deep breath and nodded. "Yeah." He took another bite and knew he had to stop home, if only for a few minutes. "Thanks."

"No problem." She took his plates and squeezed his shoulder. "Good luck."

His belly full, he got up and found an empty spot to flow out into the swarm. After orienting himself, he headed straight for Atlanta, then got his bearings again and made for the 'burbs. The hop took him about an hour and a half, and he landed in his own backyard. The wash hung out on the clothesline, flapping gently in a light breeze. The herb and vegetable garden seemed fine. Her sunflowers would be dropping seeds soon.

Inside, a shadow passed behind the kitchen curtains. Despite the girl's suggestion, he'd been hoping she might not be here. She deserved a full explanation, and he didn't have long enough to give it to her. Hanging his head, he trudged around to the front door. At least he could avoid adding scaring the crap out of her to the list of things he'd done wrong recently. The five seconds it took her to get to the front door stretched out, making them the longest of his life.

"Bobby," Momma breathed. She wrapped her arms around him, hugging him the way she did when he fell off his bike or got beat up. "They said some really terrible things."

His eyes burned as he sagged with relief and squeezed her. "I know, Momma, I'm sorry. I didn't mean to make you worry and stuff."

She let him decide when the embrace ended, then pulled back and put a hand on his cheek. Just a few inches shorter than his own five feet, nine inches, she had to look up, but he'd never felt bigger than the woman that raised him. "There's ghosts in your eyes, boy. Come on in and sit down."

"Yes, Momma." How would he explain any of this? Should he explain any of this? Could he leave it all vague? He sat down on the couch obediently. "Nice the heat broke some," he observed. The day he left had been at least ten degrees hotter, and he could never have worn a trenchcoat in that.

"Don't you try to distract me with things like that." Brenda Mitchell planted her feet on the floor and loomed over him with her arms crossed. "Those policemen said you were hauled off by Feds, that you're a terrorist, that you killed Mr. Peterson."

He winced and hung his head again. "Yes, Momma, I know. I ain't no terrorist, though, and I didn't do nothing more than punch Mr. Peterson once." This reminded him of the time he found the cookie jar broken, knocked off the counter by a gust of wind, and went ahead and ate all the cookies.

"I told you to leave him alone, boy."

Knowing that tone, he hunched down and mumbled, "I know." He scratched the back of his neck and squirmed. "I just— Never mind. I gotta ask you something, Momma." He looked up at her and sighed at how much trouble he'd caused her. It'd only get worse from here, too. "Am I adopted?"

Frowning at him, she asked, "What's that got to do with anything?"

"Something happened out there, Momma, and it's hard to explain. I ain't normal, and I'm trying to figure out why. Did you adopt me?"

She turned away to stare at...maybe another time or place. "No." Taking a deep breath, she sat down beside him and clasped her hands together in her lap. "You were born of my body, but I don't know who your daddy rightly was. To be honest, I'm not a hundred percent sure you and me are actually related by blood."

He shifted into his thinking pose and tried not to get upset. Whenever he looked at a picture of them, he figured he took more after his real father, whoever that might be. Edward came into their lives before his fourth birthday, and he never thought to ask about the mystery man before then. After, she'd always brush off any questions with an admonition to think of Edward as Dad.

One of her hands moved to settle on his. "I was young, and I fell in with a bad crowd. I wound up on the drugs, and on the street, and all that. These nice ladies scooped a bunch of us up and asked us to participate in an experimental program. They said they'd help us clean up, get some job training, give us health insurance for five years, and help us find jobs. All we had to do was be a test subject for six months.

"In the position I was in, I said yes. The experimentation was with in-vitro fertilization. They were making test tube babies, and the process was still new then. We were told the chance of actually conceiving was small, less than one percent. While I was there, I was the only one I ever saw actually get pregnant. They said they'd help me give you up for adoption if I wanted to, but I wanted to keep the baby that grew in my body. I stayed there, with those nice people, until you were six months old, then they helped me get a job and find decent child care for you."

Stunned, Bobby let his jaw hang open and stared at her. "But..." No other words came out of his mouth.

"I got no idea if they used my eggs or not, Bobby, but it don't matter to me. You're my boy. You already knew Eddie wasn't your daddy, but he raised you good anyway, and that's what matters."

Taken on its own, the story was crazy. Compared to the last few days, though, it made sense. Sort of. Why anyone would do this, he had no idea, nor could he imagine how. Sitting there, he made a choice and held up his hand. One dragon popped off the end of his thumb. "Momma, I ain't rightly human, exactly."

Her eyes went wide as she stared at the tiny creature. She crossed herself and leaned back away from him, showing the fear he'd dearly hoped she wouldn't. "They said to watch out for anything unusual, but I thought they meant you might get sick."

Swallowing down the taste of bile from her reaction, he stood with a resigned sigh. "I'm just gonna grab a few things, then I'mma go. They didn't let me out, I escaped." Out of the corner of his eye, he saw her reach for him, but stop before her hand got close enough. He fled for his bedroom, tossing the door shut behind himself, and paced its short length a few times, trying not to let that rejection sting. There wasn't time for this. He needed to be strong and get to Baton Rouge, where he'd pick up another guy, then New Orleans, then Little Rock.

This room belonged to his old life. Souvenir beer and soda bottles wouldn't help him. Neither would his high school yearbooks or pictures from parties at work. Clothes would be helpful, he figured, and he stuffed a few pairs of socks and underwear into his coat pockets. He grabbed a keychain flashlight and all the spare cash he kept in a drawer. Since it fit, he took a spare shirt and a bandanna. The FBI still had his best shoes and jeans, and his wallet. Maybe someday, he'd take them back.

For the rest, he hoped Momma would hold onto it. All this would get sorted, eventually. He had to believe that, just as he had to believe Momma would overcome her reaction. The alternative meant a lifetime on the run, always looking over his shoulder. Shaking his head to banish those thoughts, he tried to think of anything else that might be useful in the house. The doorbell rang, making him think of the small tool set in the garage he'd used to repair it a few weeks ago. One part paranoid and one part curious, he cracked his bedroom door open to hear as Momma opened the door.

"Ma'am, we saw your son walk inside. We need to take him into custody."

He watched Momma draw herself up and point her finger at them. "You got a lot of nerve, staking out my house to watch for my boy coming back."

"Ma'am, it's important. He's wanted for—"

"I don't give a damn what he's wanted for. He's an ungrateful bastard of a boy, and he swiped money from my purse and ran out the back five minutes ago. You want to actually catch him, you best be on your way." She slammed the door in their faces and hurried to his room, holding out money. "Boy, you take this and you get going. They're gonna bust in here, probably, and it'll be best for me if you're gone by then."

Heart full of...something, he couldn't decide what, Bobby hugged his Momma and kissed her cheek. "I love you, Momma. Put my stuff in boxes, yeah? I'll be back sometime for it."

She smiled and ruffled his hair. "Get going, boy. Stay safe."

He hurried to the window and popped the screen out. Without waiting for her to leave, he dissolved into dragons and they spiraled up and out. Seeing her expression of awe, this time with no crossing herself, filled his heart, and he knew it had been the right choice to stop. Nothing like a hug from Momma to make everything seem better.

On top of everything else, she gave him money, and he knew she couldn't afford to do that. The top bill had been a twenty, so he had at least thirty-five dollars now. If he really needed something, he could get it, one way or another. And he could do his laundry. Should he chance the bank? His savings account had almost three thousand dollars he'd been saving up to someday get a car. No, he'd leave that for now. Odds were, he'd get stuck there, and that would only make things worse. 'Escaped terrorist robs bank', the headline would read. Besides, he had no ID to get the money with anyway.

He put Atlanta behind him, hopefully not for the last time, and headed west. Trying to judge how long he could go without eating had him stopping several times along the way. After doing this several times, it seemed to him that he could go two to three hours between meals. Dumpsters near eateries saved him, over and over. So many people tossed so much perfectly edible food, especially bakeries.

By the time he hit Baton Rouge, the sun had disappeared. Time to look up Andrew Roulet and give him the spiel. It took half an hour to find a gas station with a map he could open up and use to find an address. The little old lady behind the register gave him a dirty look for doing it. He ignored her and took care to fold it up properly before putting it back.

Andrew had had the not-nightmare experience, but hadn't noticed any kind of superpower. Bobby's story horrified him. The dragons fascinated him. When he stuck his hand into the cloud made by Bobby's arm, they all snapped back to Bobby, and while he stayed touching that arm, Bobby couldn't make even one dragon pop out. With that, Andrew let him eat and crash on the couch and started packing up to move himself to Colorado. In the morning, Bobby made sure he had the directions right, wished him luck, and took the short hop to New Orleans.

CHAPTER 8

"'Scuse me, ma'am, I'm looking for Raymond Beller." Bobby stood on the porch of a crappy old house, one that had managed to survive Katrina. From the outside it looked fine, at least. In a relative sort of way, anyhow. This neighborhood had a lot of houses that needed serious repairs, alongside a handful of empty lots with scattered debris. These folks had to be barely scraping along to ignore the damage for so many years.

The young black woman who answered the door when he knocked wore a gray uniform dress, marking her as likely to be a hotel maid. Her belly showed just enough of a bump that he felt confident guessing she might be pregnant. What caught his attention were her bloodshot eyes, and the way her shoulders sagged. "Are you a cop?"

Given his clothes and week's worth of beard, Bobby couldn't imagine why she might think that. Also, given the area, it surprised him she'd ask with hope instead of suspicion. "No, ma'am. I'm just—"

She reached out and touched his arm hesitantly, interrupting him. "Please stop calling me 'ma'am'. It's Belinda."

Bobby nodded, now more confused by her. "Yes, ma'am. Belinda. Maybe you noticed I got the same eyes as him?" When she nodded, he kept going. "That's why I'm looking for him. I just want to talk to him about that. Is he here, or at work, maybe? If you tell me where he works, I can go find him there instead and stop bugging you."

"I don't know where he is." She crossed her arms and leaned against the door frame. "He never came home from work last night. I called all the hospitals, the morgue, the cops, his work, friends, everywhere, but he's just gone. Nobody saw anything, nobody knows anything. Gone." She snapped her fingers. "Just like that. Left work for the day and disappeared. Cops won't look into it," she spat, "because there's no sign of foul play and he hasn't been missing for twenty-four hours yet."

Bobby paled. Two days ago, they tried to grab Jasmine and Jayce warned them. Yesterday, someone took Raymond Beller. It couldn't be a coincidence. Had he warned Andrew in time? He had to get out of here and get to the next name. Now. They started a race to collect people at Jasmine's apartment without knowing it. "I'm sorry."

Belinda seemed nice. He didn't want to know anything else about her. Didn't want to know about that baby, didn't want to know if she was his wife or just his girlfriend, or even his sister staying with him. Didn't want to know how she'd manage to make ends meet without him around. Didn't want to know. He stumbled a few steps back, watching her frown at him. "I'm sorry," he said again, not sure what he was sorry for.

He took off running without a backward glance and didn't stop until he got far enough away to be sure she wouldn't follow or find him by cruising the neighborhood. He pulled out his phone and called Hannah. She needed to know.

"Hi Bobby," Hannah said, cheerful and bright. "What's up?"

"Raymond Beller, in New Orleans? He's missing."

"Missing? Missing how?"

"Just gone. Belinda— Um, his girl, she said he just up and vanished like smoke in the wind. Yesterday, after work." He doubled over, panic keeping him from being able to catch his breath.

"Okay, Bobby. Calm down. It's not your fault. Nobody saw any-thing?"

He shook his head, then remembered she couldn't see that. "No. She called around to everywhere she could think of already. I ain't gonna find nothing by doing it all over again."

"No, you won't. Just get yourself to the next one, Bobby. He's gone. We'll find him, but we need a clue to where he is first."

He glanced around, expecting to see a suit tailing him. Instead, he saw few locals ignoring him. "Okay. Right. Just gotta focus."

"I'm on my way to Colorado right now, okay? Sam and I—she's from New York city—split from Jayce, he's going up to Boston on the train. Have you sent anyone to the base yet?"

"Yeah. One so far. He left from Baton Rouge maybe an hour or two ago." He should have come to New Orleans first. Except Raymond went missing early yesterday, and he couldn't have gotten here that fast, not even by skipping Momma's house. Damn.

"Okay, we'll do our best to make good speed, then. Watch your back, Bobby. If you find someone who can keep up with you, consider teaming up so you're not alone."

"Yeah. That's a good idea. Thanks."

"I'll see you soon, Bobby."

"Yeah." He hung up and dropped the phone back into his pocket. Panic helped nothing. Taking a deep breath, he tried to think about it more. The suits had been able to grab a SWAT team, so they must have plenty of resources. They reached New Orleans faster than he did, so they probably had access to at least one plane. Did the guys running the lab send out hit teams as soon as they noticed the four of them went missing? Man, would he love to get one of them strapped to a board naked. See how they like it.

Shaking off thoughts that led to dark places, he took another deep breath and burst into the swarm. Time to get himself to Little Rock. Two of them lived there, Elizabeth Caulfield and Daniel Jarvis, at the same address.

The flight took him less than four hours, and he had plenty of time to force himself to calm down. Nothing could make the dragons fly faster, or make the suits go slower. He had to get there and deal with whatever he found. If he got lucky, he'd reach everyone on his list in the nick of time.

Elizabeth and Daniel's house sat outside the city limits of Little Rock, by itself in a semi-rural area. Tucked in behind a bunch of trees, it reminded him of the kind of place teenagers went to in a horror movie. The walls needed paint, the roof had partially collapsed in one corner, the roof needed shingles here and there, a few shutters hung from just one point instead of two, some windows had been boarded up, and the porch didn't look anything like safe to walk on. A cracked tire hung on a frayed rope from a big oak tree and a rusty old car without tires sat on blocks off to one side. Momma would tsk at the state of the yard especially, with weeds and grass higher than his waist in some places. He'd never seen dandelions that big before.

Bobby landed and re-formed next to the mailbox on the road, stuffing his hands into the pockets of his trenchcoat. Movies, he sternly reminded himself, had nothing to do with real life. People who lived in places like this usually suffered from poverty more than insanity. At least it had no dead rodents hanging from the roof or trees. If he saw something like, he thought he might turn around and walk away. Duty or no, he hadn't igned up to collect crazy people.

Taking a deep breath, one that brought him the scent of dry earth and old leaves and damp wood, he forced himself to the front door. At the porch, he tested each step before putting his weight on it. It had no button for a bell, so he gulped and knocked. His prayers hadn't been paid much attention recently, but he offered one up to not encounter a serial killer here.

Daniel's appearance reminded Bobby a lot of himself. They had the same hair, eyes, facial structure, coloring, height, and build. Looking at him felt a lot like looking in a mirror, except Daniel seemed to have tiny differences that made him more rough and rugged, in the way he suspected a lot of women preferred. "Who're you?" From his raised brow, Bobby figured Daniel noticed that, too.

"Name's Bobby. You must be Daniel Jarvis. Is Elizabeth Caulfield here, too?"

Daniel's eyes narrowed and his brow furrowed. "Dan. What's it to ya?" His Southern accent even sounded similar to Bobby's.

"Dan, then. I'm here because we all got the same eyes, and stuff's happening on account of that. I'd really rather just tell you both the whole story at once, if that's alright. You're both in danger, though, you ought to know that right off."

"Danger? From who?" Dan peered around at the bushes and trees, maybe thinking he'd spot ninjas lurking there.

Bobby shrugged. "I ain't rightly sure who they are. Can I come in and explain to you and Lizzie? What I do know, I'll tell you everything."

Dan looked Bobby over critically, then he shrugged and stood aside to let him in. "Sure, whatever. Lizzie! C'mere," he hollered into the house.

The girl that stepped into view through a nearby doorway had fat red curls dripping off her head to frame a face with high cheekbones and a delicate, pert nose. Her faded red tank top left her fire engine red bra straps visible, and her tight little denim miniskirt made her legs seem a mile long. "Yeah? Who's this?"

Bobby stared as she draped an arm over Dan's shoulders and rubbed against his side. He'd seen girls like this before. In porn. On her, the exotic eyes enhanced everything and his gaze wound up falling from her full, pouting lips down to her chest. She stood with it thrust out, on display. If he wanted to, he could look right down her shirt.

Dan said something, but he missed it. Lizzie smiled at him, then Dan shoved her away and smacked her on the ass. "Sorry, she's just messing with you."

"What? Oh. Right. Sorry," Bobby coughed and looked down, "I just never seen a girl like that in real life before."

He laughed. "She's a wildfire in the sack, too."

Lizzie slipped around behind Dan and stuck her hands in the front pockets of his jeans. Peeking out over his shoulder, she let her eyes travel down Bobby's body, taking him in the same way he'd done to her. "What did you come to tell us?"

Her gaze unnerved him. Although it seemed like Dan controlled her, he got the feeling she actually ran the show between them. More than that, though, she watched him like a predator: a cat hiding in plain sight to catch a mouse. To heck with that; he wasn't a mouse, he was a swarm of dragons. He straightened and pulled the list out of his pocket.

They listened while he told them the whole story, from getting arrested to finding out Raymond was missing. "So, here's my proof." He let his whole left hand dissolve into dragons that buzzed the room before re-forming into him again.

"Lizzie can start fires with her mind," Dan said with a shrug. He made it sound as noteworthy as a talent for playing the piano. "I can't do anything special yet. Haven't had that waking up sweaty thing yet. Sounds like I will at some point."

She could start fires with her mind. Bobby tried not to think too hard about that. Girl like that could probably already get most anything she wanted by posing and pouting. Now she could blow stuff up, too. "We're all going to this place in Colorado, to meet up and make decisions and defend ourselves together."

"I don't wanna be part of a freak brigade," Lizzie sneered. She slipped her hand out of Dan's pocket and stuck it down the front of his jeans. "Dan, you promised we'd go do something fun soon."

Dan smirked and kept his eyes on Bobby, maybe used to her grabbing him while he tried to do something else. Crazy thing to get used to. "This could be something fun. You like road trips, baby."

Bobby looked away and coughed, hoping to cover how disturbing he found the pair of them. "If'n you stay here, uh, odds are good they'll come for you. Maybe, um, maybe you can defend yourselves and all, but it'd be better for all of us if they don't get a good idea what we all can do for as long as possible." He rubbed his forehead, unable to stop himself from imagining Lizzie doing all sorts of other things, to him and Dan both, and bothered by that. "It's possible we're all half brothers and sisters, so, this is, well, it's about family."

"We can just go see what it's like, baby, and if it sucks, we can leave."

"Is that true?" Lizzie stared at him, her eyes piercing and sharp. "If we don't like it, we can leave?"

Bobby nodded. "Not like we could stop you. We ain't the government or nothing." He pulled out the page with his copy of the directions to the place and offered it to them. "This is where everybody is. You wanna make a copy of that, you can decide for yourselves while I go on to the next person on the list. Don't let nobody know where you're going or lose the directions or nothing."

Dan took the page and read it over. "You got better handwriting than me, baby, go take care of that."

"Sure." Lizzie snatched the paper with a mild scowl and swished her butt out of the room.

Bobby watched her go, unable to tear his eyes away. When she turned a corner, he scratched the back of his neck and found Dan smirking at him with his arms crossed over his chest. "You think you'll go?"

"Yeah." Dan nodded. "She's just being obnoxious 'cause I told her not to play with you. Once we're on the road, she'll get into it."

Whatever 'play' meant to Lizzie, Bobby thought he ought to be grateful to Dan for putting him off limits for it. "Only name I can really give you for sure is Hannah. She seems to be good at the organization thing, so she's the one that's acting kinda in charge, but she ain't really in charge, so don't give her no crap for that."

"Cool." Dan nodded again and shook hands with Bobby. "It's cool you're out doing this. Coulda just run for the hills yourself and left the rest of us to swing in the wind. Says something about a man when he risks his own butt for total strangers."

"'Specially when it's a nice, tight butt," Lizzie said, returning already. She walked into Bobby's personal space and thumped his paper onto his chest. She got so close he could smell peppermint on her breath. "You look just like Dan, you know." Her tongue flicked out. "I could mistake you for him easy." She squealed and danced away backwards.

Dan's arm pulled her back by the waistband of her skirt until she thumped into his chest. "No, baby, you couldn't." He kissed her neck and wrapped an arm around her waist, holding her close and tight.

"I'll get going, then. See you there, I guess." He backed out, pulling the door shut to the sound of Lizzie moaning. As he hurried to the road, a repressed shiver worked its way across his entire body. People didn't normally creep him out, but those two did. Jasmine was nice, he reminded himself, and so was Hannah. With thirty-five of them, some being freakish shouldn't come as a big shock.

Feeling dirty, he rubbed his hands on his jeans, then broke apart into the swarm. If he ever wound up in the position where a hot girl sticking her hand down his pants happened so often he ignored it to get other things done, he wanted to be put out of his misery. Dallas, he had to get to Dallas. Pulling out his list, he checked the name: Stephen Cant.

He sent up a prayer for Stephen to be less creepy.

CHAPTER 9

Three hours later, Bobby walked up to the front door of a grand two story house in a wealthy neighborhood. Stephen's house, like many of the others in this Dallas development, had a wraparound porch and a manicured yard with a patch of green grass. His stomach rumbled, threatening to embarrass him in front of whatever society person happened to answer the door. He judged getting to Stephen as more important than eating. Besides, he might be able to wrangle a meal out of the guy.

An older lady answered the door. Her clothes, a light tan pantsuit with a light blue blouse and pearls, marked her as someone who probably had an important job, like a lawyer or a doctor or an executive. "Can I..." Her light green eyes zeroed in on his own and she sucked in a breath. "Stephen isn't here."

"Okay." Bobby stared at her, blinking.

She put a hand on her pearls and frowned. "Are you his brother?"

He figured that for a weird question to come from the woman he presumed to be Stephen's momma. Stifling a shrug, he ran with it anyway. "Yes, ma'am. Know where I can find him?"

"I'm sorry," she breathed, "so sorry. I didn't know he had one."

Still lost, Bobby raised his brow. "You didn't know he had a place to stay?"

She shook her head sadly. "No, a brother. I would have adopted you both if I'd known."

This conversation suddenly made much more sense. "Oh. It's alright, ma'am. I just really need to find him and I don't know where he's gone. It's kinda urgent-like."

"Of course." She gave him an address. "It's our church, I've been going there for a very long time. He's always felt at home there. Pastor Chris can help you."

"Thank you, ma'am." Bobby turned away.

"Are you hungry?"

Her voice made him stop and look back to see a grimace of guilt on her face. She wrung her hands together and seemed to desperate to atone for some sin. Although he really did want something to eat, he figured finding Stephen rated higher than his stomach. "Not really, no, but thanks for the offer. Is there something I can deliver to Stephen for you, though?"

Her lip quivered and her eyes crinkled, giving him the impression she might burst into tears at any moment. She nodded and disappeared, then stepped back into sight with a brown leather purse. He walked back to the door while she rooted through it. The wad of cash she pressed into his hand felt thicker than he'd ever had before. "Take it, use it for both of you."

Only a few days ago he had nothing at all, not even clothes. Looking down at the twenty folded over more bills, he had an urge to give it back. He'd lied to her, at least a tiny bit, and inadvertently given her guilt. This money felt like it came from a dishonest place. When he stole, he preferred to do it because he had no other choice. She owed him nothing, no matter what she thought.

On the other hand, Stephen didn't deserve to be deprived of money his momma wanted him to have for lack of being here to take it. He tucked it into his pocket. "I swear on my Daddy's grave he'll get this."

She covered her mouth and he noticed her eyes watering. "Tell him I love him, very much, all of us do, and we miss him. We all hope he finds what he's looking for. A phone call every so often to let us know he's okay would be— We'd all really like that."

"Yes, ma'am," he ducked his head. "I'll see about getting him to call. I'm sure he's fine." He really ought to see about calling Momma himself once in a while. It had to be hard on her, not knowing. On the other hand, some form of cops had to be tapping her phone, maybe even those suits.

She nodded and kept watching him with that unhappy, pitying smile. Not wanting to see that anymore, or to take anything else from her, he turned and walked away. From the sidewalk, he tossed a wave over his shoulder, then hurried up the street. Her behavior puzzled him, in part. What happened to Stephen that she adopted him and felt that much guilt for missing his brother?

Around the corner, he ducked behind a tree and broke apart into dragons. He re-formed half an hour later, down the street from the Second Baptist Church of Dallas. The neighborhood contrasted sharply with the one where Stephen's momma lived. It had tiny little houses with tiny little yards, many in need of paint and sweeping and minor repairs. None of them had grass. He wondered how the Cants went from this church to that neighborhood, and why they never switched churches to a closer one.

The church, a plain brick building with no ornate decoration, fit in with its neighbors. The landscaping had weeds and needed mowing, the lone fir tree had dead branches in need of pruning. Black plastic covered one window. Without the sign and a couple of crosses here and there, he might have mistaken it for a struggling business of some kind, or a small, underfunded school.

Finding the front door unlocked, he walked into a single large room with stacks of folded chairs leaning against one wall with a microphone stand, folding tables leaning against the other wall, and an empty, footed bathtub at one end. It had three other doors, two marked as restrooms and the third with a piece of paper taped to it that read 'Kitchen'. At the end opposite the bathtub, an area had been blocked off with half-height bookshelves. He saw small bean bag chairs, battered books, a worn shag throw rug over the industrial pseudo-marble floor, and bins in cubbyholes with toys poking out.

On his hands and knees with yellow rubber gloves, a sponge, a spray bottle, and a roll of paper towels, a man in jeans and a white button-down shirt worked hard to clean something off that piece of carpet. He looked up at the soft chime made by the door opening. Friendly green eyes under shaggy brown hair smiled at Bobby in welcome. Sitting up on his feet and swiping the back of his arm across his forehead, he said, "Hi there, I'm Pastor Chris, can I help you?"

"I surely hope so, Pastor." Bobby stuck his hands in his trenchcoat pockets and echoed the Pastor's smile. "I'm looking for Stephen Cant. His momma said he might be here, or you might know where to find him."

"Ah." His smile faded. "Why are you looking for him?"

Bobby shrugged, wondering if that tension in his voice meant the Pastor had him hidden in the basement for some reason. "It's complicated. I gotta talk to him about stuff."

Pastor Chris scanned Bobby from head to toe and nodded. "Life is full of complicated stuff."

"I s'pose that's true."

"If you'd like to talk about it, I can listen."

"Not really." Bobby reached up and scratched his beard. "I dunno. I just—" Unwilling to keep looking at Chris while he tried to ignore the things tumbling around in his head, he swept his eyes around the room, hoping to find a distraction. The makeshift altar grabbed his attention. "How come you don't got no crucifix inside here?"

Pastor Chris smirked. "Because, fool that I am, I spend the church money on other things, like bills and an aide for the day care I run here."

"You don't got no church ladies to run a bake sale for it, huh?"

"I do," Chris chuckled, "but there are always more important things than decorations that need the money. I haven't even been able to replace the window yet." He gestured to the black plastic as he pulled his rubber gloves off and stood up. "If you're willing to finish cleaning this up for me, I'd be happy to share my dinner table with you."

Bobby had no interest in taking anything away from this tiny, cash-strapped church. He could graze elsewhere. "How about if I do that, you tell me where to find Stephen?"

Chris nodded, disappointment showing. "Alright, I'll tell you what I can. Would you like anything at all, though?"

"Nah, save it for yourself. 'Sides, I ain't as raggedy as I look."

"That's comforting." Chris grinned and passed Bobby the rubber gloves. As he did, his eyes flicked to Bobby's. "What's your name?"

"Bobby. I'm Stephen's half-brother." It seemed safest to stick to the same maybe-kinda-lie he told Stephen's momma. He pulled the gloves on and knelt down to see what he'd gotten himself into.

"It's grape juice. I'm mostly worried about ants." Chris stood there and watched Bobby get to work. "I didn't know he had a half-brother."

"Yeah, he don't, neither. I didn't 'til a few days ago."

"So you came to meet him?"

"Yeah, that's part of it."

"Hm." Chris paced away, leaving him to the work. It took no skill, only elbow grease. Several minutes later, he decided he'd done as much as a body could do. Chris came back out of the kitchen with a tray that he set on the floor while pulling out a table and two chairs. "Looks like my timing is good."

"If you get ants, it ain't gonna be because of this." He pulled off the gloves and picked up all the cleaning supplies. Eyeing the second chair and the plate set in front of it, he sighed. "You don't gotta feed me."

"At least have a glass of water. You can take something with you if you want. Set that stuff by the kitchen door and come sit with me. Eating alone gets tiresome after a while."

"This is why you can't afford nothing," Bobby shook his head and gave him half a smirk. He could smell the lasagna and it made his stomach growl. Once that gave him away, he sat down and picked up a fork. Along with a large slab of lasagna, he'd been given a biscuit and a small salad with two fat cherry tomatoes. No sense letting this go to waste.

"Charity is something we can all afford to give, no matter how much we have." For a few minutes, neither spoke, both busy with the food. Chris watched him eat with a pleased smile. "There's a bathroom here if you want to wash up when you're done. It has a shower."

Bobby had to cough to keep himself from choking at how that struck him. "Do I really look that rough around the edges?"

Chris smiled kindly. "A little, yes. You mostly look like you've had a rough break recently."

"I ain't really that bad off, not really. I mean, it ain't no picnic, but I ain't starving or nothing."

"What happened?"

He wanted to help. Bobby had somehow managed to stumble across another of what he'd always thought to be a rare breed: people who see others in need and try to do something about it. This Pastor had nothing in common with the one he'd grown up listening to. Pastor Adam talked about how God punished fags with diseases. When a girl he knew got knocked up, Pastor Adam spent a sermon pointing at her and calling her a slut in league with the Devil. He said she got pregnant as a punishment from The Lord.

That man presided over holiday charity events, but the few times Bobby volunteered to help, the Pastor never showed up and the church ladies took care of everything. Thinking back on everything Pastor Adam did and said, he couldn't recall any personal acts of charity the man did. Everyone sinned and needed to repent by giving him money. His church had stained glass windows and mahogany pews.

Bobby sighed and stared at his water glass. He'd already gotten tired of explaining about the superpowers, and still had to do it several times. Still, other things weighed on his mind, and a priest could maybe help with that. This particular pastor seemed suited to it, anyway. "Do you think stuff happens the way it's gonna happen, and nothing we can do about it, or are we really running our own lives for ourselves?"

Pastor Chris's brow popped up in surprise. He took half a minute to finish the bite in his mouth, chewing slowly enough that Bobby suspected him to be stalling for time while he decided how to answer. "God did give us free will, making it a struggle to do the right thing when we could do what's easy or convenient instead. That's why faith is important, it shows us the right path."

Poking his fork into the lasagna, Bobby frowned. "What if there's more'n one right path, or all of 'em suck? What if what I'm choosing is 'tween saving this guy or that guy? How does a body pick at times like that?"

"The road to Heaven isn't achieved through perfection, it's through doing the best that you can with what you have, and helping those who are less fortunate than yourself. Some will tell you it means following God's laws like they're the only things that matter, but I say, listen to your heart. It knows what's right. Do unto others as you'd have them do unto you. We're all in this world together and should act like it."

His frown growing deeper, Bobby said, "You sound kinda like a Democrat."

Chris laughed quietly, covering his mouth with his napkin. "I rather think I sound like a decent human being, but everyone is entitled to his own opinion."

"God's got a plan, though, right? They always say that."

"The only thing I'm truly certain of is that I feel Christ in my heart, there to guide me when I feel weak, warm me when I'm cold. Whether there's actually a plan or not..." He shrugged. "We are to God like ants are to men. Comprehending something on such a vastly different scale is chancy, at best. Use the mind He gave you, the heart He gave you, the hands He gave you. Think, listen, act. Preferably more or less in that order."

Bobby smirked. "If Pastor Adam heard you say all that, he'd call you a blasphemer."

"Not everyone interprets his pastoral duties the same way."

Nodding, Bobby stuffed the last bite of lasagna in his mouth. He broke the biscuit apart and used the pieces to mop up the last of the sauce before eating them. No matter how weird Chris might be, he offered up a good meal, and Bobby leaned back in his chair to tell him so. The door opening with a soft chime interrupted him.

In walked a man, wearing jeans and a hoodie, the hood pulled up and covering his face. He hopped out of the sunlight while the door closed and shook his hand with a hiss of pain. "I need gloves," the newcomer muttered.

Chris smiled at this person. "I'll see if I can find some, Stephen. There's a box of winter clothes in the basement."

Bobby narrowed his eyes at Chris, knowing he'd been snookered. "Why'n heckbiscuits didn't you just say he'd show here?"

Stephen pulled his hood down, revealing pale skin and short platinum-blonde hair. As expected, he had the icy blue eyes. One of his nearly invisible eyebrows arched up in mild amusement. "'Heck biscuits'?"

"You looked like you needed a friendly ear," Chris said with a restrained grin. "I'll let you two talk." He gathered up the plates and cups, taking them to the kitchen on his tray.

"What do you want from me?" He had a very mild Southern twang, much lighter than Bobby's. His one hand nearly glowed with a lobster red sunburn.

"I got a story to tell you. Might as well have a seat. It'll take a few minutes." When Stephen shrugged and obliged, Bobby told him the whole thing, from start to end. At this point, he could tell it without getting sidetracked or winding up on tangents. It took him about five minutes to lay everything out for Stephen.

"About a month ago, I woke up like you said." Stephen frowned as he spoke, looking down at his hands. The sunburn had faded to a light pink. "It was... I had this crazy thirst, like nothing I'd ever felt before. I spent that night with my girlfriend, and when I looked at her right then, I wanted her so bad I could taste it. I reached out to mess around and she was light as a feather." He paused and Bobby watched his face contort while he grappled with something, maybe whatever happened next. "I'm a vampire."

"Seriously?"

"Yeah. I drink blood, I'm unusually strong, I can fly, heal myself, the whole thing."

"Dang." Bobby lifted his hand and finally got to the demonstration part, letting his hand fall into dragons. "Don't look like holy ground bothers you. How about garlic?"

Stephen stared at the dragons. One landed on his hand and walked across it, sniffing his flesh. "No, nothing repels me that didn't already before. I never really liked garlic much, though. How many of these are there?"

"Lots. More'n I could count." Bobby sat back in his chair and watched the dragons, too. He never left them to their own devices. The bunch of them flitted around and investigated everything with curiosity and wonder. They stuck together for the most part, not straying more than a foot or so from the nearest other dragon, but otherwise spread out and got into everything nearby. "You leave behind fang marks?"

"No." Stephen kept watching the dragon on his hand as it ducked its head up his sleeve and chirped. "My saliva somehow removes the minor injury. It also seems to be a sort of aphrodisiac, or maybe just overloads the brain. Where do your clothes go?"

"No clue. The girl what can turn into a squirrel, hers go with her, too. One second, there's a fully clothed girl standing there. Next, a fuzzy little squirrel." Bobby shrugged. He couldn't think of any other questions for the moment. "You gonna head to Colorado?" So Stephen couldn't use the dragons as a distraction to evade the question, he called them back. They obeyed without hesitation.

Stephen tapped his thumb on the table a few times. "Seems I wasn't very hard to find."

"Not really, no."

"Unless you want some company, yeah, I guess so."

Leaning back, Bobby recalled Hannah suggesting that very thing. It sounded like a good idea then, and still did now. His back might not need watching as much as some other folks, but he could use the company. "How fast can you fly?"

"About a hundred miles an hour, give or take. You?"

"Same. Yeah, come with me, that's cool." He scratched his beard. "It's kinda late on for tonight, though, you maybe want to stop in and tell your family you're okay? Your momma was pretty upset."

Stephen sighed and raked a hand through his hair. "I left to protect them. From me. I don't want to accidentally kill one of them. They're better off without me around, at least until I can get some kind of reliable control over this."

Bobby pulled his phone out and set it on the table. "Least give 'em a call."

Reaching out, Stephen put two fingers on the phone and pulled it closer. He stared at it for several long seconds, then pushed it away again. "Not now."

"Don't wait too long."

Stephen sighed again, now hanging his head. "Next pay phone I see."

"Speaking of pay phones, your momma gave me this." Bobby pulled out the wad of cash, trading it for the phone.

The stack sat for three or four seconds with Stephen peered at it suspiciously. He finally sighed and swiped the money, then flipped through the bills. "Christ, this is four hundred dollars, what did you tell her?"

Dang. "She asked if I was your brother, and I said yes."

"Ah." He peeled off the outer two twenties and left them on the table for Pastor Chris. "She must have assumed you were in the house I was taken out of when she adopted me. I can see how that might make her feel guilty enough to shove this at you." Standing up, he nodded for Bobby to come with him into the kitchen. Pastor Chris stood washing dishes in the industrial kitchen. "Bobby's staying in the basement with me tonight, we're leaving in the morning. Neither of us will be back."

"Are you sure? Because you know you're always welcome here."

"He's like me."

Chris's brow flew up. "You're a vampire, too?"

Bobby cracked a grin. "No, I ain't. But I ain't all human, neither, just the same as Stephen. If'n you don't mind, I'd rather keep what I can do to myself."

"Of course." Chris nodded and gestured for them to use the door Stephen headed for. "Whatever it is, don't let it be a burden so heavy you can only look down at your own feet."

Unable to think of a response, Bobby nodded and followed Stephen downstairs. The basement had boxes stacked in groups, all of them neatly labeled. This bunch had Christmas decorations, that bunch had pageant costumes, Easter stuff, and some with donated clothes. It also had a couch with blankets and a pillow on it, and two easy chairs that looked squishy and comfy.

"So, you sleep still, huh? Wasn't expecting that."

Stephen snorted. "Yes, I still sleep."

Chuckling, Bobby settled himself into one of the chairs. It had a lever that he cranked to stretch out with a footrest. Yeah, he could sleep here. "Hey, it's a fair question. What about sunlight? I saw your hand before."

Stephen threw a blanket at Bobby and sank down on the couch. He held up the burned hand, now as pale as the rest of him. "I've always burned easily. It's much worse now. A quick flash of full sunlight turns my skin red, a full minute in it makes me blister. I don't want to know what longer than that does. Sunblock still works, though."

"Why're you walking around in daylight and sleeping at night, then?"

Stephen shrugged. "It's what I'm used to, I guess. A lot of businesses are only open during the day. Besides, it's easier to meet prey that isn't skanky whores."

Bobby stared at him, trying to decide if he wanted to get into the 'prey' issue or not. No, he didn't. "Maybe we ought to go at dusk, then, get as far as we can before sunup tomorrow."

"Suits me. Dusk is in about four hours. Where are we going, anyway?"

Pulling out his list, Bobby checked. He hadn't read it enough times to memorize it yet. "Austin first, then Phoenix."

Stephen gave a low whistle. "Austin to Phoenix is a long haul. We might want to stop somewhere between. El Paso, maybe. At least for a meal."

"I gotta stop to eat every few hours anyway."

CHAPTER 10

Comfortable and safe, Bobby fell asleep within seconds of closing his eyes. At dusk, Stephen shook him awake, ready to go with a pack on his back. On the way out, Bobby paused in the kitchen to grab two bananas and stuff them in his pocket. His belly stayed quiet for now, so he put off eating in favor of getting to Austin as soon as possible. He'd eat there.

The swarm streamed up into the air and Stephen followed. He floated upwards with his body limp. When they reached an altitude high enough to pass over skyscrapers, he shifted to being hunched over in what appeared to be relaxed comfort. He had the dragons surround the vampire to make sure he didn't wander off course by not looking.

Less than two hours later, Stephen touched back down the same way he took off. The second he re-formed, Bobby gave him a funny look. "Why d'you fly like that? It looks…weird."

"How should I fly?" Stephen cracked a half-grin. "With my arms out, like Superman? Or maybe I should flap my arms." He demonstrated, proving it looked stupid.

"Don't you gotta do nothing to fly?"

"Like what?"

"I dunno," Bobby shrugged, "something."

Stephen barked out a laugh. "No, it's a lot like making myself run.

Just have to want to do it."

"Huh." Bobby shrugged and dropped the subject. "I usually find a gas station, they always got maps." He snorted. "Listen to me. 'Usually', like this is something I do all the time."

Clapping him on the back, Stephen chuckled. "Don't worry about it, Bobby. Let's just destroy Christopher's life and get our asses to Phoenix to keep spreading the love."

Bobby rolled his eyes. "Yeah, I think that's a gas station up there."

Half an hour later, Stephen rang the doorbell for the upper of two apartments over an 'adult toy' store. "I could get used to living with a location like this." He nodded to indicate a bar across the street, and a nightclub next door to it. "Target rich environment."

"I can't see no reason to complain much, neither." They heard footsteps inside. Bobby pulled out a banana and stuffed his face with it.

One of theirs opened the door. He had the swarthy complexion of Hispanic heritage, with dark hair. In good shape, he stood taller than Bobby, but not quite up to Stephen's 6 foot 2. "Can I help you gentlemen?" The guy had a queer, girly-sounding voice, and he looked them both over the same way Bobby had been known to check out a shapely girl.

"Uh, yeah." Bobby heard someplace that about ten percent of all people turned out gay. It still never occurred to him that members of their group would be. All his life, he'd been told gays were gross and an abomination. Christopher instantly repulsed him. At the same time, they might be half-brothers or cousins, which meant family. Nothing in the world meant more than family. He had no idea what to think or feel.

Christopher's eyes went flat and he pursed his lips. "My mistake," he told Stephen, turning his shoulder to deliberately snub Bobby. "There's only one gentleman here."

Mouth open to say something, Bobby stopped because Stephen elbowed him in the side. "We came to warn you that someone may be interested in abducting you because of the unusual abilities all of us with these unusual eyes have." Stephen tapped his temple.

Christopher sniffed. "Take your jokes someplace else." He slammed the door shut.

"Way to go, genius."

"What?" Confused by the exchange, Bobby looked from Stephen to his half-eaten banana. "I didn't say nothing."

Stephen's mouth twitched with amusement. "What do you want to do? I got the impression leaving people behind was out of the question until they understand the risk they're taking by doing so."

"Yeah. I dunno. Nobody never slammed the door in my face before." Food had none of these complications, so Bobby finished the banana, tossing the peel into the open dumpster below them. One look inside it and he had no interest in checking it for food.

"You know, you didn't actually say anything. He reacted kind of strongly for just the comical expression on your face."

"Gee, thanks."

"I'm just saying," Stephen grinned, "that maybe he can read minds or something. I sometimes get weird little bursts of inspiration about my prey—"

"Do you have to say 'prey'?"

Stephen ignored him. "I just suddenly know the name of a person they care about, or what they do for a living, or other little bits of information."

"Your point?"

"It's completely possible he saw something in your head, only he isn't aware it's happening."

"Great." Bobby harrumphed and gripped the handrail of the stairs, staring out at nothing in particular. "Maybe you should just talk to him, then. All I can think about when I see a fag is how gross it all is."

Stephen rubbed his chin in silence for several seconds. Finally, he said, "I know a lot of people who think that. It's really normal down here. Well, not in Austin so much, so I've heard, but yeah. Still, he's one of us, and that doesn't change just because he happens to like guys."

Bobby grunted in annoyance. "'S'not like I'm standing here calling him a pervert or nothing. Just something I was taught ain't right, and I was keeping it to myself."

"Go do something for fifteen minutes." Stephen waved vaguely towards the street. "I'll meet you out front."

"Yeah." Bobby sighed and hopped down the steps. He knew very well that gay people were still people. Pastor Adam used to say they perverted God's will. He called them dirty all the time and railed about the stories of Sodom and Gomorrah. The first time Bobby remembered him explaining gay sex, he'd been eleven, and the pictures disturbed him. Without that last part, Bobby thought he'd care about it roughly as much as he cared about the supposed damnation premarital sex insured. Now he thought about it, though, Pastor Adam focused on men and ignored the idea of lesbians, which struck him as weird.

Whatever. So long as he didn't have to think about it, he didn't care. Having a guy right there in his face made him think about it. He leaned against the wall of the building with his hands in his pants pockets, watching people walk past. A few people walking by looked him over suspiciously. A few minutes later, an ordinary guy in a rumpled suit stopped a few feet away.

"Um, hi." He glanced around nervously. "I've, uh, never done this before." The guy stuffed his hands in his pockets and wouldn't look Bobby in the eye.

After looking around for someone else the guy might be talking to, Bobby stared at him. "Done what?"

"Um, are you a cop?"

"No." Was this guy—?

The guy's shoulders relaxed "Oh, good. Because that would just be —" He chuckled apprehensively. "Yeah. Um, so." His eyes roved down Bobby's body. When Christopher did it, Bobby got the impression he'd been appraised and found pleasant to look at. When this guy did it, he felt more like a slab of meat being judged for a meal. "Is a hundred bucks enough?"

Hot damn. Compared to Christopher, this guy made him want to take a shower forever. If this was how girls felt when he leered at them, he'd never, ever do it again. Putting his hands up, he stepped away from the building and noticed the display he'd been standing in front of. This store didn't hide its light under a bushel. Combined with his own appearance right now, he knew he'd brought this on himself. Punching this guy in the face would be downright rude. "Man, if you gotta pay to get laid, you need to seriously rethink things about your life. I ain't selling what you're trying to buy."

"Oh my gosh." The guy blushed so hard his face glowed. "I'm so sorry."

Bobby grunted with disinterest and noticed a black SUV over the guy's shoulder, parked across the street. He peered at it and thought the license plate seemed weird, but it was too far away to get a good look.

"Are you selling drugs, then?"

"What?" Bobby watched two men in dark suits get out of the car, then saw they wore sunglasses despite the darkness. He waved the guy off. "No, go on and git. I ain't selling nothing." When he saw two more suits step out of the SUV, he knew something had to be up. Guys in suits showing up to Christopher's neighborhood couldn't be a coincidence.

"Nobody just stands around here." The guy didn't seem nervous anymore.

Bobby waved the guy off and walked around the corner of the building, intending to hurry up the stairs to Christopher's door.

"Stop." The unmistakable sound of a gun cocking got Bobby's attention.

Raising his hands, he stopped and turned around. "I ain't selling nothing, really."

"Who do you work for?"

"What? I don't work for nobody. Who'n heckbiscuits you think I am?"

The guy gave him a flat, unimpressed look. "I'm the one asking questions."

"I don't got time for this." Bobby had no interest in finding out what getting shot felt like. He burst into a cloud of dragons and sent them streaking upward, looking for a way inside Christopher's apartment. That guy's mouth fell open and he gawped, which Bobby considered to be better than shooting or screaming. The swarm noticed the suits huddled in a small group. One of them pointed to the porn shop, so he knew they had to hurry.

Desperate to get inside, the dragons found an open window. The horde destroyed the screen and poured through. He re-formed from the feet up in the room where Stephen and Christopher sat at a small table, talking. "Suits coming, out on the street. We gotta git, now. Sorry about the screen."

Christopher's mouth fell open, gaping at Bobby.

Stephen nodded. "We have five minutes for him to pack a bag?"

"Nope. More like one for him to grab his wallet. Can you fly him out the window or something?" Bobby checked out the window and saw the suits hurrying across the street. "They're here, right down there."

"Christopher, you have sixty seconds to grab whatever you need, then were leaving. Don't bring your phone." When Christopher didn't move, Stephen slammed his hand on the table. "This is life and death."

Christopher jumped with a squeak and scrambled to his feet. "Right. Money, I guess." He hurried out of the room.

Bobby pulled the torn screen out of the window. "Can you get through this? You got them shoulders."

"Yeah, I think so."

"Can you grab some stuff outta the fridge for me? I ain't got nowhere to stick it, and I'm already hungry."

Stephen grimaced in distaste, but sighed and went into the kitchen. "What do you want to do with him? He doesn't have any powers he's aware of. I think its mental, but whatever it might be, he definitely can't fly."

"Christopher, you got a car someplace aside from right here?"

"Yes, I keep it at my parents' house. Parking around here is a bitch." He emerged from the bedroom with a small pack and frowned at Stephen rifling through his fridge. The doorbell rang. Bobby put himself between Christopher and the door.

"Ignore it. Where's your folks' place? Far?"

"A few miles."

"We can take you that far." Stephen slung his own pack, then he slipped in behind Christopher and grabbed him around the waist.

Christopher squeaked and his eyes popped wide and scared as Stephen lifted him off the ground and hauled him through the window. The swarm followed along behind them both.

"I feel like Lois Lane!"

"I'm more Dracula than Superman."

"Whatever!"

CHAPTER 11

When they landed at a nice house in the suburbs, Bobby gave Christopher the directions to the place in Colorado. He avoided touching the other man and tried not to think about gay sex. In return, Christopher wrinkled his nose and took notes without commenting. He and Stephen kept the drop-off short, taking off again as soon as they could.

They struck for El Paso, figuring to stop for the day so Stephen could hide from the daylight. While he could turn his body to avoid burning, they had to worry about being seen. High enough to be invisible from the ground probably meant high enough to be seen from an airplane or helicopter. Best to play it safe.

"Dang, I'm starving." These words spilled out of Bobby's mouth the second he re-formed in an alley. They'd stopped once in the middle of nowhere so Bobby could devour the food Stephen swiped from Christopher's fridge. By now, the sun had been up for nearly an hour, and he did his best to keep them in the shade of buildings as they walked through the city.

"I suppose it seems ridiculous," Stephen said as he adjusted the hood of his sweatshirt, "but I'm incredibly jealous of your...ability."

Bobby plucked a half rotten apple out of a garbage can and looked it over. The other half was fine. "Says the guy able to carry a backpack."

"To the guy who can eat regular food." Stephen's eyes locked onto and tracked a woman passing not far away. "I need to feed. I also need to not be charged with rape or any other form of assault."

Bobby took a bite from the good side of the apple and followed Stephen's gaze to a heavy-set middle aged lady. She pulled a wheeled basket of full cloth shopping bags behind her. Either Stephen had different tastes in women, or appearance didn't matter much. Given this was about food, the latter struck him as more likely. "How 'bout chomping on a guy?"

Stephen sneered with distaste. "It's too much like sex."

Bobby's chewing faltered. "Oh."

"And now you see my dilemma." Stephen snorted. "No offense, but having you with me isn't going to make this easier. We should make a plan to meet someplace later."

"I'm gonna look for the crappiest part of town and bunk down with the homeless folk. Maybe hit a soup kitchen if'n I can find one."

Stephen grimaced. "You want to stay with people who may very well rob you in your sleep?"

Bobby snorted. "So long as I don't show I got any money, all of 'em got more'n I look like I do. You might have trouble there on account of the pack, but not if it's clear we're running together. Risking two guys ain't worth it."

"Were you homeless?" Stephen put his hands up. "You just seem like you know how they think and operate."

Shrugging, Bobby said, "I had some friends in school what were. Parents lost their jobs, and they didn't have no place to go."

"Ah. I'll find you there, then." They shook hands and Stephen jogged across the street, chasing after that woman.

Bobby kept walking, grazing on what he found in garbage cans along the way. He checked with a couple in raggedy clothes under a highway bridge, and they pointed him in the right direction. The houses got progressively shabbier until he found a wide alley with weathered, beaten faces, shopping carts, and mounds of rags.

At the other end of the alley, he found an abandoned warehouse lot with shanties made of cardboard and garbage leaning against the building. Shopping carts full of stuff had been parked here and there, and they had barrels scattered around. Bobby guessed the cops left them alone so long as they didn't squat inside the building.

He walked through the gauntlet, head down and hands in his pockets, listening to them try to ward him off. There were no drugs here, they said, no hookers, and no social services. Kids didn't belong here. Get out while you still can. Go find a job, a girl, a life. If only things could be that simple again.

"You need a place to sit for a little bit, kid?"

Bobby looked up, expecting to find a man with disturbing, greedy eyes. Instead, the speaker turned out to be a thin, grizzled old man, bundled up in multiple blankets despite the warm weather. If he hoped for someone to take advantage of, it didn't show. Besides, he'd get a lot more than he bargained for if he tried that with Bobby, or Stephen when he showed up. "Yeah, thanks."

"You're kind of young for a place like this." He set out a ratty old cushion and gestured to it. As he withdrew his hand, he coughed and tried to cover his mouth with his elbow. Bobby saw a gob of blood on the sleeve when he pulled it away from his mouth.

"Just passing through." Bobby shrugged and sat down. "Ain't got enough money to stay someplace fancy. You know, with showers and beds." He flashed the old man a friendly smile.

The man chuckled. It turned into more coughing and he hacked a dark gobbet of crap off to the side. "You have a name, kid? Mine's Kurt."

"Bobby. That's a nasty cough you got, Kurt."

"Yeah, it'll kill me someday." Kurt chuckled. "Where you headed for that you're just passing through?"

Unwilling to reveal anything about his plans, Bobby shrugged. "Someplace else."

"Mmhmm." He offered Bobby a small packet of peanut butter, one with the seal still intact. "You've got unusual eyes."

Figuring that refusing a gift would be taken poorly, Bobby accepted the packet and opened it. "Yeah, I guess. So folks tell me, anyhow."

Kurt nodded and went quiet, his eyes glazing over. A commotion at the other end of the shantytown broke the silence. Bobby looked up and saw Stephen with his gloves on and hood pulled up, stalking down the line, a swagger to his steps. It made him look like a seriously bad dude who stepped out of a comic book and any second now, he'd pull a sword to start battling ninjas or werewolves. The locals reacted like scared puppies.

Bobby stood up and got Stephen's attention with a two-handed wave. "Where'd you learn to walk like that?"

Stephen smirked. "Nightmares."

With a short and a shake of his head, Bobby gestured for Stephen to sit with him. "This is Kurt, he's being decent."

"Hi, Kurt, I'm Stephen."

Kurt nodded absently, still staring at nothing. His head kept bobbing until he watched Stephen sit down and focused on him. "I've seen eyes like yours before." His voice sounded misty and distant.

"Oh yeah? Where was that?" Odd that he hadn't mentioned it before, but Bobby figured he might as well see where this led. The guy probably saw a poster with elves on it and had lost enough marbles to believe it had been real.

Kurt shook his head violently and started coughing again. More blood smeared onto his sleeve. "Top secret. They'll fire me if I tell you, Aaron. I want to tell you, but I just can't."

Stephen and Bobby both blinked in surprise at the response and looked at each other. Covering his mouth to shield it from Kurt's view, Stephen whispered, "Keep going, sounds worth pursuing."

Keep going, he said. Bobby rubbed his face and tried to think about how they did this kind of thing on TV. "Can't you even say what kind of work it is?"

Kurt shook his head and looked pained. "Someday, you'll understand. They have to keep it a secret, son. Sometimes, the government keeps a secret to protect us, because the knowledge would get people killed, a lot of people."

"I wouldn't ever tell anyone, you know that. I just...I want—" Bobby paused, forcing himself not to fill the space with 'um' and 'uh'. He took a flying leap and guessed that when Kurt said 'son', he meant Aaron had been his actual son's name. "I want to know about what you do, about who you are."

Tears formed in Kurt's eyes, his face filled with pride. "I know you do, just— When you're older— If you really want to know about this, you'll have to get yourself into the Army and be able to get the highest possible security clearance. The project is called Maze Beset, remember that, but don't ask for it by name. Tell them you want to work on the same program as your old man, they'll understand."

Glancing over at Stephen, Bobby saw the vampire's mouth hanging open in shock. His own seemed to be doing the same thing, and he snapped it shut. Kurt worked on a secret military program where he saw eyes like theirs, a long time ago. How long ago? It couldn't have been recent. He reached over and shook Kurt's shoulder gently. "Kurt, wake up, man, you kinda drifted off there."

"What?" More coughing produced a little splat of black stuff on the ground. "Huh?"

"How long you been out here, Kurt?"

Kurt took a deep breath and shook his head. "Years and years."

"You sound like a pretty smart guy, though. How'd you wind up on the streets?"

Kurt hunched in on himself and said nothing for several long seconds. "It was a car accident," he whispered. "Belinda— My wife. She didn't usually drive, but it was my retirement party. I drank more than I should have. They said so long as I kept my mouth shut, everything would be fine. I could just be with my wife, we could do the things we never got to do because of my job. We were going to travel, see the world. But she was dead, they killed her. It should have been me. I ran for it, ran for my life. Such a coward."

Bobby put his hand on Kurt's shoulder, trying to be friendly and supportive. "How long?"

"I don't know." Tears spilled down his cheeks and he coughed more. "I was sixty. Twenty years ago, maybe."

Twenty years on the streets would wear anybody down to nothing, even someone fifty years younger. Bobby frowned and thought about Kurt's son, a man whose mother died and father disappeared. "What about Aaron? Where's he?"

Kurt shook his head, too busy crying and coughing to answer the question. Bobby put his arm around Kurt's shoulder, wondering if the hand of God sent him to this particular man at this particular time.

"Kurt," Stephen said gently, "can you just tell us your last name?"

He managed to rasp out "Donner". Another minute or so later, he said, "God forgive me, I see her eyes in my nightmares. Your eyes." An especially harsh coughing fit wracked his body and Bobby held on. He and Stephen looked at each other behind his back. From his taut expression, Bobby figured they must be thinking the same thing: 'her eyes'. Were they all siblings after all? Could 'she' be their mother, their real mother?

They sat with Kurt while he slowly calmed down and fell asleep, probably exhausted by the memories and coughing. Bobby felt ready to collapse himself, from watching and from not sleeping enough last night. "I'm about to fall over, too."

Stephen yawned. "Yeah, I at least need a nap." The two of them, neither talking about what they just learned, moved Kurt under his crude little shelter in case the weather soured. He had enough space so long as neither of them stretched out, so both stayed under it with him, falling asleep without issue.

When Stephen woke Bobby up later, Kurt lay dead.

CHAPTER 12

"That's Camellia's place." Stephen gave a jerk of his head to indicate the tiny beige faux-adobe house with the flat roof as they approached it. The tiny front yard had rocks instead of grass, some scraggly weeds and cacti poking through it here and there. All the houses on this block had the same small income, southwestern feel. No garages here—some of the driveways had beat up old cars in them, but hers didn't.

"It's dark."

"Some people sleep at night. It's after ten."

Bobby's stomach growled. "No wonder I'm hungry."

"You're always hungry."

"So're you."

"Touché."

Stephen rang the doorbell and knocked, tamping down the grin Bobby provoked. Neither had anything in particular to say while they waited, so they stood there in silence for a solid minute. Stephen hit the doorbell again, and they waited another minute or so.

"Don't think she's there."

Stephen peered in through the front window. He rattled the doorknob and found it locked. "We should break in and take a look around."

"What?" Bobby's brow jumped up in shocked surprise. "We can't do that. It's her house."

"How else are we going to be sure she hasn't been grabbed already?"

"But—"

Stephen cut him off with a roll of his eyes and a wave of his hand. "If she's there but just sleeps like the dead, we apologize and explain we were concerned she'd been grabbed. If she's not there, but there's no sign of any-thing nefarious, we wait for her to get home and do the same. Honestly, Bobby, did you really think you'd manage to always find people at home when you happen to get there?"

Bobby opened his mouth to protest again. Given their purpose here, what Stephen said made sense. He shut his mouth. Momma was pretty clear about messing with another person's house. Sure, he'd broken a few laws in his youth. It'd all been about spray paint and messing around, not stealing or smashing things, or hurting people. Except...he stole a car a few days ago, along with a radio, a baton, and a few other things. As far as lines to not be crossed were concerned, this horse had already run out of the barn at full speed. "Okay, fine," he sighed. "I don't know nothing about breaking into a house, though."

"Are you implying that I do?" Stephen chuckled. "Well check for an open window, and if there isn't one..." He shrugged and paced around the house without finishing the statement.

If there wasn't one, they were screwed, because he didn't have the first clue how to pick a lock. Bobby stayed by the door, looking up and down the street to check if any neighboring curtains twitched. All the other houses had the lights off, except two with the gentle glow of television bleeding around the drapes. He saw no sign of movement.

Half a minute later, Stephen came around the other side of the house. "Nothing. She doesn't have very many windows. It's even smaller than it looks, too. From what I saw, it's a bedroom, a bathroom, and the rest is all one space. Mom would have a fit at the sight of the kitchen. It's smaller than her closet."

Bobby snorted. "Okay, smart guy, so how do we get in, then?"

His eyes still on the house, scanning up and down it, Stephen paused and pointed up. "Can you get a dragon into that?"

His finger directed Bobby's attention to a vent on the roof with small openings, and he instantly felt stupid for not thinking of it first. "Let's find out." One dragon popped off his thumb and flew up there. Since he wasn't sure what would happen or how much they could handle autonomously, he focused on it. His mind slid into it. He became the dragon and its little mind served as his co-pilot. Or maybe the other way around, because it knew how to move the body around a lot better than he did.

The vent had a screen inside it, but the dragon knew what to do about that from Christopher's place. His dragon chewed open a hole in the screen, doing real damage faster than Bobby could realize Camellia might not appreciate that. The vent connected to a metal tube that went to the swamp cooler, which the dragon squeezed past.

Inside the house, the dragon flew around, orienting itself, then located the front door. Bobby set it to the task of unlocking the knob, noting the deadbolt wasn't thrown, then let the dragon go to get it done without his interference. Back in his own body, he blinked and noticed Stephen watching him. "What's it look like when I do that?"

"It's adorable." Stephen grinned broadly. "You look like you're thinking very hard. Either that, or taking a dump."

Unamused, Bobby smacked Stephen in the arm. "I'll get a second opinion." His dragon got excited, which he took to mean that it got the job done. He reached over and opened the door.

"Excellent. I'll turn you into a ne'er-do-well yet."

Bobby snorted and took his dragon back into himself as they paced inside. While Stephen walked through the main room, looking around, Bobby poked his head into the bedroom. "She ain't here."

"There's a few things tossed around, but that could be from her hurrying. Hey, she's cute. There's some pics on the fridge."

Moving into the bedroom, Bobby checked the closet and under the bed, finding two empty suitcases and no sign of anything missing. "She's got a computer in here." A laptop perched on her minimalist black plastic desk, screen flipped open and plugged in. A tiny green light glowed steady, though the screen was dark. On the off chance it might be turned on, he pressed the spacebar.

"She's got plenty of food, so she wasn't planning on going anyplace. Woman must know how to cook, there's no doggie bags."

The laptop's fan whirred into action and the screen blinked on. He saw an image of himself, as seen by the built-in camera. Given the angle and his height, Bobby noticed a stain on his left pants pocket. "She seem like the type to be careless enough to leave her laptop running?"

A beat passed before Stephen answered, "Not really. If I assume the small signs of disturbance are from someone else intruding, then no, not at all. She's got her leftovers labeled and dated."

"Yeah, her bed is made, her desk is neat, it's all tidy and stuff. You know how to use computers? I'm not really all that up on this stuff. I didn't even have a cellphone."

"Barbarian," Stephen said with a sniff of disdain as he walked in and shooed Bobby out of the way. "So, using the webcam, were we, Camellia? What were you taking pictures of?" He sat down in her chair.

"You do that, I'm gonna eat." Without waiting for a response, Bobby went out and poked through the fridge. God bless labels and microwaves. As he slid something labeled 'turkey vegetable tetrazzini' in dainty handwriting into the nuke-o-matic, Stephen called out.

"I think she was taken by suits."

"Oh yeah, why'zat?" He punched buttons on the microwave and started it.

"She got a picture of one."

Bobby blinked and rushed into the bedroom. "Seriously?" He peered at the the screen. Sitting in the same chair Stephen now occupied, he saw the girl in the pictures on the fridge, a perky brunette with blond streaks in her shoulder-length hair, the same icy blue eyes, a cute little nose, and a big smile. She showed off a tattoo on her shoulder blade, of a rose.

Behind her, in the doorway, a man in a dark suit and sunglasses held a syringe ready to use. The guy's face looked blank, impassive, uninterested. Just another day at the office. More chilling, Bobby recognized that jaw from the group that showed up at Christopher's apartment. Camellia had no idea what was about to happen to her, and he reached out to touch the screen, wanting to warn her.

Stephen looked up at Bobby. "The image timestamp is from today, about five hours ago. They've only had her that long. We only missed her by that much."

If only they'd...what? Not slept? Not paused in El Paso? Not met Kurt? "Weren't nothing we could do to get here faster'n we did."

"Yeah." Stephen nodded in grim agreement, turned back to the laptop. "You eat, I'm going to see if there's anything to tell if her power is active or not and what it might be."

CHAPTER 13

Phoenix lit a fire under Bobby and Stephen to get to LA as quickly as possible, and they arrived before nightfall. The city of angels was home to three different members of their group, so they split up to each grab one and meet back up at the third. Bobby met Tiana, a zoologist working at the zoo who could talk to animals with her mind. She had to be the most attractive black woman he'd ever met, and he took another moment to boggle at how pretty everyone on the list had turned out to be so far.

"Tiana didn't want to leave her job," Bobby told Stephen as they walked to the front door of Matthew Garrison's apartment, "but I told her we'd have a ton of wild animals at the new place, and she said she'd think about it. Also, we can crash at her place tonight if we need to. You?"

"Javier was so eager to go along he almost tried to jump on my back so I could fly him away," Stephen snorted. "I could see why, too. His girl-friend is a bitch. She's knocked up and pals with his mom. Could hear her screeching from a block away. I did him a favor and bit her to take the edge off her temper. He'll get himself out there if he has to walk." He reached up and knocked on the door. "Hopefully without her."

Bobby snorted, though he wasn't so sure one of them abandoning a pregnant girlfriend should be hoped for. They waited about three minutes for someone to answer the door. "Shoot, I guess we gotta do this the hard way."

Stephen sighed and nodded for Bobby to get on with it.

Four dragons came off his hand and flew around the place, looking for any way in they could find. A neighbor opened their door and they dove in, looking for air vents to go through the ductwork. About ten minutes later, while Stephen and Bobby stood around trying to look innocent and harmless, the locks on the door clicked open. Bobby opened the door and walked in, the dragons reattaching to him. "I gotta say, until you had the idea in Phoenix, I never woulda thought to do that on my own."

"You just have to think like a rapist."

"I'm gonna pretend you didn't just say something that messed up."

With a light sigh, Stephen said, "Sorry. It's hard to get sex off my mind since this happened. A lot of what I can do is wrapped up in it. When I get really desperate for blood, my mind conjures up— Let's just say some of what goes on in here," he tapped his head with a finger as they looked around the apartment, "isn't about cute little bunnies and fuzzy duckies."

"Message received and understood," Bobby replied absently. He flipped through the mail sitting on the counter, then checked the fridge. Since he was there and could use a bite, he grabbed a swiftly spoiling banana to eat it.

"There's a messy serial killer in LA," Stephen noted as he picked up a newspaper and looked it over. "Funny, this is from a week ago. And it's only the front page section. This next one is from two weeks ago." He flipped through the stack on the table. "Offhand, I'd say either Matthew is the killer, or he's pals with a victim." Looking up, he rolled his eyes to see Bobby drinking milk from a cup. "Must you always eat in front of me?"

"I'm hungry. Flying all over the place like that takes a lot of energy, it don't just come from nowhere." He chugged down the rest of what was in the glass and rinsed it out in the sink, then put it in the dishwasher with the other dirty dishes there. "If he's killing people, that makes this more complicated."

Stephen waved dismissively. "Let's find out a little more about who our boy actually is before we decide who he might be. I'm just saying that him collecting these particular papers is suggestive."

"Yeah, yeah." Bobby started looking through drawers and cabinets. He saw a box of cereal and started munching on it while he kept looking around. Half an hour later, they knew he'd been discharged from the military about six months ago. He'd been having trouble holding down a job, his bills were all late, and he had a girlfriend. It looked like the girlfriend might be dead. Their apartment had evidence of a woman living in it, but also not. Nothing in the bathroom looked like it belonged to a woman, but decorations around the place that pointed to a feminine hand. The fridge had bachelor food in it, but the cabinets had stuff that didn't match up.

At least they knew they had the right guy. A picture of the two of them in a classy frame hung on the wall. They were a cute couple, both good looking and happy.

"I think our guy has some problems." Stephen walked out of the bathroom carrying two different prescription pill bottles. "I'm guessing he didn't leave the Marines just because his tour was up. I have no idea what these drugs are, but they can't be for anything shiny or happy. The names are too long."

"D'you get the feeling like he just crashes here and that's it?"

Looking around, Stephen shrugged. "Maybe he's just a neat freak."

Bobby sighed in frustration. "None of this really tells us where to find him."

"We could just wait until he comes home. Everything points to him sleeping here regularly."

"I s'pose. If he's out there killing folks, though, are we a little guilty for not finding him and stopping him?" Bobby looked in the fridge again and grabbed a box of Chinese takeout, sniffed it, and started eating it cold with his fingers. He dropped himself into a chair with that.

Stephen grimaced in utter disgust and sat down where he wouldn't have to watch Bobby eat. Both would be in sight of anyone opening the door. "No. I feel no guilt whatsoever for not being psychic or an experienced investigator."

Before answering. Bobby finishing chewing his mouthful of lo mein. "Fair enough. What about sending him to all the others if he's a serial killer?"

"I would feel some amount of guilt about him killing them, yes, I will admit that."

"I meant, maybe we shouldn't send him there."

Stephen steepled his fingers. "No. Regular cops won't be able to stop him, if they can even find him. Depending upon what his superpowers are, anyway. If I was out killing people, they'd likely never find me unless I chose my victims based upon a personal connection to me. If it was you, the same, and I'm sure for many of the others, as well. If you really want to stop him from killing people, sending him there is likely the only way it'll happen. Just call ahead and warn them."

Bobby nodded while he ate, seeing the point, and the wisdom. "We are kinda dangerous, ain't we. Nobody could stop me if'n I wanted to rob houses and stuff."

"I would make an unstoppable serial killer," Stephen agreed.

The memory of that one suit's brains splattered on the wall and floor surfaced, and Bobby set the empty food box aside. Alice's episode came to mind soon after, then the ease with which Ai stole what she needed. His mind wandered down the worst case scenario of the ones he knew about, and he saw bodies and destruction and looting. He let out a somber sigh.

"Yes, it is a little disturbing to realize the only thing really preventing you from taking whatever you want is your own commitment to morality."

Bobby nodded, finding the statement close enough to his thoughts to be the same. "If he won't go, there ain't a whole lot we can do about that."

"Untrue. I can take him forcibly. You can go on to the rest on your own."

"I s'pose that's the best option." He had something else to say, but the sound of someone unlocking the door interrupted him, and they both went still. The door opened. Someone slipped inside and plastered himself against the door, panting.

Bobby recognized Matthew from the photos. He wore jeans and nothing else. Blood had been smeared and splashed across his chest and arms, and his eyes stared out, wide and horrified. It took him a moment to notice the pair of them. In the space of perhaps two seconds, the jeans disappeared, his body grew muscles and fur and claws, and his head reshaped with a fanged snout. He shot upwards to nine feet tall, turning into the scariest damn werewolf Bobby had ever seen.

While Bobby blew out into dragons, terrified this thing would maul him, Stephen remained sitting with his legs crossed and hands laced together in his lap. "How apropos that a vampire and a werewolf should fight this close to Hollywood. With dragons, to boot. I wonder if we'll attract any orcs or fairies."

Matthew made a snarling, barking noise and jumped at Stephen. The vampire surged up to meet the werewolf. Bobby, unable to get into it much without causing a problem for Stephen, got the dragons to open the door a crack so ten could slip out and keep watch. If someone came to this door, he wanted to know about it before they arrived and got involved.

Stephen and Matthew seemed an even match, each strong enough to hold the other back. To try to help the odds, the dragons went in for the werewolf's legs. His little critters scratched and scraped against Matthew's furry flesh, finding it tougher than anything they'd encountered before. With them so ineffectual, he pulled the dragons out to keep them safe.

Furniture flew and fists smashed into the wall. Stephen threw the werewolf into the fridge, rocking it back and denting the wall. Matthew returned the favor by tossing the vampire through an inner wall, putting Stephen in the bedroom. They did what Bobby thought of as wrasslin', except for the fangs and claws and superhuman strength. It carried them back through the apartment, wrecking it as they went, until Stephen got thrown through a window and Matthew chased after, like a dog going after a stick.

With it now public, they stood a very real chance of this scrap getting noticed by the neighbors. If the noise hadn't already prompted a call to the cops, looking out a window and seeing this spectacle surely would. He could almost imagine the call to the police. 'Officer, there's two costumed freaks wrasslin' around outside, making a heckuva ruckus!' Or however the locals would say that. The swarm followed them out, keeping a watch all around.

Matthew filled the air with giant angry dog noises. Stephen hissed, reminding Bobby of a riled-up cat. Claws flew and fangs crunched. With every injury inflicted, each of them healed over. In Stephen's case, the wounds knitting seemed to take something out of him, tiring him, or depleting something. Despite that, every time the werewolf tossed him, he righted himself and plowed back in, pushing Mathew back towards the apartment.

A police car screamed onto the scene, brakes screeching as it halted sideways to block their passage farther down the street. Bobby saw it coming and couldn't think of anything to do about it. As helpless as any other bystander, he watched and hoped the situation might clear enough for him to see a way to interject himself. This feeling reminded him of how he felt when that needle went into his leg at Jasmine's apartment, except that this just kept going on and he didn't get the luxury of blacking out for any part of it.

Jumping out of the cruiser, a cop held his gun out and shouted for the two men to freeze and get on the ground. The command drew Matthew's attention. He threw Stephen again and bounded for the flashing lights of the police car. Bobby couldn't let the cop get hurt just for being the one to show up. He dove at the officer and re-formed right in front of him, willing to take the hit. Matthew slammed into him claws first. The impact made his body disperse into dragons again, and Matthew fell forward, splaying on the ground at the cop's feet.

Dragons dove in and buzzed Matthew's head. Although it kept him from being able to see any other targets, it made him freak out more, and he scraped at the air around his head. This distraction gave Stephen a chance to grab the cop and toss him out of the way. The cop stumbled aside and fired into the fray, emptying his clip at the impossible scene. Stephen twisted and dropped to his knees. Still on the ground, Matthew's body jumped as bullets slammed into it.

The werewolf stopped fighting to lie on the ground panting. On all fours now, Stephen coughed and spat out a mouthful of blood. Bobby panicked. One of his dragons had been crushed by a bullet—he could see it over there. What would happen when he re-formed? He had no idea, and didn't know what to do. He couldn't stay in the swarm forever; he needed to sleep and eat, and he couldn't do either as all dragons. Would he just not have a fingertip anymore? Would there be a bullet hole in a random place on his body?

Part of the swarm noticed the cop changing his clip and moving forward to threaten Stephen. The rest focused on the broken body of the little dragon on the ground several feet away. He heard Stephen say, "You moron, you have no idea what you've just involved yourself in." Did he mean to convince the cop he'd stumbled into some kind of secret vampire-werewolf war?

Dozens of dragons surrounded the broken one—and it was broken, he saw, not injured—to pick it up and... Eat it? Part of him rebelled at the notion of his dragons being cannibals. The rest freaked out about the 'broken' part. He was made of robots, tiny robots shaped like dragons. Tiny robots shaped like dragons that ate metal and each other. What did that make him? Was he even human anymore? Had he ever been?

The cop's voice, shaky and shocky, called for an ambulance, presumably over his radio. He ejected the clip from his gun and slammed a fresh on in. "I really don't care about whatever crazy thing you're doing out here, lie down on the ground and put your hands behind your head."

"Like that's going to happen." Stephen sat up on his feet and spat a bullet out. It bounced and rolled to the cop's shoe. "You want to shoot me again?" Spreading his arms out wide in invitation, he gave the cop a wide-eyed glare, his nostrils flared. "Go ahead and shoot me."

Another cop car screamed into sight, snapping Bobby out of his panic. They had bigger problems than his confusion about himself. He re-formed and dropped down next to Matthew, checking him over. "He's alive." He had to clench his jaw to deal with agony in his hand. "I think he's healing." A quick check of himself revealed no missing parts and no holes or other injuries. The loss of a dragon seemed to have translated into sharp pain in his left hand and nothing else.

"Lovely." Stephen spat another bullet at the cop.

Slapping his second hand onto his gun to steady it, the cop's mouth dropped open and he took labored breaths. "What are you?"

Matthew's eyes snapped open and he focused on Bobby. His clawed hand shot up to grab him by the neck, but he exploded into dragons again to avoid the problem. Growling, the werewolf picked up the nearby cop car and tossed it, sending it rolling down the street.

The second cop car switched into reverse to speed away from Matthew. It drew his attention, and he turned to chase it.

"I'm going to call him unwilling, Bobby. You should get out of here and I'll handle this. And yes, I'm sure." Stephen lurched to his feet, smacking the first cop aside hard enough to knock him for a loop. He jumped onto Matthew's back before he reached the second cop car and sank his fangs into the werewolf's neck.

Matthew flailed about to dislodge him, with no success. They lifted off the ground, moving upwards under Stephen's power, and Matthew's struggles weakened as they rose beyond the range of the street lights.

At that point, with one cop senseless and the other staring up, slack-jawed, Bobby took off. Stephen would get Matthew to their new base, and they'd handle him one way or another. These two cops would have to figure out what to put into a report. Good luck to them. Bobby had no intention of sticking around long enough to be questioned or charged with anything.

Thank God Stephen had been here, because Bobby couldn't have contained Matthew on his own, nor could he have picked him up and carried him away. He offered a quiet prayer to never find himself in that position without someone like Stephen around. People could get hurt or killed. No one deserved that.

CHAPTER 14

Bobby flew an hour north, then found a hole to curl up in near the coast. He slept until the garbage truck woke him up around dawn by picking up the dumpster he slept against. Before he had a chance to take in his surroundings, it slammed back down into him, sending dragons scattering. Half a block away, he re-formed and called Hannah while foraging for food.

"Good to hear from you. How are things going?"

"Sorry I ain't called since El Paso. Camellia in Phoenix got took. There's Javier and Tiana headed your way. Also, Stephen from Dallas is coming back with Matthew who didn't rightly want to go, exactly. I dunno, maybe he will when he wakes up. We hadta beat him into submission. Two cops and a buncha folks saw us, I think. Stephen and Matthew had a fight on the street."

"They...what?"

"It weren't our fault." Bobby could hear himself whining and made an effort to stop that. "There's something wrong with Matthew, we think he's been killing people and he's got meds and stuff. Andrew might want to keep a close eye on him when they get there."

"I see. So you know, the others have found four more gone missing in the past week, and we lost contact with Jasmine and Will. Are you alright?"

"Me? Yeah, sure." He frowned at the news. Of the group, Jasmine seemed the nicest, and he hated to think of her locked up somehow. "Got a rude wakeup call this morning, but I'm fine. Looking to head out to Honolulu soon as I find a map so I'm sure I'm going the right way."

"Actually, can you go north first? Ai is having some trouble in Portland. So, can you pop up to San Jose first? Her name is Lily Wislen, and I've got an address for you."

One sigh later, Bobby found himself nodding. "Yeah, sure. It ain't that much outta my way, I guess." He had nothing to write down the address, but figured he could remember it that far.

"It's about three hundred miles north. Follow the coast, or there's a highway that goes up the middle of the state. And thanks, Bobby, you're a champ. We'll have a bed waiting for you when you get here, promise."

"That's something, I s'pose, though I'd rather have a good meal."

"I'll see what we can do."

"Yeah. Stephen's got some news about a Kurt Donner. Don't let him forget to tell you." Bobby hung up, sorry he'd called. Not really, but a little. Now he had to think about Jasmine trussed up and getting tortured, in addition to knowing he'd have to go farther before seeing his new home and being able to rest in safety for a few nights.

Maybe he'd get lucky and this Lily would be able to fly to Hawaii with him, to keep it from being boring. Anything could happen, right? Depending on how far Hawaii actually was, maybe he could crash at her place and get an actual good night of sleep first. Eat a good meal, too. The dumpster-diving diet featured an awful lot of bread and not much meat, and he missed fresh food a lot. A nice, crisp, whole apple would really hit the spot right now, so would some medium-well steak with mashed potatoes and gravy.

Before he could get caught up in food fantasies, Bobby reminded himself that he had money. If he wanted to, he could eat a real meal every day. It seemed wise to not do that and hold onto it, in case of some kind of emergency. Like...he had no idea, but something could come up that required money and put him in a world of hurt without.

Setting the notion aside, he blew out into the swarm and flew north at top speed. He followed the coast from several thousand feet up and watched the sun climb upwards. By the time he reached San Jose and found a map, a clock in the convenience store told him the trip had taken about three hours.

Lily lived in a nice neighborhood, so far as he could see. It reminded him of Stephen's momma's house, only more green. It had that same upper middle class, homeowner's association, everybody uses the same guys to cut the grass feel to it. Either Lily still lived with her folks, or she did pretty darn well for herself.

Trying not to feel grossly out of place, he found a place to land and re-form, then walked up her street. Curtains twitched as he passed them. When he turned up the stone path to her front door, it felt like a hundred people must be watching him. He knocked and stuck his hands in his pockets, hoping no one called the cops while he waited.

Nobody answered. This place probably had an alarm system, so he peered in through the window instead of sending dragons to break in for him. He saw nice living room furniture with toddler toys strewn about. If that kid's momma turned out to be Lily, she wasn't coming to Hawaii with him, even if she could snap her fingers and be there.

"Who are you?"

Caught in the act of peeking in, Bobby turned around and held up his hands. The woman standing there with two toddlers peeking out from behind her legs couldn't be Lily. The little boy, though, had to be her son. Cute little thing had a mop of brown hair and the icy blue eyes. Funny, he hadn't really thought to wonder if the eyes would get passed on as-is to their kids. Apparently, they would.

"I'm looking for Lily. Was hoping she'd be home, but life don't seem to work out the way I'd like most of the time." He noticed the woman's eyes flicking to his own, then she put a hand protectively on the boy's head. The boy gave him a shy little smile.

"If you actually knew her, you'd know she's working today."

He pulled out the 'aw shucks', getting the impression this might be Lily's sister or close friend. "I didn't say I know her, ma'am, it's just real important I talk to her as soon as possible. Where's she work?"

The woman backed away, pushing the two toddlers along behind her. "You must be crazy if you think I'm going to tell you that."

"I ain't here to hurt nobody." Bobby took a step after her. When she flinched, he stopped and stuffed his hands into his pockets. "I ain't crazy, neither. You seen the eyes. We're related somehow, and part of why I'm here is to figure that out." He almost asked after the boy, but thought that would probably make her run and call the police, maybe with a screech. "My name's Bobby. I just want to talk to her, nothing else, I swear on my daddy's grave."

She frowned and looked down at the boy. He nodded to her, so she sighed and nodded, too. "She works at the Wislen Garden Center."

"Thank you kindly, ma'am. I appreciate it." He, of course, had no clue where that was. Asking directions seemed like pushing her a little too far. Besides, he saw a gas station around the corner where he could ask anyway.

To his surprise, when he started walking, she said, "It's that way." When he looked back, she pointed in the opposite direction that he'd chosen to walk. He tipped an imaginary hat to her in thanks and turned that way, moving at a brisk walk. A block away, he dove behind a tree and burst into dragons to get a higher vantage point.

The Wislen family business wasn't hard to find. He walked into the place and looked around at the plants and decorative pots and things. Momma would like to be able to wander around and buy stuff here. The yard ornaments weren't so much her thing, but they had flowers he never saw before that he knew she'd like. Those big red ones the size of dinner plates would catch her eye for sure.

"Can I help you?"

He looked up to find the owner of that soft, sweet voice and found himself face to face with icy blue eyes. Long brown hair framed a delicate, pretty face, and she took his breath away. None of the other women had done that, and he couldn't explain why she did. For a long few moments, he stood and stared at her, gawping like an idiot.

Her pleasant smile dimmed. It shook him out of his stupor. "Lily Wislen, I need to talk to you."

The smile dropped away completely, and he wanted to punch himself for doing that to her. "Thatcher."

Oh. She was married. He blinked and scratched the back of his neck. Disappointment crushed him back to reality. "Sorry, ma'am. Mrs. Thatcher. I still gotta talk to you." He tapped on his temple to indicate his eyes. "It's important. No joke."

She reached up with a slim hand and brushed her hair back. For Bobby, the world slowed down and the pink polish on her nails flashed in the sunshine. Her gaze swept the area, then she pointed discreetly to the front gate. "I'll meet you out there in a few minutes. I just need to tell my boss I'm taking a break."

"Yeah, sure." He bobbed his head and watched her turn around and walk away. Out of all the women he met on this wild ride so far, only she pushed all his buttons at once, making it hard to think. Naturally, she was married, probably happily. She'd have a tall, strong, handsome guy. He'd be a really great person, the kind of guy Bobby could never hate or measure up to. He might even be that guy over there, talking to a couple by the rosebushes.

Shaking his head to knock the stupid out, he ambled to the front gate, finding a curb to sit his butt on while he waited however long she decided to make him wait. For all he knew, she would go about her job for another hour before actually coming out to talk to him. Heck, she might just dismiss him entirely so he'd be still sitting out here after the place closed, not realizing she'd slipped out the back to get rescued by her Mr. Thatcher around the corner. The thought put a sour frown on his face, right up until she walked out and sat next to him five minutes later.

"You have fifteen minutes."

Pleasantly surprised by her joining him so quickly, Bobby nodded his understanding. He pulled his much crumpled list from his pocket and offered it to her. "About a week ago, me and three others got grabbed and shoved into a lab where we were experimented on. We escaped and found this list on the way out. We're going across the country, looking up everyone on that list to tell 'em you're in danger. Far as I know, seven of 'em gone missing in the past few days, we think they got took by government agents, and are right now being experimented on just like the four of us were. I don't know if they're for sure gonna come for you, but I'm here to warn you and offer a place to go where it should be safe. Even if they find us there, we're all willing to fight together to stay free and safe."

Lily listened to him. She found her own name on the list and ran her finger over it. Leaning close, she whispered to him, "Why are they doing it?"

"Not rightly sure, but all of us have these eyes, and so far, most of us have some kind of weird and crazy ability, like a super power. Not gonna pull mine out here in broad daylight, but if you got something you can do, you're not crazy, promise."

She sagged against him with relief. "Oh, thank God." Her head rested on his shoulder.

As much as he wanted her to lean on him, he coughed. "Ain't your husband gonna get a little tetchy if'n you do that?"

"I doubt it." She lifted her head back up with a sigh anyway. "He's been dead for a little over two years. I have a son. If I can't bring him, I won't go anywhere."

Oh. That changed things. He tried to hide how his heart swelled. "You can bring him, sure. I haven't been to the place we're taking up yet, so I can't say what we got for amenities yet, but yeah, bring him. He's got the eyes, right? They'd take him, so you should bring him."

She sat bolt upright, her body tensed and ready to run. "When are they coming?"

"I got no clue." Wanting to reassure her, he put a hand on her arm. It bolstered his resolve when she didn't pull away or brush him off. "The one in Phoenix was gone already when I got there a coupla days ago, but all three in LA were still there. No idea how they're deciding who to take in what order."

"They can't take him, I won't let them." She stood up and hurried back in through the gate.

Bobby stood up and stretched. His work was mostly done here. This momma had protective tiger written all over her now, and she'd take her cub to a promise of safety. As much as he wanted to stay and get to know her, he had to give her directions and get his own to Hawaii. Maybe on that flight, he could think about why he reacted to her so strongly.

She jogged out with her keys two minutes later, and her blue sedan got them back to her house in ten minutes. He saw no black SUVs or cops, or anything. She ran to the house next door anyway, and came out about ten minutes later carrying the little boy Bobby saw earlier. Holding him possessively and protectively, she squeezed him they'd been parted for a week or a month instead of a few hours. It made him want to call Momma.

"This is my friend Bobby," Lily told the boy. "Bobby, this is Sebastian."

"Nice to meetcha all proper-like," Bobby said with a wave.

"Bobby scared Auntie Allie," Sebastian announced, his small voice grave and accusing.

"Hum. I didn't mean to. Was just looking for your momma." He had a thought to leave it at that while Lily unlocked the front door of her house and led him inside, but he wanted Sebastian on his side. Besides, he had a cousin with a boy that reminded him of this kid. "Some bad men want to hurt your momma, and I'm trying to protect her from them."

His little eyes went wide. "Are you a policeman?"

Bobby grinned. "Nope, I'm a superhero."

The boy's mouth made a little 'o' of delight. Lily, on the other hand, rolled her eyes at him. The corners of her mouth tugged upwards, though, so she didn't think too poorly of him for it. "Bobby is going to help us pack up some things in Mommy's car so we can take a trip to a place where the bad men won't find us. You know what would be a big help?" She set the boy down on the stairs. "If you could go pull your most favorite clothes out of your dresser and your most favorite toys out of your bin, and put them all in a pile, that would help a lot."

"Okay, Mommy!" Sebastian raced up the stairs, using his hands and feet.

Watching the little boy move with such enthusiasm and determination made Bobby grin. "How old is he?"

"I'd love to chat and do the whole 'get to know you' routine," she said as she bustled into the kitchen, "but maybe that could wait until we're in the car?"

He followed her, his eyes drifting downwards. "Oh, I ain't coming in the car." And that was a damned shame. Driving that far with her might mean being able to snuggle up overnight, and he'd liked the feel of her head on his shoulder. He'd liked that a lot. "I got another stop to make before I get to go to the farm. I was wondering if I could get you to look up on the internet how far it is from here to Hawaii, though, because I gotta get my scrawny butt there next."

Lily turned from pulling food out of the cabinets, probably meant for the trip. "It's over two thousand miles from here. We went there once when I was a kid, it's like a five hour flight."

Bobby's mouth slipped open, then he shut it. On maps, they always put it right below the 48 states, so he never thought of it as far away. He figured it would be maybe four or five hundred miles, a thousand at the most. At his speed, it would take him an entire day to get there, and he'd be so tired and hungry when he got there, he'd fall flat on his face.

"Dangit." At that moment, he realized he hadn't yet shown her his ability, so he held out his hand and let five dragons detach. "I was gonna fly there," he explained, "but that's too far for me. I can only go about a hundred miles an hour."

She sucked in a surprised breath and stared. One of the dragons decided to walk on the counter, sniffing it, and she put her hand out next to it. The dragon sniffed her hand, then climbed up on it and walked all over it as she turned it around. "Wow. This is nothing like what I can do."

"Yeah, I ain't seen nobody else with anything quite like this yet. They kinda got their own minds, but they're me, too. It's hard to explain."

She chuckled. "If that's the best you can do, it must be."

By focusing down on that one dragon, Bobby got to vicariously explore her hand, noting the wedding ring still on it, the dirt under her short fingernails, the softness of her skin, a few freckles, and how delicate her fingers really were. "Yeah. Um, maybe I could find the number of the one out there and call before I find a way to get myself out there. Make sure she ain't abducted, too."

"Um." She pulled her hand to herself, and Bobby, sensing her sudden discomfort, got the dragon to hop off. "I can boot up a computer for you to use, I guess."

"Thanks, I'd appreciate that." Any idiot could look a person up on the internet, right? He called his dragons back and sat down where she pointed to try to find Maisie Polape. Weird sounding name, so maybe not too common. After finding a browser, he tried very hard to ignore the attractive woman in the room so he could punch the name into the search bar. It came back with only a few results. Halfway down the page, the hits only had one name or the other.

The first link went to the Honolulu Star-Advertiser, the paper out that way. It had an article about how Maisie Polape went missing last night. A leaden feeling settled in his gut, making him sit and read the whole thing. She'd been out with her boyfriend, it said, and he got hit from behind. When he came to, Maisie was gone. He saw nothing. The police were already investigating it as an abduction.

Why were the cops looking into it if the government snatched her? Maybe they did that as a cover, and they'd 'investigate' for a little while, give up and call it a cold case. Still, why not just arrest her? Then again, none of the other missing people had been arrested so far as the families knew. These people had enough skill to abduct a person without leaving witnesses, and either no connection to the police, or no interest in keeping the cops out of it.

"I think you should hurry," he said. Getting out of the chair, he found the kitchen empty. A plastic box full of food sat on the counter, and Lily must've left while he read the article and panicked. At least he now knew he had no need to figure out how to get to Hawaii and back. On reflection, he probably could have taken a plane out there and back, depending upon how much it cost. Or, heck, maybe he could fly in the baggage compartment if he stayed in the swarm the whole time. He shut down the computer and pulled out his phone to let Hannah know about Maisie while looking around the house for Lily.

As he passed the front door, he noticed movement on the wall, a shadow tracking across it. Hannah picked up the phone as he hurried to the front window and peered out around the side. The sight made him pale and pull back quickly, hoping the two guys in suits hadn't seen him. Two long heartbeats later, the doorbell rang.

"Hannah," he murmured into the phone, "there's guys in suits here, I'm at Lily's place." He took the stairs two at a time to go intercept Lily on her way to answer the door. "Maisie got took last night, according to the paper. It's so far, I decided to check first. If you don't hear from me again today, it's cause I'm took." Without giving her a chance to respond, he snapped the phone shut and stopped short of colliding with Lily. "It's them, they're here, now, to grab you up. What's your power?"

To her credit, she blanched without panicking. "I can make things out of nothing. Simple things, like hand tools, toys, that sort of thing."

Nothing leaped to mind for how to make that useful in this situation. "You stay here, keep packing up, keep Sebastian close. I'm gonna see if'n I can get rid of them, one way or another. Make up a bag of what you gotta take if you gotta go with just one bag, keep that close, but keep working anyway, just in case." He took her hand and pressed the phone into it. "Hannah is speed dial one."

She nodded and ran to her son. He hurried down the steps to answer the door. Halfway down, the door smashed open. Two men in suits stepped inside with guns out and ready, sweeping them around the room. He had no Stephen or Jayce around to handle this kind of thing, so he'd have to do it himself. Lily could help, except she needed to keep Sebastian safe. Who knew how many men these guys actually had. They could send someone to circle around back and swipe the kid while these guys in the front kept them busy. Not acceptable.

In sight of the door, Bobby put his hands up rather than bothering to hide and draw them upstairs. Both suits pointed their handguns straight at him. Not a lot of choices presented themselves. He picked the best thing he could think of an committed to it. "I sent her away already, you're too late."

"Then what are you doing here?" It bothered him a tiny bit that these suits had normal voices. With the sunglasses hiding their identities so much, they ought to have creepy voices, or say crazy stuff, or something.

Bobby shrugged. "Packing some of her crap, using the bathroom, that kinda thing. Y'all made it so I ain't exactly got lots of funding and all."

"What's your name?" Presented with an obvious target, they both focused on him. Good.

"That's a kinda personal question. How's about you tell me who you're working for, and I'll tell my name."

"Are you going to come quietly, or are we going to have to shoot you?"

He took a moment to think about that, and made sure they could tell he thought about it. "You know, I ain't rightly sure. Last time I got shot, it bruised up my hand something fierce, so I'd say it ain't much fun, but I don't rightly think it's gonna kill me like it would you guys." Saying that out loud gave him more confidence. He took the steps down slowly, keeping his hands up. "That kinda leaves me with not so much of a need to avoid it as a regular person might. A regular person such as yourself. I mean, you're hunting us with guns? Really? Didn't we make it pretty clear that ain't gonna cut it?"

"Mitchell," the second suit said into his sleeve, probably into a microphone of some kind. "It's Mitchell."

"Shoot, you figured out who I am." He needed to make sure any bullets that got fired went nowhere near Lily and Sebastian. If he acted cocky, it might draw them out. Outside, he might be able to figure out a way to knock them down for a while. An old-fashioned fist to the face might work. "Well, I guess I ain't got nothing left to bargain with. 'Course, I know where they went, but you probably don't care about that."

"You're lying."

Bobby shrugged and forced himself to keep going down the stairs. They couldn't hurt him, not really. This fear bubbling in his belly came from what their masters had done to him. Knowing that didn't really slow his heart down. It kept beating a million miles a minute, ready to back him up the second he needed to fly into an adrenaline fueled frenzy. "Suit yourself." Did adrenaline affect the dragons? Interesting question.

He pushed past the first suit, shoving him aside with his shoulder. Stepping past that man put him between the two of them. It felt stupid and crazy and vulnerable. The other suit holstered his gun, too. Behind him, he noticed movement, too late to do anything about it. The first suit jammed something into his back, and it buzzed and clicked.

A hot poker drove into his lower back. His body tightened, voltage sending him into spasms. His hands burst into dragons. His arms followed as he tried to scream and made only a weird whining noise. As more dragons fought their way free, the swarm flew into a blind rage. Stuck in a dizzying fog of pain, Bobby had no control over them. An eternity later, the swarm calmed down and let him re-form, his hands burning with agony.

Both men lay limp on the floor, covered with scorchmarks, and tiny bites and scratches. Their clothes had been shredded, with the damage focused around their hands and less frenzied across the rest of their bodies. Their faces hadn't been spared at all, and their eyes— He covered his mouth with a hand, tasting bile. He did this, not Alice or Jayce or Stephen. His dragons, which were him, killed two men. They wanted to hurt him and others, so he'd done it in self-defense, but he still killed them.

Scrambling to get away from them, he stumbled into the nearest bathroom and splashed water on his face. Both his hands hurt even worse than last night, and he wondered how badly the dragons had been damaged by the jolt. Like any other bathroom, this one had a mirror over the sink, and he stared at himself in it.

"I did that." He gripped the sink with both hands and groaned from the pain. "It was me, no one else. I gotta live with it. It was my fault." Just like killing those homeless people had been Alice's fault. "You dumbass. It had to happen eventually, but you just kept going, like you're invincible and perfect and all that, but you're not. You're just a guy with a gun who ain't figured out how to use it yet."

He splashed more water on his face and grabbed a towel, drying his face as he hurried back to the stairs. One foot on the bottom step, he froze at the sound of a car door slamming shut, then an engine roaring. Out the door in a second, he caught sight of a black SUV peeling away, another suit in the driver's seat. This one, he recognized. Austin, Phoenix, now San Jose, that guy got around, and fast. Though he wore sunglasses, Bobby thought it likely the suit saw him, too.

Part of him wanted to chase that guy down and demand to know where Jasmine had been taken. Terrified he'd kill that one, too, he ran back into the house. They had to get out of here. Would the suit call for backup or just let them go? How long would it take him to get backup? What would they bring?

Heckbiscuits, they had two dead bodies lying on the floor. As soon as anyone else walked through that door, they'd freak and call the cops. Taking the stairs two at a time, he ran up and called out. "Lily, they're...I— Um. It's safe for now. You don't want to let Sebastian see, though. I...it was kinda an accident."

The door cracked open and Lily peeked out. "Are you okay?"

"More or less, yeah. They had a taser, it stings, but I'm okay. They really...uh, they ain't getting up."

She nodded and let out a tiny sigh of relief, then her face clouded. "We should pack up the car and go, then, before they're missed."

"Yeah, uh, too late for that. We gotta move. Is it okay if I come with you after all? I don't need to go to Hawaii, as it turns out."

As a response, she opened the door and hugged him. It came as a surprise, one he needed badly. He wrapped his arms around her and held on tight. "Thank you," she whispered. "If you hadn't been here, they would've taken us."

The apology he intended to deliver for doing something so horrible as killing two people in her house died under the weight of her gratitude. "Nah, you'da done alright." With her this close, he wanted to kiss her. While he thought about that, trying to decide if he ought to or not, she pulled away. To cover up his disappointment, he crouched down to Sebastian's level.

"Hey, buddy, we gotta load up the car and go away, right? There's something at the bottom of the stairs, though, and I don't want you to see it. There's a..." He faltered, trying to figure out how to explain without explaining. "Here, just lemme carry you down the stairs and out to the car, okay?"

Sebastian looked to his mother, who paused for a second, then nodded. He put out his arms and let Bobby pick him up, and Bobby turned the boy's head into his neck, then covered the one angle he might be able to still see from. Lily followed behind him as he carried the boy down the stairs and stepped over the bodies. He heard her sharp intake of breath, then they both reached the car. Sebastian's car seat had already been strapped down in the back seat, so he settled the boy inside it.

"I'll bring stuff out, just tell me what to grab." Ten minutes or so later, she started the car and the three of them set out. With the one suit knowing exactly what had happened here, Bobby decided not to waste time trying to hide the bodies. He shoved them aside so he shut the front door and left it at that. His hands hurt. He did it all anyway, without complaint. Instead, he clenched his jaw and soldiered through it. His daddy would be proud.

Chapter 15

Once they reached the freeway, Lily turned on some soft jazz for Sebastian's amusement. Bobby hadn't had nearly enough good sleep over the past few days to resist that assault. Secure, warm, and comfortable enough, he passed out. He woke up to Lily shaking his shoulder.

"I hate to wake you, but I had to stop for Sebastian. We're just south of Stockton." She left him in the car and hurried around to Sebastian's door to let him out of his seat.

Blinking and rubbing his eyes, Bobby got out and stood up. "Dang, I was really wiped."

"Sebastian didn't want to wake you up or we would have stopped sooner." Lily held the boy's hand to walk him to the building. "He needs to use the bathroom."

"Sounds like a plan to me. I can take him into the men's room if you like."

"Sebastian, do you want to go into the boy's room with Bobby, or the girl's room with me?"

The boy looked from one to the other and said, "Mama, please."

Bobby cracked a grin. "Ain't nothing like the honesty of a little kid." In the bathroom, he took the time to run his head under the faucet, the closest he'd gotten to a shower since being arrested. As he walked back to the car with a handful of spare paper towels, he remembered he hadn't called Hannah back yet. She must be worried to all heck. First Jasmine, now him. He groped around for his phone, started to panic, then recalled handing it over to Lily. At the time, he'd done it in case the suits managed to grab him somehow.

He found Lily making peanut butter and jelly sandwiches, a little one for Sebastian, and a full size one for him. He took his with reverent gratitude. "You got no idea how much I need this." He took the first bite with unfeigned and unrestrained joy at the simple pleasure of fresh food prepared specifically for him. Though he wanted to use the phone, he wanted to eat much more. Five more minutes wouldn't break Hannah. He sat down on the curb nearby and watched Lily make a sandwich for herself.

Sebastian sat next to him, enjoying his own sandwich. "Mama is pretty."

"Ayup." He nodded while he swallowed his bite. His gaze traveled from her feet up to her hips and he sighed with contentment. "She sure is."

Lily glanced over her shoulder as she screwed the lid back on the peanut butter. Knowing he'd been caught staring at her behind, Bobby looked down at his sandwich.

"Bobby's eyes are like my eyes, like Mama's eyes."

"Ayup, they sure are. That's why I'm here, kinda."

"Bobby talks funny."

Bobby snorted. "I'm from Georgia. This is how we talk down thataway. You talk funny from where I'm sitting."

Sebastian giggled and managed to smear peanut butter on his nose. Like he knew it would, a paper towel came in handy. Bobby used one to wipe the kid's face off, managing despite him squirming and blowing raspberries.

"Aw, quit yer grousing, boy." Bobby tapped him on the nose with a finger and stuck out his tongue. "You do that to my Momma, and she'd tan your hide. How old are you, anyway?"

"Two and a half." He held up three fingers.

Lily sat down with her sandwich, putting Sebastian between her and Bobby. "Not until September. His birthday is in March."

"You don't seem old enough to have a boy his age."

"I got pregnant right after I graduated high school." Lily sighed. "Got married then, too. His father enlisted, though, and was killed in action about a month before Sebastian was born."

Stunned, Bobby gaped at her. "He had a wife like you, and a baby on the way, and he enlisted?"

She stared off at nothing. "We didn't know there was a baby on the way when he did it. He thought if we were married, I'd be able to live near him easier. Then they sent him to Afghanistan, and he never came back." Her thumb fiddled with her wedding ring. "Besides that, though, he just had to do it. He wanted to...he said he felt like he had something to prove, to himself and to his own father."

He nodded, because he understood. He didn't share it, because he didn't feel like going off to die would make his father proud, but he understood it. "My daddy was a Marine. He died in Afghanistan, too, when I was twelve." He had nothing else to offer on the subject and couldn't figure out how to feel about her story. Plain as day, she still loved the guy. That might not leave much room for anyone else.

For several minutes, nobody said anything. Bobby polished off his sandwich and wiped his hands. "That really did hit the spot." He stood and stretched his arms up.

"You didn't say where we're actually going, just Colorado. Do you have more specific directions than that?"

"Yes, ma'am, but I think Sebastian here needs to be rambunctious. He's a boy, after all. I'll go take care of that." He picked the boy up and carted him to a grassy space, where he chased Sebastian around and threw him up in the air. They wrestled around on the ground enough to get the boy shrieking with joy while stopping short of making him puke his food back up.

When they'd gotten back on the road, he picked up his phone where Lily left it for him and made the call. "Sorry I didn't call sooner, it was complicated and then I fell asleep."

"We were about ready to write you and Lily off."

"We're both fine. On the road to you right now. I...um, those two suits, they—" Bobby frowned, not wanting to admit what he did.

"Did you have to kill them?"

He sighed heavily. "Yeah."

"Jayce had to take two down, also."

"They're gonna come for us with big guns, you know that, don'tcha?"

"It's been on our minds, yes."

"Did Stephen get there yet?"

"No. Where are you? How long do you think it'll be until you get here?"

"I dunno. Lily has a little kid. We gotta stop a lot for him, probably. Just leaving Stockton right now."

Hannah left a long pause. "She has a kid?"

"Yeah, he has the eyes. Cute as a button, too."

"That's really interesting."

"If'n you say so. Do you want me to check in again before we get there?"

"No, just call if anything goes wrong."

"Alrighty. See ya soon." He hung up and watched the scenery go by.

Several quiet seconds later, Lily asked, "Who's Stephen?"

"He's a vampire." That sounded all kinds of wrong, so he quickly added, "Not a real vampire. I mean, he doesn't much like sunlight, drinks blood now instead of eating, is mighty strong, heals real fast, and can fly, maybe can do a few other things. But it's not like there's a lot of them out there and he was infected or turned or whatever, he's like us. There's a guy that's basically a werewolf, too."

"And Hannah?"

"She can make a shield with her mind, sort of like what you can do, only with blue stuff that I think is pure energy."

"How many people are on that list?"

"Thirty-five. At least seven have been nabbed by guys like those two suits, we think. No idea who they are or who they're working for. Why they want us, though, that seems pretty clear."

Lily's eyes flicked up to her rear-view mirror, giving her a view of her son. He cheerfully scribbled with crayons all over a coloring book from the box of toys and snacks next to his seat. "They can't do that to Sebastian. I won't let them."

In that moment, hearing her steely determination, he wanted to reach over and put a hand on her leg. Wary of her husband's ghost, he didn't do it. "Neither will I. Ain't right for nobody, doubly so for a little kid, triply so on account I like this particular one."

"Thank you for playing with him like that. His uncle tries, but he's got daughters. He's kind of restrained."

"No problem. I remember needing that sorta thing when I was little.

Was that the guy I saw at the garden place? His uncle, I mean."

"My big brother, yeah. He lives next door with his wife and three daughters."

"That musta been the lady I met when I went to your house first."

"Auntie Allie and Kaitlin," Sebastian supplied, proving he'd been listening.

"And we just left them all behind." Lily sighed again. "My parents, too. They've been really great about Sebastian, and his father. I feel like crap for just leaving like that."

"The alternative was waiting around to see how long it took them to send more goons with bigger guns." Bobby shut his mouth and watched the world go by, trying not to think too hard about how the dragons went out of his control, or what actually happened to his consciousness. Until then, he'd thought they were under his control unless he let them loose.

Now he knew they had enough autonomy to shut him out. One small point stuck out to keep him feeling sane: they had to all go into a rage for it to happen. He knew, somehow, that they'd still obey him so long as the majority of the swarm had no driving need to do anything in particular. Now that he thought about it, they couldn't force him into the swarm, either. He'd burst into it every time either because he wanted to, or to save his life.

With those moderately cheering thoughts, he settled back and let the radio blank his mind. The landscape shifted from one kind of farm to another, with towns planted here and there. At some point, that gave way to hills and trees, then mountains. They passed a sign announcing a turn for Lake Tahoe.

"Mama, I wanna stop."

"Okay, little man, we'll go for the next rest stop, but I don't know how long it'll be." She flashed Bobby a pleading look.

He nodded and turned enough to see the boy. "You know what, buddy, I got a cousin about your age, and he likes dinosaurs. D'you like dinosaurs?"

"Rawr!" Sebastian made claws with both his hands.

"I'll take that as a yes." Where Sebastian couldn't see, he popped a dragon off his thumb. It flew back to entertain the boy. " This here is a dragon, which is a lot like a dinosaur. You gotta be careful, though, because it's only a little bitty one. A big one, you could smack it all you wanted, and nothing would happen, but this one, it's real easy to hurt 'cause it's so small."

Sebastian watched it fly around him with delight, then land on his pudgy little hand and flex its tiny wings for him. "Baby dinosaur!" The dragon played for and with Sebastian, keeping him distracted. When the novelty started to wear off, he sent a second and a third in as reinforcements. They kept the boy from needing to stop for another hour. By then, Bobby wanted to stop, too, and so did Lily.

Bobby needed the roughhousing at least as much as Sebastian did, and the little boy's shrieks of laughter and joy buoyed his own spirits. After a dinner of bananas, granola bars, and more peanut butter and jelly sandwiches, Bobby drove. They had to stop one more time before Sebastian fell asleep in his chair and Bobby focused on getting them there in one piece. When he noticed himself nodding off, he pulled off the road and let himself sleep. Lily barely woke when he shut off the engine.

He woke up when his phone rang. Grabbing it, he rolled out of the car as fast as he could to let Lily and Sebastian sleep. While he intended to say 'hello', it came out as "Ungha?"

"Where are you?" Hannah's voice struck his foggy brain as urgent and concerned.

Rubbing his eyes with a thumb and finger, he yawned and collected his wits. "Um, just past the border into Utah from Nevada, on..." He'd seen so many signs with so many numbers, he had to think about it. "I-80, I think. The one that goes through Reno."

"Really? How fast do you think you can get back to Reno?"

"What'n heckbiscuits for?" He finally opened his eyes and saw the bare hint of orangey-pink in the east, and knew he couldn't have had more than four or five hours of sleep.

"Ai went to get her pickup in Reno. She got there about ten minutes ago, just as two suits were hauling Anita into a black SUV, probably unconscious. She tried to intervene, but they got away and are now on 80, headed straight towards you."

"Seriously?"

"Yeah."

"Damn, we coulda stopped there last night."

Hannah sighed. "But you didn't, so move on. Can you go back and maybe ambush the SUV or something? Ai is following them, but can't really do anything to stop the car while she's running at that speed. She can, apparently, talk on the phone, but that's about all she can spare concentration for."

"Just a sec." Bobby pulled in a deep breath and rubbed his face. This meant he had to leave Lily and Sebastian, because he couldn't put the boy into that kind of situation. It burned to let them go. If Ai needed his help, though, then that had to come first. "Yeah, okay. Can somebody there do some math and get me an idea where to stop and wait? I go about 100 miles per hour."

"I'll check. Hang on."

While he waited, Bobby peered back into the car. In the dim light, he saw Lily rubbing her eyes and Sebastian stretching his little arms out. He opened the door and ducked his head in. "I gotta go help another one of us, so you'll have to go on from here without me."

"Are they okay?"

"We'll see. Hey, buddy, you sleep okay?"

The boy made some inarticulate noises, then strained against his seat, trying to get out. His struggles prompted Lily to get out of the car and unbuckle him. "Mama, I gotta potty."

"Bobby," Hannah said into his ear, "best guess is to make for Elko and intercept them there."

At the same time, Lily looked around. "There's no bathroom here, can you hold it?"

"Got it," Bobby told Hannah, then he snapped the phone shut. She'd call Ai and set that up, because none of them had anybody else's numbers. Stuffing the phone away, he paced around the car to Sebastian. "I'll take him off the side of the road here."

Lily grimaced in distaste. "There could be a rest area just up the road."

He rolled his eyes and snorted at her. "We're boys, Lily. C'mon, buddy, lemme show you what to do when there's no bathroom nearby."

Sebastian hesitated, then he took Bobby's and walked with him down the shoulder. For miles around in all directions, he saw nothing but flat, boring desert. He would have preferred a corn field or some bushes to screen them. They had to take what they could get, and the sun hadn't really lit up the sky yet, so Bobby just turned his back on Lily and the car. He took heart that the boy followed along with him this time, not refusing in favor of his mother.

"Using a bathroom is better, of course," he told the boy as they paced back to the car. "When you gotta go, you gotta go." He crouched down to talk to Sebastian at his eye level. "I gotta go help somebody else, so it's just you and your momma for the next while. Remember that all this driving is about getting away from bad guys who want to do bad things to her. It ain't fun to go this far without stopping much, but when you get to where you're going, you'll have time to run around like crazy, okay?"

Sebastian nodded, then threw his arms around Bobby's neck, almost knocking him off balance. "Okay. Be careful."

Bobby squeezed him tightly, sorry to have to leave them both. "I surely will." He let go and gave the boy a solemn nod. "I'll see you again soon." Standing up, he tousled the boy's hair and turned to find Lily right beside him. "Um, yeah, so." Should he hug her, too? Shake her hand? He'd punch a guy in the arm.

She solved the problem for him by stepping in and wrapping her arms around him. "Thank you for everything. We wouldn't have gotten this far without you." Only a few inches shorter than him, her cheek rested on his shoulder.

Her body warmed him, and a powerful urge to kiss her bubbled up. He pushed it aside, knowing they both needed to get going. In opposite directions. "Just doing my part. Keep it no more'n five over the limit, and remember not to use a credit or debit card. You got cash for gas?" Reaching back, he opened the door for Sebastian.

"A little, probably not enough." Her eyes watched his mouth. Or he might have imagined that.

He put his arm around her shoulders and walked her to the driver's side door. Digging into his coat pocket, Bobby produced the money his momma gave him way back in Atlanta. "Here, take this. Should see you there."

She flipped through the bills. "Bobby, this is two hundred dollars, I don't need this much."

Dang, Momma gave him two hundred dollars? Why in heckbiscuits did she have that much lying around? Was she expecting him to break out and need cash to run for it? "It's fine." He waved it off and opened the door for her. "I been alright with nothing so far." He pulled out his list and the written directions for how to get to the base site and handed them over. "Don't need these no more, so you take 'em."

For a long moment, she stood there, looking at him. A light breeze lifted her hair, and the floating wisps glowed in the early morning sunshine. He had trouble catching his breath and caught himself leaning in. They still had no time for that. Before his mouth could say anything stupid, he stepped back and hurried around to buckle Sebastian in. "Take good care of your Momma, and be good, buddy."

The boy gave him a high five. Bobby shut the door and watched Lily signal, speed up, get back on the highway, and drive off. If he stood there, this road ran so straight and flat he'd probably be able to see her for a long time. Wondering if he'd made the right choice with Lily, he turned away and burst into the swarm. They had to reach Elko before that SUV did.

Behind him, the swarm watched car speed away. He had to stop thinking about her for now. Ai needed him, and so did the girl in the car. Forcing himself to watch the ground race past below, he settled into a hazy, bored zone and let the dragons do the flying.

Two hours later, he stopped in Elko and wandered from dumpster to dumpster. Nothing he found came close to the meals Lily set him up with, despite the fact he found half a roast beef sandwich. Woman had a way with peanut butter. Something about her made simple, plain food taste better and go down easier.

Hannah hadn't called, and the SUV didn't show up, so he burst into the swarm again and looked for a good place to set up an ambush along the road. Traffic ran light on the highway this morning. He dropped down to the southwest of the city, where the westbound lanes separated from the eastbound with a berm between. As he settled, he noticed the dragons nudging about food.

To keep them quiet, he re-formed and sat on the side of the road. He pulled a banana out of his pocket and ate that. It made him think of Lily again. When she'd handed him that banana yesterday, he noticed the softness of her skin. Something about her flipped all his switches. Having her there made it easy to forget about the two dead—

Nope, now he thought about the men he killed. The dragons, which were him, but not, took control when some of them got seriously hurt. His hands still ached from it, and driving yesterday had been rough because of it. He pushed through that to get things done, but they still hurt. The part where they ate the broken dragon still bothered him, too.

Here he sat, waiting for more men to come and be killed by him. Was he actually planning to kill them? It seemed more like he intended to hurt them in a way they could recover from. That explained why he chose a spot this far from the nearest city, so they'd have to wait a while before any actual help would arrive when they called. Realistically, though, he came out here to kill them, and should admit it to himself. These men were doing something wrong, whether they knew it or not, and he had to stop them, one way or another.

Where did they even get this many guys in suits? Goons R Us? For that matter, who was 'they'? Some part of the government, certainly. Kurt said it was military, but that happened a long time ago. It could be anybody now. If the FBI actually knew about all of this, would they try to stop it? What about the President or Congress?

He hopped to his feet and paced, thoughts swirling around in circles. Too many questions to think about popped in his head, but at least they took his mind off the fact he killed people and planned to do it again. What if he took one of these guys prisoner and questioned him? He and Ai and the one from Reno could hold him down and demand answers. If either suit knew anything, they could probably force him to cough it up.

What was he willing to do to get that information? Thinking back to movies he'd seen that showed or hinted at things that could be done to a person, he scratched the back of his neck. They always had assorted sizes and shapes of small blades, plus scary-looking things with purposes he could only guess at. Would just smacking him around be enough? What if they had tasers?

His phone ringing provided a welcome interruption. "Yeah?"

"Ai just passed exit 261. Are you in Elko yet?"

"I'm west of it, waiting by the side of the road. A bit past exit 271. Ten miles means about ten minutes, yeah? I'll be ready." Snapping the phone shut, he peered down the road. No way would he see something ten miles off here, not with the way the road followed around the hills. He popped one dragon off and sent it up to keep an eye out.

One car whipped past him, then another and another. The dragon got his attention, and he saw a black SUV coming up the road with a cloud of dirt kicked up along the side of the road in its wake. The dirt had to be Ai. He dipped his hands in his trenchcoat pockets and pulled out two handfuls of broken glass he'd gathered in Elko, then tossed it all onto the road. In case that didn't work, he blew out into the swarm so he could follow it.

The car sped over the glass and none of the tires blew out. His next tactic had the dragons diving under the vehicle. They grabbed the undercarriage and wriggled around, looking for parts to eat or break or poke holes into. Half the swarm got its fill of metal, and one clump of dragons punched a hole into the gas tank. The liquid splashed out, leaving a line on the road and spraying over at least a quarter of the little critters.

The vehicle sputtered and died, then coasted off to the side of the road. It rolled to a stop on the shoulder, and Bobby let the dragons keep wriggling through the innards, eating what they wanted. With this snack, they'd staved off hunger for a while.

He heard a car door open. One foot in a dress shoe, connected to a leg wearing suit pants, stepped out of the passenger side and crunched on the loose gravel. Rushing air kicked dirt up into a cloud and a male voice grunted in surprised pain. Bobby called the dragons out, sending them streaming out of the exhaust pipe, the front grille, and the undercarriage. Part of the swarm immediately surrounded a man in a suit.

Ai dropped down in front of the car, panting and drooping. Her eyelids hung heavy with dark circles ringing them. Dirt covered her body in a thin layer, and tiny streaks of blood on her exposed skin pointed to minor cuts. Traveling her way did a number on her. "There's four of them," she whispered.

The rest of the car doors opened, and Bobby gulped when he saw they all had tasers, guns, and one even had a net. A net? Who did these people think they— Five dragons freaked out, trapped under the net. Flames billowed out in a ball around a clump of dragons hit by a taser, igniting the gas covering them. One of the men swung a bat through the air, hitting several dragons. He heard someone say, "It's Mitchell!"

If he did nothing, the dragons would boil into a rage and murder all four of these men. He panicked, grasping to keep them from pushing him away. Their tug-of-war took time, and the suits spent it zapping and smashing dragons. Though he felt no pain like this, he suspected re-forming would beat the heckbiscuits out of him.

Bobby felt like he only had two choices. Either he let them keep going and the dragons all got smashed, or he re-formed and kept control and hoped Ai could handle this. He did want to live, thank you very much —he wanted to at least live long enough to find out what he could have with Lily, if anything. Living to watch Sebastian grow up would be kind of nice, too.

He re-formed kneeling on the ground beside the car, bruised, battered, and beaten. Everything hurt, from head to toe, and his left arm ended at his wrist. The suit with the net dropped it to the ground and stomped on the struggling bunch of them before letting them go to rejoin Bobby. Several struggled to fly, hopping along the ground with wings too damaged for proper flight.

Blood trickled down from his nose, and the nearest suit slammed the baseball bat into his head. It hit with a crack, the dragons too scared of being crushed to fly apart again. Lying on the ground, unable to get up but still conscious, Bobby heard tasers sparking all around. He saw Ai crumple nearby, twitching.

"And Dazai," another agent sneered.

Something else hit him in the back of the head and everything went black.

CHAPTER 16

"You're quite a troublemaker, Mitchell. Where have you been send-ing everyone? Where are Hannah and Alice?"

Feeling like crap all over, Bobby tried to move his hands without suc-cess. Something held them down, and it hurt too much to struggle against it. He opened his eyes and cringed away from the too bright light in his face. "Go to Hell." He wanted to go swarm, even though they probably all needed time to recover as much as he did. Nothing happened. He figured the suits had pushed him past the point where he could do it.

"I heard Georgia boys were polite. I guess that's just another stereo-type."

Something touched his side, then explosive pain rocked his body hard enough to make him scream. The crackle of electricity registered after the fact. He lay there, gulping air and now realizing his feet had been tied down, too. In the back of his mind, a tickle told him he had one dragon loose, on dragon watching this being done to him and gripped with enough angry terror to fill a bucket.

"Where are the others, Mitchell?"

"Go to Hell," he ground out again between gritted teeth.

"Well, we have Dazai, too. She'll probably tell us whatever we want to know when we're through with her."

Bobby's eyes snapped open to glare at the suit. The light stabbed his head with spikes of agony, but he ignored that to focus on delivering his message. "Keep your hands off her," he growled.

"Put three patriotic men in a room with a female terror suspect, and you never know what might happen." The suit's mouth curled into a cruel smirk of satisfaction. "You've been injected with a muscle relaxant. We have reason to believe it will prevent you from using your freak ability, so you get to lie here and listen." The suit stood up and opened the door of what must be a bedroom in a house. He had no idea how they found a house, set it up, and got here fast enough for him to wake up and still feel this awful.

With the door open, he could hear someone whimpering and sniffling. It had to be Ai or the other girl. Either way, he wanted to kill these four men for causing it.

"The thing about Miss Dazai is that once she's tied down, she isn't going anywhere." The suit nodded to someone outside the room, then he crossed his arms leaned against the door frame.

"Get away from me," Ai said, a warble of fear in her voice. She whimpered and Bobby heard cloth ripping. "Stop," she begged, "please don't." She sucked in a breath, and it sounded like she'd begun to cry.

"Don't you dare touch her!" Bobby shouted with all he had, straining to free himself. He could feel the dragons still under his skin, but none could break free.

"Just answer the questions, and this all stops. Where are the others going?"

This couldn't be happening. No one really did this kind of thing, not in the States. Bobby stared at the suit, torn between disbelief and rage. "Let her go. She don't know nothing. It's all me, I'm the only one what knows. You let her go, and I'll tell you anything you want to know."

"No!" Ai cried. "Bobby, don't tell them anything."

How could he lie here and listen to that? He liked Ai, she was nice and friendly and a decent person. She didn't deserve anything like this. No one did. Had he really thought about doing it to someone else not so long ago? Listening to her crying and begging for them to stop, those men disgusted him. That he wanted to return the favor disgusted him more.

He shut his eyes and breathed deeply, trying to push away Ai's voice. It would give him nightmares later. No, he wouldn't torture any of these men, not even for a minute. "I'm going to kill you. All of you."

The suit snorted. "I seriously doubt that, Mitchell."

Something still held his dragons in check, frustrating him and forcing tears of sympathy out of his eyes. He stopped trying to ignore the noises and let them in to fuel his anger. If he couldn't take it in her stead, he would listen. For being unable to stop it, he'd have memories of her screams and tears as penance.

"You sick fucks," a new female voice snarled.

Bobby's eyes snapped open and he strained to see the person he guessed must be the Reno girl, Anita. He watched the suit in the doorway turn in surprise and pull out a gun and saw little else.

Something crashed in the other room and the suit fired his gun. He kept firing and ran to the side. Whatever Anita could do, he doubted she could dodge bullets, leaving Bobby with little hope for rescue. Heavy things scraped across the floor, wood cracked, men grunted and groaned, and gunshots rang out. A nightstand sailed past the door, giving Bobby an idea of what happened out there.

With one last crash, the gunfire stopped, leaving Bobby's ears ringing. "Come on," Anita said, barely loud enough for him to hear, "we've got to get out of here before they wake up."

"We can't leave Bobby."

Anita growled in the back of her throat. "Fine, I'll get him. Stay here." A Hispanic woman with the eyes appeared in the doorway. She hurried in and bent to unbuckling the straps holding him down.

"Anita?" He sagged to make freeing him easier. "What'd they do to her?"

Anita clenched her jaw. "Why didn't you save her?"

"They drugged me." With one hand now free, so he reached for the strap on his other wrist. Clumsy and stupid, his fingers fumbled with the buckle. Not willing to go to Ai unprepared, he persisted. "What'd they do to her?"

She stopped and glared at him, her nostrils flaring. "They didn't have time to rape her yet, but were going in that direction. She's mostly cut up some. You let it happen."

As if he didn't have enough guilt banging around inside his head already. She had to go and add an extra pile to the heap. He already knew he let this happen. It had been his idea to attack the car there, and his choice to attack it the way he did. Bobby growled at her. "You wanna blame me, fine. Get her out and I'll make my own way from here."

"Fine." She tossed open the strap on his right foot and shot to her feet, then stormed out.

"What about Bobby?" Ai whimpered and hiccuped.

"He'll catch up when he's ready to be a man," Anita sneered. "You need medical attention, let's go."

What did she expect him to do? Was it not clear he would have smashed skulls if he could have? Every inch of his body ached, especially his head, and he couldn't even manage to free his hand. Sagging back to take a short breather, he called out, "Take care of yourself, Ai. You're strong, remember that."

He heard a faraway door open and shut. If he called the one loose dragon back, would the drugs make it reattach? Probably, so he couldn't chance it. He returned to freeing himself and managed to slide his hand free when he heard someone groan in the other room. Sitting up, he attacked the strap on his ankle. His hands still refused to do what he wanted, and he had to slow down to accomplish anything.

A suit staggered into the doorway. This one had been the driver at Lily's house. "Left you behind, huh?" Small cuts on his face oozed blood, and he held his side with one hand, a gun pointed at the floor with the other. "Still going to be loyal to those bitches?"

"Least I ain't a rapist." He kept working on the cuff around his ankle.

"It's a fine line, you know. But really, none of you are actually human. We can do whatever we want to all of you."

"I'm still an American citizen. So is she." Stupid, stupid fingers took far too long.

"Technicality. Cats and dogs aren't citizens, even though they live here. You just are because you look human enough to pass for one"

"I ain't a cat nor a dog."

"Close enough."

The buckle came loose and he looked up into the barrel of that gun. In his current condition, a BB gun could probably kill him. He froze and gulped.

"Think you're faster than a bullet, Mitchell?"

His dragons still wouldn't come out to play. "If'n you don't think I'm human, why d'you keep using my last name? That's my daddy's name."

The suit chuckled. "Cute. Hands up or you get shot."

With another gulp, Bobby slowly raised his hands. For now, he'd have to do what this guy said. Why did he have to mouth off at Anita? Oh, right, because she blamed him for what these assholes did to Ai. His eyes danced from the gun to the man and back again as he thought about taking the chance. Another voice groaned out there. Two guys with guns sounded like way more than he could handle right now. Besides, the hospitality here sucked.

Adrenaline pumped through him, easing the pain all over his body. Ducking to one side, he swung an arm out to push the gun aside. It went off. He lunged. They scuffled over the gun, both in equally bad shape. Bobby heard another gunshot. Something stabbed him in the side and he felt himself go pale. No matter how much he wanted to keep going, to keep fighting, his body wouldn't let him. It had been beaten, battered, and now broken, and it couldn't take any more.

Staggering back, Bobby grunted as the suit shot him again. He collapsed and felt unconsciousness creeping up over him, so he reached out to the one lone dragon that managed to stay apart. It perched outside the window, claws around the upper edge and dangling down to watch. Somehow, he found himself in there with it, and he watched the suit nudge his body with a shoe, watching himself not react. This beat everything else he'd ever done or seen for weird, no contest.

The suit holstered his gun under his jacket and knelt beside Bobby's body. He tucked two fingers under his chin to check for a pulse, then ripped Bobby's shirt off. His muffled voice called out for the others and he covered the two the injuries he just inflicted, applying pressure to both. So, they wanted him alive. Had to appreciate the guy not putting a bullet in his brain and leaving it at that.

Hannah needed to know what happened here. His current assets: one tiny robot dragon with no ability to speak. It could, instead, make cute little dragon noises. Now that he paid attention, this tiny robot dragon had enough rage to kill someone fifty times over. Its claws had dug into the metal it held onto so hard they punched holes in it. In fairness, he had a powerful urge to gut these four men, too.

Getting a message to Hannah felt remote and impossible under these conditions. Freeing himself had to be his next best option. Thinking of it that way confused him, so he settled on thinking of it as freeing his body. The dragon preferred to do that, and let its rage simmer down to a manageable level to help.

From this vantage point, he watched another suit hurry in with a medical kit. Together, they worked on keeping his body from bleeding to death. Neither of them tried to pull the bullets out or sew anything up. Instead, they focused on using powders and applying gauze and bandages.

The problem of freeing his body occupied his mind while they worked. Actually, freeing it now would be stupid. He'd be unconscious, unable to accomplish anything and at their mercy. Waiting until it got real treatment and woke up struck him as a better plan, since he couldn't go swarm until that happened. In the meantime, he would keep track of it, listen in, and try to find a way to contact Hannah. This plan sucked. It was still a plan, and better than no plan.

For this plan to work, he needed to be able to hear what they said. Thankfully, the dragon understood it needed to stay apart from the swarm for now, so he could count on its help. Never mind the weirdness of that. This was not the time to be dealing with the absurdity his life had become. This was the time to be dealing with the crap in front of him. He directed the dragon to fly all around the house and find a way inside.

As soon as they saw the tiny dragon, they'd recognize it. If even one of them noticed the weird shape of his finger, they knew he had a dragon loose. There would be no element of surprise here, and no hiding in plain sight. This dragon had to stay out of sight, and had to do it where he could listen in and follow them. The possibility existed that they wouldn't think he could have his mind in the one missing dragon, which gave him a slight advantage.

The dragon found a vent in the eaves of the two-story house and crawled inside, then flew through it and found the dryer vent with no dryer connected to it. The laundry room had no washer, either. That meant no one lived in this house. How did they get here? Where was 'here'? The questions gnawed at his brain. Mind. Whatever. They gnawed. He flitted through the house from ledge to shelf, keeping track of the best hiding spots.

All the action had taken place upstairs, so he stopped on the moulding at the top of the doorway closest to the bottom of the stairs. Unless a suit shone a light up here, they should remain unnoticed. With so little furniture and decoration, the voices carried, so he heard the suits talking. In fact, it had such a small amount of anything, he wondered where Anita had found anything to throw around.

"Why did you even shoot him a second time? You could have just pistol whipped him." Bobby decided to call this voice Suit One, it being the first one he heard well enough to make out the words. He spoke in a clean baritone with no obvious accent.

"You saw the pictures from San Jose." As already noted from his brief conversation earlier, Suit Two also had no accent. Did they train these guys that way? "They didn't do his handiwork justice."

"He was doped up and couldn't do that right now. Christ, that's why we aren't dead now."

"Just call it in and get us another ride."

"You think the girls took the car?"

Suit Two snorted. "Of course they did. They'd be stupid not to. These things may not be human, but they aren't stupid. If we've learned anything by now, it's that underestimating them will get us all killed. We're just lucky Martinez only beat the crap out of us."

Another voice groaned and debris shifted.

Digital tones announced an outgoing phone call. Suit One spoke. "Dazai and Martinez got away. Mitchell is in custody, but seriously injured. He's been shot twice. ... Yes, sir, but Dazai and Martinez took our vehicle. ... No, sir. ... He's stable for the moment, but we need to move. This location has been compromised. We could all use some medical attention, we didn't let them go quietly or anything. ... Yes, sir. ... Understood."

"Did anybody get the number of that Mack truck?" Suit Three, also accent-free, joined the conversation as a pained tenor. "Jesus, I think she broke my goddamned arm."

"Barnes is still out," Suit Two said. "Check on him."

"Someone will be here in half an hour," Suit One said. "Privek is pissed."

Was that FBI Special Agent Steve Privek? The one that originally arrested Bobby a million years ago, on the other side of the world? Privek apparently had been slumming it by picking Bobby up, or maybe got a promotion from doing it with whatever freaky organization they all worked for. It couldn't really be the FBI. The country his daddy fought and died for wouldn't let the FBI do things like this. He hoped not, anyway.

"No shit," Suit Two growled. "We'll be lucky if it isn't a cleaning crew."

"Barnes is dead," Suit One announced. "We should blame him."

"Seconded." Suit Three grunted with pain.

Suit Two said, "Agreed. He was in charge of keeping Martinez subdued. His judgment on the subject allowed her to get free, and that's how she overpowered us and got away."

"Shooting Mitchell twice is all on you, though," Suit One snapped.

"Whatever. He was still a threat. At least we have him."

"Assuming he lives," Suit One snapped.

"He'll live." Along with Suit Two's voice, Bobby heard the sound of latex snapping, probably him pulling off gloves. "He'll never be a quarterback, but he'll live."

They moved on to tending Suit Three, who Bobby learned had a name of 'Walker' when Suit Two told him to stop whining. Whatever injuries he had, they seriously hurt. Bobby figured these guys had one thing in common with his daddy: they didn't bitch and moan about minor injuries. If they made noise, it damned well hurt. Walker made a lot of noise.

It took them fifteen minutes to get Bobby's and Barnes's bodies down the stairs and within easy reach of the garage. Walker had to go slow and cradled his arm. After that, Suit Two walked around the house, dousing it with clear liquid from a large canister they must have brought along with them.

At the same time, Suit One went through Barnes's coat in the kitchen, where Bobby could see it. He pulled out four different badges from four different agencies, checking each one and setting them in a stack. When he'd checked all the pockets, he slid them in an already half-full bag, along with a set of keys, a pack of gum, and a few other small items. Bobby's own trenchcoat could be in the bag, though he doubted it.

With that done, Suit Two pulled Bobby's cheap cellphone out of a pocket and futzed with it. It had only one number in memory and the call log, and he punched a button to dial it. If only he could warn Hannah somehow, or at least hear the other end.

"Yeah, I got clear, sorry to make you worry." Suit Two did a reasonably good impression of Bobby's voice. He listened in disgust, praying for Hannah to see through the ruse before she revealed anything. "I'm pretty messed up, but I'll heal. Are the girls okay? ... Good, good." He stood there for several seconds without saying anything. "Hello?" He growled in the back of his throat and snapped the phone shut. "She hung up on me."

Bobby would have breathed a sigh of relief if he could have. The dragon kept its head and didn't let him make any noise.

Suit Two showed the phone to Suit One. "Trace the number down. It looks like he's called it plenty of times. We should be able to get a fix on it."

Suit One pulled out his own smartphone and tapped on it several times while checking the number on the flip phone. "Assuming they don't smash it. Someone just pointed out they aren't stupid not too long ago."

A thumping noise cut off the conversation and made both suits look up. "Our ride is here," Suit Two said, snapping the phone shut and tossing it into the bag. The two of them headed to the front door. Bobby followed along, doing his best to stay out of sight.

Completely out of place in this nice, normal neighborhood, a sizable cargo helicopter landed in the middle of the street. Since they clearly intended to load his body into it, Bobby turned his attention to the task of getting into it unseen and finding a hiding place for the flight. Men in military camouflage hopped out and left the door open, and everyone kept their heads down, making his job easy. The dragon fought the wind from the rotors to come around the other side and swoop in over the top.

From his perch under the pilot's seat, the dragon could see part of the instrument panel. Bobby had no idea what any of the knobs, dials, and gauges meant. He did, however, figure out that one near the middle was a clock. Their flight lasted fifteen minutes and thirty-five seconds. It landed at some kind of military facility, one with hangars and an airfield, and some really enormous mountains in the distance.

This was not Elko. No one would be stupid enough to put an airport along a road that wound through the mountains, and these particular mountains didn't look like anything he saw flying over and near Elko. Until he got a better view or saw a sign, he had no guess for his location, other than 'not Elko'. That meant he might have been unconscious longer than he thought.

Soldiers hefted his body onto a stretcher, then into a building. He sent the dragon slipping in through the doors. From the way they shouted and gestured wildly, he gathered the medical facility and personnel only rarely saw gunshot wounds. They carried Walker in right behind him. Strangely, the soldiers accepted the suits without challenge, referring to them as 'sir'. He might have missed them flashing badges.

How in the heckbiscuits could he possibly escape this place? After surgery, they'd keep him so pumped full of drugs he couldn't burst into the swarm until the suits came and took him again. That meant he needed to get away on foot. From a military base. With suits on site. Assuming he ever woke up before they found a better way to restrain him.

He shelved that problem in favor of getting more information. There might be a way to get a message out. Besides, if the suits stayed more than another day at that facility in Virginia, he'd eat his boot. Knowing the four of them got out, they'd be sugar frosted stupid to keep using it. That meant the others they'd nabbed could be here. Jasmine could be in the basement.

Two hours later, the dragon had flown through the entire duct system of the building with nothing of interest to report. When he found his body again, a doctor was still working on him. The next time he went swarm, this would get translated into generic pain. They, of course, didn't know that. Even if they did, they wanted him unable to go swarm anyway. What did they even want him for at this point? They already spent five days doing whatever they wanted, and had plenty of his blood and whatever else they decided to take while he wasn't conscious. Why not kill him?

The dragon settled in at the vent over the surgical suite. He watched the doctor pull a lump of bloody lead out of his shoulder and drop it with a clang into a metal pan. It bothered him to wonder what purpose they possibly could have for him now. Thinking about it made the dragon surly, so he stopped. At least, he noted with some small satisfaction, they hadn't removed his jeans or boots. When he left here, it wouldn't have to be in a hospital gown.

When both wounds had been taken care of, the doctor let a soldier come in and wheel his body out. The surgeon followed at first, talking to the nurse. Because he wanted to hear what the man said, Bobby had the dragon follow along in the ducts, rushing from vent to vent. The nurse nodded in a bored, disinterested way at his instructions until he used numbers and words Bobby had never heard before, which he assumed to be drugs and dosages.

Along the way, they ran into Suit One and Two. The doctor sighed when he saw them and stopped while the gurney kept going. With the dragon confident it could find his body no matter what, Bobby also stopped to listen.

"Just the man we were looking for." Suit Two smiled, reminding

Bobby of a viper. "What's the prognosis?"

Doc nodded. "He'll be fine, eventually. Nothing major damaged, just muscle and a rib."

"Excellent news. How long until we can have him back?"

"At least twenty-four hours," Doc said. "Mind, I'm saying 'at least'. If anything goes wrong before then, he's staying longer. We'll know more with certainty when he wakes up."

The two suits exchanged looks, their eyebrows raising up over their sunglasses. "We want him kept sedated." At this point, he had no doubt Suit Two wore the pants for his team.

"That's not in his best interests—"

Suit One gave the doctor a winning smile as he cut him off. "We're more concerned about the best interests of the US government. If he escapes, that would be...bad."

"He's in the middle of an Air Force base." Doc rolled his eyes. "We'll post a guard outside his door, he won't get away in his condition."

"I can appreciate your position, doctor, I really can." Suit Two's voice grated for how syrupy sweet he slathered on the sugar. "That man has already killed three of our agents when he should have been easy to subdue, and is a known terrorist." Three? They put Anita's handiwork on him? "We're much more concerned about the safety of everyone else here at the base than we are about his best interests. So long as he can be interrogated, that's all that matters."

Doc sighed and raked his surgical cap off to reveal short, graying black hair. "Fine." He crumpled the cap and jabbed a finger at Suit Two's chest. "But in twenty-four hours, we're waking him up, at least for an hour, to see what condition he's really in."

Suit Two shrugged, unmoved. "No problem. We'll be back in twenty-four hours, then."

Doc glared at their backs as they turned and walked away. Bobby had to decide which to follow. He wanted to hear what Doc said to the nurse, but he also wanted to know what the suits would say outside. If only he had two dragons, then he could listen to both. Before he made a decision, the dragon chose to follow the suits. They left the building, and he followed them out the top of the door, tail whipping out as it closed. The suits moved away from the door, finding a spot between buildings where Suit Two lit up a cigarette. Bobby perched in a nearby shrub to listen.

"I'll make sure he's dosed, you set up transport to the depot." Suit Two checked his watch. "It's just after one now, so I'll want to slip the stuff into his IV around noon tomorrow. I'll stop in on the way to lunch."

"Sounds like a plan," Suit One nodded. "Man, Mitchell better be worth the trouble. He's a serious pain in the ass, not easy like Milani was."

"Tell me about it. This time tomorrow, though, he'll be down for the count and hopefully on his way to being tucked in with the rest of them."

Suit One turned his gaze out to the airfield and stuck his hands in his pockets. "Playing them off each other might have been a mistake."

"No, that was the right way to go. Martinez just wasn't secured well enough. Mitchell would've broken when Dazai was actually raped. They still think they're human."

Suit One grunted in assent. "You hungry?"

"Starving."

Uninterested in watching them eat, Bobby let them walk off without following. The dragon's claws had crunched the small branch it perched on, and he found its anger difficult to separate from his own. Yeah, he still thought of himself as human. He'd grown up human and so had the rest of them. Whatever they'd become, they still deserved to be treated like people, not animals.

Thinking about this got him nowhere. In twenty-three hours, his body would be dosed with something, probably the drug that inhibited his ability to break into the swarm. He needed to prevent that. At the same time, his body needed to rest and heal. So, he needed to figure out how to do that, then kill some time.

His dragon noted it had gotten hungry, so he added finding something for it to eat to his to-do list. Knowing he prioritized that, it flew off in search of food. It sniffed around and found some spare parts in a hangar to devour. As he flitted around the base, he passed a sign marked 'Hill Air Force Base'. He'd never heard of it. Most Marine bases, he'd recognize, but not Air Force.

Before he could come up with any better ideas, he needed to know where he was. He and the dragon climbed into the sky to get an aerial view. The base sat on the north side of a large city, one with a major highway running through the middle of it. Huge mountains to the east and a giant lake to the west gave him a strong suspicion for his location.

They dove into the city, looking for signs. Sure enough, he passed one confirming he'd been taken close to Salt Lake City. If he remembered geography right, Utah was next to Colorado. Could he reach home base and get back in about twenty hours? Even if he could, would it be worth going? What would he do, have the dragon pantomime everything or try to hold a pencil three times its size?

He had to try. If he never tried, he'd never know what might've been. Besides, he'd be able to find his body again even if he got back late. Maybe he'd miss this chance, but there would be another one. At some point, his body would wind up in a position where one dragon could manage to free it. He had to believe that. Otherwise, he might as well give up and die now.

Turning east, they went up and beat those little wings as fast as they could handle. It flew high enough to go over the mountains that must be the Rockies. From that vantage point, he saw the ribbon of Interstate 80 winding along. He kept it to his left. Understanding the importance of this trip, the dragon pushed itself as hard as it could, and Bobby had no idea how fast it managed to go.

Up here, with nothing and no one around and the dragon doing all the work, Bobby's mind wandered. He started with watching puffs of cloud, moved to tracing the contours of the land, and wound up hoping Momma wasn't worrying about him too much. She deserved better than him for a son. All his life, he'd given her a hard time. Maybe he did it because deep down, he knew he didn't belong to her.

He had weird eyes. He could turn into tiny robot dragons. The suits made it clear they thought that made him something other than human. What if they were right? Did that mean he had no right to call himself a citizen? They took his blood and did tests. Did they find some proof? God, if he wasn't human, what was he? What were they all?

The dragon didn't actually say 'shut up, I'm concentrating', but the impulse came through loud and clear. Bobby quit thinking so hard and watched the land slide by underneath. To think, he spent his time moping over Mandy not too long ago. He wasn't even sure how long had passed since then. Two weeks, maybe. He'd liked her, sure. Compared to everything that happened since Privek arrested him, she meant nothing. That thought threatened to spiral into those same topics he already annoyed the dragon with, so he cut it all off again and made an effort to just be and enjoy the scenery.

CHAPTER 17

Bobby guessed it took four or five hours to fly from Salt Lake City, Utah to their plot of land south and east of Fort Morgan, Colorado. When he got close, they had to follow the roads, using the directions he'd memorized to find the right place. They zoomed up a tree-lined driveway to find a decrepit farmhouse in the middle of renovations. The barn off to the side looked much worse than the one in the picture had. He had no doubts, though, that he came to the right place.

Matthew unloaded boxes from a van, straining with the effort. Despite not seeing him much without his fur, he recognized the werewolf immediately. Until the moment he saw a familiar face, he had no idea how much he needed one. Matthew, though, couldn't help him right now. Bobby needed someone who would instantly recognize the dragon as being part of him. The werewolf had been focused on Stephen the whole time.

With no real idea about the layout or where anyone in particular might be, Bobby let the dragon wander. Eventually, he'd find someone that could help. It took a slow, lazy circle around the house. In the back, some Asian guy sat on the ground, eyes closed and hands in the dirt. Dan and Lizzie, hands all over each other, slipped into the woods surrounding the house. They'd be no help, and he had no interest in watching them get naked and sweaty together.

Voices came from inside the house, promising better results that way. As he neared the closest window, the back door slammed open. A little boy barreled out, naked and shrieking with glee. The sight made him want to laugh. Even better, Lily would be along shortly to collect Sebastian. He chased the boy down and dropped into his sight. Sebastian stopped and recognized it, then put out his little hand. The dragon landed and chirped a greeting at him.

"Bobby! Mama, Bobby is here!" Sebastian turned around and ran back to his mother. Even with a red bandanna over her hair, she took Bobby's breath away. If he could have one wish right now, it would be to climb out of this dragon and be there to take her in his arms. He'd wrangle the boy for her, too.

She peered all around. "Where? I don't see him." When her son presented the dragon, she bent down and wrapped an arm around the boy to prevent him from getting away again. "Bobby?"

The dragon trilled, trying to get her attention. She kept twisting around, waiting for him to come walking around the corner. A minute later, she shrugged and picked Sebastian up. The boy squirmed and wriggled, and she had to abandon the search in favor of handling him. He did have to admit that getting the naked kid into clothes rated higher than him. Sort of.

"Hannah," she called out as she opened the farmhouse door, "one of Bobby's dragons is here," The inside of the building had more to recommend it than the outside. They'd put up a fresh coat of paint and scrubbed the floors so far.

"I'm in the meeting room," Hannah's voice called out.

The dragon leaped off Sebastian's hand to follow her voice up the hallway. It passed a large kitchen with a picnic table and Andrew stirring a large pot hanging over an actual fire.

"I've got Seb—" Lily stopped and smiled. "Oh, it's heading for you."

Bobby had to give them all a lot of credit for what they'd done so far with a place that must have been a real dump. They didn't seem to have electricity yet, and still managed to get the place well on its way to livable in a short time. Lots of hands willing to help at least part of the time made a big impact.

Another hall branched from the first one, and he kept going until he found a large space. A wall running across the middle of it had been half smashed, and a thin layer of white dust covered everything. Stephen yanked a sledgehammer out of the plaster and drywall with a grin on his face. Good to see him able to help out in a way that amused him. Hannah stood near the door, using her force field to catch the debris he pulled away. They had an ancient, rust covered wheelbarrow she dumped it all into.

"Just one of his dragons?" Stephen set the sledge aside and wiped dust and plaster off his face with his gray shirt. "He won't be able to talk through it. We'll have to ask it yes/no questions. Oy, dragon!"

Thank God. Bobby nudged the dragon to land on Stephen's hand. It danced in a circle and trilled at him. Much to Bobby's surprise, it also belched out a tiny puff of fire.

Stephen flinched away and put his other hand up. "Okay, okay, you got my attention. Christ, don't do that again." He smirked. "Okay, Lassie. What is it, girl? Is Timmy down a well?"

The dragon stuck its tongue out at Stephen, then nodded. Bobby had no idea these things even had tongues. Also, he appreciated that it translated what he thought the best it could.

A grin flashed on Stephen's face, then he schooled his face into a frown. "Is Bobby in trouble?" Nod. "Is he hurt?" Nod. "Damn. How are we going to figure out where he is?"

"A map? I'll see what I've got." Hannah hurried out of the room.

"Can you lead us to him?" Nod. "How many hours did it take you to fly here, little guy? Can you tell me that with fingers or claws or whatever?"

Without knowing the time, Bobby had no clue how long it took. He saw Stepehen's watch on his other wrist and had the dragon walk to where it would be. There, it sniffed and prodded until Stephen got the hint and held up his other hand sot he dragon could see the watch face. At his direction, the little dragon held up four claws, curling the thumb partway under.

"More than four but less than five?" Nod. "Okay. Bobby can go about the same speed as me, that'll put him someplace between four and five hundred miles away, give or take. Is there a time limit? Is Bobby going to be moved in some amount of time?" Nod. "Hm. If you have any ideas about how to express that, I'm paying attention here."

How should he explain noon? It took Bobby a few seconds of furious thought to come up with something. The dragon rolled onto its back and showed him twelve little claws.

Stephen's lips moved while he counted. "Twelve? Midnight or noon? Er, is it midnight?" Shake. "Noon tomorrow?" Nod. "I can get that far by then. Violet can, too. Actually, we could drive that far. Is Jasmine there?" Shake. Stephen sighed and shook his own head. "We'll find them, all of them."

"I hope he's still in America." Hannah rushed in with a simple map of the country, showing only state borders and capitals.

"Four to five hundred miles away, so yeah, he should be."

"Huh." She crouched down and set the map on the floor so the dragon could walk on it.

He jumped down and scurried to Salt Lake City, tapping north of it with a claw.

"Salt Lake. Okay. If we had internet, we could get more specific, but that's close enough for right now. Let's see, we need to make sure there's at least one person with defensive ability here, and we're not taking anyone who can't handle a fight. I wish Jayce was here already."

"We smashed all the phones," Stephen explained to Bobby. "A suit called with yours. Er, Bobby's. Hell," he turned his attention to Hannah, "I don't even know if he's in there or it's just the dragon. Anyway. You stay here, I'll take Lizzie and Dan, Violet, and—"

"Not Violet, she has no idea how to fight. All she can do that we know of is fly."

"I'll go." Matthew stood in the doorway. He had a quieter, more intense voice than Bobby expected from listening to him roar.

Stephen pursed his lips. "No offense, but I'm not so sure that's a good idea."

"None taken, and I agree, but I'm going. If there's going to be a fight, I should be there."

Hannah frowned and stood. "I'll go talk to Andrew."

"Wait." Stephen put out a hand to prevent her from getting up. His eyes stayed on Matthew. "I can handle it."

"This is going to be messy enough already." Hannah sighed and rubbed her neck. "At least bring an insurance policy."

Bobby saw Matthew and Stephen exchange tiny nods. Seemed like they'd connected on the trip up here. From his perch, that seemed a good thing. "I'm enough of an insurance policy. We'll be fine. No need to put Andrew in harm's way. He can't fight, either."

"Oh, whatever." Hannah rolled her eyes. "I'll go find Alice, then, and Lizzie and Dan. Anyone else?"

"Andrea," both men said at the same time.

Hannah sighed. "Please don't kill any more people than you have to. That's all I'm going to say." She left the room without waiting for a response.

"People are going to die." Matthew said it flatly, as a statement of fact.

"Yeah." Stephen nodded. "We'll wait here so we don't have to wait around there too long. Let's see." He turned to the map and ran his finger over the basic route despite the lack of roads on the page. "This drive will probably be, what? Eight or nine hours? Be ready to leave at midnight. Let's push it a little, but not cut it too close."

"Twelve hours to make a nine hour drive?" Matthew fiddled with his watch. "Sounds reasonable." The two men shared a look, and Bobby thought something else passed between them. With a curt nod, Matthew left the room.

Bobby stuck with Stephen as he explained what they knew to Lizzie, Dan, Alice, and Andrea. Andrea reminded him of an underwear model, with frothy brown curls and cinnamon skin. It might have had something to do with the tight little shorts she wore. Even so, despite getting an eyeful of three different attractive women at once, Bobby's thoughts still strayed to Lily. He wanted to curl up with her and never let her go.

Stephen watched the four of them go to prepare and sighed. "I will never get tired of watching that," he muttered, his eyes firmly on Andrea's backside.

Bobby had to admit the view could be much worse. The dragon trilled his agreement, provoking a smirk from Stephen.

"Hey, you have a minute?" A girl with a ton of freckles and straight red hair in a bob cut poked her head around the corner. Her ears had five hundred piercings filled with different colored studs. Back home, Bobby called a girl like that 'freaky'. He'd since developed a whole new definition of that word, and chose instead 'different'.

Stephen saw her and smiled. "Sure, Kaitlin, what's up?"

She stepped into the room, showing off an outfit that hurt Bobby's head: orange and pink striped tights, a black pleated miniskirt, fuzzy purple slippers, an orange tank top, and a gray hoodie with the zipper halfway undone. 'Different' definitely covered Kaitlin.

"I heard Hannah saying some of you are going out to rescue Bobby?" As she got closer, Bobby put her height at about five foot nothing.

"Yeah." He quirked an eyebrow at her. "You want to come?"

"Hell no." She waved her hand, dismissing the idea as crazy or stupid. "I just thought you might want some guidance. Oh, hey, is that one of his dragons? Can I hold it?"

"That's kind of up to it, not me." How true. "And yeah, that would be great. Thanks."

Bobby urged the dragon over to another girl who wanted to touch the cute dragon. She held him up high enough so the dragon could touch her nose, then shut her eyes. Figuring she might be using a power, he sat patiently, tail wrapped around the dragon's feet. A minute or so later, her eyes snapped open.

"Don't speed on 80 in Wyoming. He's on a military base with planes. Don't expect him to be able to help. Jayce will be here just after ten tonight and you should bring him. Don't take Hannah's van. There are three suits, don't let any of them get away." She offered Stephen the dragon back, then paused with her other hand up, finger extended to make him wait. "Don't go through the front gate, and watch out for the little girl inside the building: pigtails, red shoes, red dress. Protect her at all costs."

While the dragon hopped back to Stephen's shoulder, he repeated everything back to her, and she corrected him when he made a mistake. "Will do. I just love saving little girls." The words came out creepy, leaving Bobby—and Kaitlin, probably—with the impression that he meant to add 'for snacking' on the end.

"She's important." Kaitlin grabbed his arm and yanked him closer, her whole expression steely and daring him to try something. "Really important. She has to live and see you guys as big damn heroes."

All traces of humor gone in an instant, he nodded. "I get it."

"Okay." She let go and gave him a satisfied smile. "Good luck."

He tipped an imaginary hat at her and left the room. Bobby watched him stuff a change of clothes in a bag, studiously avoid the kitchen, field a few questions from the others, then return to the work of smashing through that interior wall. Just when he thought he'd have to figure out how to pass the time without his mind buzzing or distracting Lily from her boy too much, the dragon settled on a shelf and shut down. Everything went black.

The dragon came awake again. Surprised to find himself still in the dragon, Bobby accidentally made it yawn and stretch. It tumbled and brushed on something, revealing it had been scooped up by a hand. He found himself eye to eye with Stephen. "Are we ready to go?"

Bobby trilled and stamped, then flared his wings and jumped into the air.

"We didn't get all dressed up for nothing," Jayce said with a smirk.

Warm relief flooded through Bobby at his voice. Nothing like hearing the rock-steady sound of someone he knew and trusted. He flitted to Stephen's shoulder and chirped a greeting for Jayce.

"Is that Bobby in there, or just the dragon?" Jayce flashed him a confident grin and climbed into a van.

Stephen slid into the driver's seat. "I don't know, and actually, I'm not sure I want to know. I mean, thinking about that is a little mind-blowing. Sure, we all defy the laws of physics already, but that's just going way, way past logic and into crazy."

Jayce chuckled. The rest of the van gave up a few snorts and chortles. "Because getting your nourishment from blood isn't way past logic and into crazy."

"It's only crazy," Andrea's light Tennessee drawl said, "when it hasn't been written about in umpteen books already."

Bobby checked the rest of the passengers and smiled when he saw Alice. No matter how big a pain she'd been, familiar faces made everything seem better. Noticing him, she gave the dragon a wave and a pleasant smile. He lifted a claw and waved back.

Lizzie sat across Dan's lap, both of the refusing to use seat belts. Andrea, sitting beside Alice, now wore black leggings and leaned against the window. Matthew lounged across the back, arms crossed and eyes shut. When Stephen started the engine, he faced front again.

Lily ran out the front door in a green flannel robe she clutched shut. Standing on the front stoop, she waved, her hair mussed and eyes drooping. She must have gone to bed already, but made sure to wake up for this. Through Stephen's open window, he heard her say, "Be careful and bring him back safe!"

Stephen gave her a thumbs-up out the window, and she smiled. It held enough worry to crush Bobby for doing that to her.

"Awww." Lizzie's rough alto voice crooned from the back. "She's so cute. Probably jump him the second he gets back."

Bobby ignored her. Sort of. Aside from the guilt, seeing her make a special effort for him... He didn't get warm or flush or blush or sigh, but he felt like if he had his body, he'd definitely do at least one of those. He'd also follow through on all the other impulses by taking her in his arms and finally kissing her.

Alice sighed. "Doesn't it bother you the slightest bit that we might all be siblings?"

Dan grinned. It bothered Bobby how much he and Dan looked alike. It crossed his mind that the two of them might have the same real parents, making them full brothers. "Honey, we grew up as brother and sister. Mom had me and adopted Lizzie two years later. She called us a matched pair." He kissed Lizzie's neck. "We so totally are."

"And if we are related by blood, who cares?" Lizzie raked her fingernails across his scalp to brush his hair behind his ear. "It's not like we're planning on having kids and a white picket fence."

"I want a dog, though. I like dogs." Dan grinned and kissed Lizzie hungrily. The rest of the group, aside from Matthew who seemed to be asleep, either rolled their eyes or grimaced.

Leaning forward, Andrea said, "I dunno. I mean, no offense to you two, but I'm just not that interested in any of the guys at the farm. Oh, sure, you're all pretty. Being at the farm is a lot like living in one of those weird perfume commercials and all. But nobody's a spark for me. I need a spark, a pop, razzle-dazzle."

"None taken," Jayce said with an amiable smile. "I'm not particularly interested, either. Nice to look at, but not interested."

Stephen, Bobby noticed, kept his mouth shut and his eyes firmly on the road. His knuckles, already normally quite pale, had gone white from his grip on the steering wheel. Odds seemed high he had one of those cute little bunnies and fuzzy duckies moments going on in his head. At least he knew those things were wrong and actively avoided following through with any of them.

With that, and Dan and Lizzie not bothering to stay quiet, the chatter in the car died. Jayce turned the radio on, flipping between stations until he found one that Andrea danced in her seat to. The pop songs blurred into each other, broken up only by commercials.

Bobby couldn't stop thinking about Lily. If she turned out to be his sister, half or full, nothing would change. Like Lizzie said, he had no plans for kids of his own. Sebastian did make him think he might be a passable daddy. That didn't mean he felt ready to raise his own from the ground up. Anyway, their problems started and ended with her dead husband.

Annoyed and bored, the dragon sent signals that he ought to shut up. It stretched its wings by buzzing the car, then settled in the ashtray and shut down before Bobby could protest. Twice, the eyes opened, rousing Bobby, when they switched drivers and filled up the gas tank. Alice took a shift, then Jayce.

The third time, the sun had come up and Jayce stopped at a gas station. After filling up, he jogged into the building and came back with a map and sandwiches. Sensing this might be more than a basic stop, Bobby made the dragon stay away when Jayce started the engine again, and he sat on the dash as he pulled the car into a shaded parking spot.

Jayce opened up the map and invited others to take a look. Lizzie and Dan chose instead to go use the bathroom. "According to the cashier, there are two bases in Utah: Hill and Dugway. Hill is just north of here, Dugway is pretty much the western half of the state."

"Kaitlin said it had planes." Stephen wore a hoodie now and sat with Andrea and Alice. "The dragon pointed to Salt Lake City."

"Probably Hill, then." Jayce looked down at the dragon. "Is it Hill?" Nod. "We should have a plan of some kind. We can try walking in the front door and asking politely, but I'm going to go ahead and guess that won't work."

Dan and Lizzie came back, disrupting the discussion. They settled onto the same bench seat again and Bobby wondered how either of them ever managed to accomplish anything. Then again, their house had been in need of enough repair that he would've been ashamed to let his Momma see it.

"Kaitlin specifically said not to use the front gate. If I fly in, I can probably find a way to get everyone else in quietly. Biggest problem, though, is the damned sun." Stephen scowled.

"I can help." Lizzie held up a black bondage mask for him. Her dress, so far as Bobby could tell, had no pockets, and he hadn't seen her reach into their bag. With a moment of reflection, he realized he'd be better off not knowing why she had it in hand.

Stephen stared at her for a long moment. His lip twitched, showing one fang. Reaching back, he grabbed it and muttered, "Thanks."

Lizzie grinned and blew him a kiss. "Can't we just blast our way in? That would be a good diversion."

Andrea rolled her eyes and shook her head. "How public do we want to get? That kind of thing is a line. Once we cross it, we can't really go back."

Alice shrugged. "It's a military base, we won't get a lot of press from it. Mostly what will happen is the suits will know that a bunch of us are working together and get an idea of how well we do that, plus they'll learn about the powers the rest of you have."

"And—" Matthew, now sitting in the front passenger seat, had to cough and clear his throat before finishing the thought. "And we'll be telling them that we'll go to the mat and pull out the stops for one of our own. They'll be more ready for us the next time it happens."

"They might also step up the effort to find us in this region, because they'll have a time frame to work with." Jayce checked the roads on the map, following them with his finger. "Since they know how long Bobby has been here, they know how far away we can't be. Maybe we should wait until the last minute to keep as much area in their search pattern as possible."

"Why did Kaitlin say not to take Hannah's van?" Stephen fiddled with the mask, giving it a dirty look. "That's the one thing she said I didn't really see the need for." He finally put it on, getting familiar with the zippers and snaps and figuring out how to make it fit best.

Everyone went quiet and Jayce started the engine. Bobby figured that since the suits knew she'd come with them, Hannah's plates had some kind of alert on them. Not only that, she had Pennsylvania plates, which would stick out in these parts. The Montana plates this van sported wouldn't get a second look.

Almost three hours later, after another stop and another close look at the map, Jayce parked the van in a residential neighborhood. Everyone piled out to walk the rest of the way. The dragon perched on Stephen's shoulder and saw him check his watch, noting the time as 11:15. With his dark hoodie, creepy mask, leather gloves, and nondescript jeans and sneakers, he looked like a serial killer. Without them to keep him sane, he could be one.

They moved in a disjointed group, Stephen keeping Jayce and

Matthew between him and the few people they passed by. A few blocks lat-er, they reached the last row of houses before the razor-wire topped chain link fence providing a wide buffer for the base. The dragon pointed at the cluster of buildings in the distance, making sure they knew not to go look-ing in the hangars.

"We'll see you on the other side." Stephen tipped an imaginary hat and grabbed Dan under the armpits. They flew up and over the fence, landing on the other side. Lizzie blew Dan a kiss and Stephen flashed a peace sign back at the group, then the two of them dashed across the open space to the nearest hangar. Anyone paying attention to this section of the perimeter would see them, no question. Bobby doubted anyone watched it all the time.

Getting into that building required pushing a button and being buzzed in, which would be harder. Security might be lax around the edges, given this base sat in the middle of the country and had a barrier against casual trespassers and dumbass kids. The actual buildings, so far as he saw before, told a different story.

Knowing what would happen in a minute or so to help defeat that security, the two men put their backs to the building Bobby pointed out for them and waited in the shade. Right on cue, an enormous, billowing bale of fire exploded at the spot where they'd left the others behind. Lizzie certainly did have a flair for the dramatic. He barely knew her, but could easily imagine her dancing around in the flames like a giddy schoolgirl in a shower of confetti.

"That's my girl," Dan murmured. He smiled as a second huge plume of fire erupted near the first.

Stephen pulled the mask off while they waited and stuffed it into a pocket. "Damn, that thing is hard to breathe through. You're sure you can make someone push a button?"

"Yeah, I'm sure."

"I should mention that I'm hungry."

"Awesome." Dan grinned, showing no sign of squeamishness. "You take down whoever gets in the way, I'll grab Bobby."

Vehicles raced across the base in time to see a third fireball explode. So far, only a few scraggly shrubs had caught fire, presenting no real threat to the base or the neighborhood around it. Andrea or Jayce would be standing next to Lizzie, reminding her not to kill anyone. Hopefully, she'd listen.

"Lizzie isn't a patient woman."

"Yeah, my girl is more of the instant gratification type."

Stephen checked his watch. "We'll give them a couple of minutes to muster everything that's going to get mustered."

"Burn, baby, burn," Dan chuckled, his eyes lighting up with glee. They watched as more and more vehicles streamed off in that direction and more and more fire shot into the sky. Any of those blasts hitting a building could demolish it. They had to be that big to attract enough attention and cause enough chaos.

Stephen tugged his hood up and patted Dan's shoulder. They rolled around the corner, slipping up to the front door. He pushed through the outer door of an enclosed entry with ease. The inner door, on the other hand, had a place to swipe a key card and a button to press to get someone to open it for them. He tapped the glass to check how solid it was, then pressed the buzzer to get someone to show themselves.

Dan scowled as no one popped into view. "It's a camera system. Sorry, can't use that."

"No problem. We can do it the hard way instead." Stephen took three steps back, then threw himself at the glass, hitting it with his shoulder. The glass cracked.

"Awesome." Dan flicked a finger at the MP stepping out into view as he drew his gun. The guy shot the glass four times. He turned the gun on himself and shot his own leg.

Stephen hit the glass with his shoulder again and smashed through it. He stopped a few feet inside the door and shook glass off himself.

Dan followed him through the hole and picked up the dropped weapon. He clucked his tongue at the guard's whimpers of pain. "Don't bitch, buddy, I coulda made you point it at your head."

When a second MP jumped into the hallway, Stephen grabbed him by the neck and threw him at the wall with enough force to leave a dent. "Lead the way, dragon." He pulled out his nightmare swagger and stalked up the corridor.

The plan Bobby heard discussed outside neglected to mention mayhem inside the building. These two seemed to have intended to do it all along anyway. On the bright side, Dan was right, he could have had the man shoot himself someplace fatal. The dragon flitted forward, trying not to think too hard about the angry path these two men had decided to carve through the staff here. Dan's gun barked several times along the way. Not one of the shots hit anything vital on anyone, suggesting he was either a lousy shot or a fantastic one, and he only aimed at men.

Less selective in his targets and methods, Stephen also avoided killing people. Some hid fast enough, the rest got his fist in their face or thrown into a wall. "If I'd known it would be this easy, I would've just come by myself." He smirked as he ignored a doorway to a room full of scared people. Several had phones out, taking pictures or tapping away.

"That wouldn't be fair, to keep all this fun to yourself." Dan tossed his empty gun behind them and caught the one that a surprised guard lobbed to him. That guard turned and punched the guy next to him in the gut. "Do we care if anyone besides the base takes pictures of us?"

"A little." Stephen backhanded a guy not quick enough to get out of his way. Bobby took a look back at the groaning bodies and debris littering the hall and realized the vampire had lost most of his control. He breezed through, treating this like a party. The guy needed cake.

Dan stopped at a doorway and stared into the room beyond it with a feral grin. The sound of several people smashing their cellphones put a bounce in his step as he moved on to the next group. More gunshots rang out and they hit the stairwell.

Damn, these two men scared the heckbiscuits out of Bobby. This seemed like a good idea up until now. He should have found a way to free himself. There would have been a window, he could have figured something out. But no, he had to go for help. The blame for all of this belonged on his shoulders. When the suits came looking for the group with a nuke, it would be his fault. If anyone got killed, that was on him.

CHAPTER 18

The dragon fluttered against the door to his room, then landed on the knob. Seeing that, Stephen grabbed the nearest nurse and put her in standard hostage headlock position. Dan opened the door and shut it behind Stephen and his guest. He held his latest gun ready to fire at anyone else coming through it.

There he lay on a gurney, wires and tubes monitoring him and keeping him alive. His body still wore those jeans and boots. Funny how they never bothered to remove either. No sheet covered his torso, leaving all his injuries available to be seen. Bandages covered the stitches, with purple bruising peeking out from underneath. His wrists had less severe bruises, and angry red burns marked where he'd been repeatedly tasered.

"Damn, you got messed up," Stephen breathed. Adjusting his grip on the nurse, he pushed her forward. "Unhook him, now."

Bobby wanted to stay out here and watch while he woke up. The dragon didn't care about that. It dove at his body and merged back with the swarm. Everything went black again. The next thing he knew, someone patted the side of his face.

"Wake up, sleeping beauty." Dan had picked up a penlight and shone it into Bobby's eyes. "Welcome back, Bobby."

Flinching away from the light, he tried to talk. "Nguh." His tongue refused to work. A moan of ecstasy attracted his attention, and he turned his head to see Stephen with his mouth locked on the nurse's neck from behind. Her eyes fluttered and her mouth hung open. Not wanting to watch that, he tried to lift his arms and found them uncooperative.

"Yeah, Kaitlin said you'd be useless. Anything burning important you want to tell us?" Dan had tucked his gun into the front of his jeans for the moment. He put an arm around Bobby's shoulders and tried to help him sit up.

Squeezing his eyes shut, he tried to think around the vampire porn happening in the corner. "Suits." It took a lot of effort to push that word out.

Failing to make much progress with getting Bobby vertical, Dan gave up. "Three, like Kaitlin said?"

The woman slumped in Stephen's arms and he let go of her neck. He licked the last smear of blood off her flesh, then set her aside and adjusted his jeans. "I needed that. I really, really needed that."

Bobby blinked repeatedly, trying to focus. "Yeah." In the movies, the drug cloud always lifted pretty fast. He could feel the edges perking up, at least. It might not be too long before he could help.

"He's a big lump."

Stephen stretched, standing up and reaching until his fingertips brushed the ceiling. "Muuuuuuuch better." He breathed deeply and cracked his neck. "Push him out on the bed and watch for a wheelchair. I'll plow the road."

"Pig." Bobby had a take a breath between the two halves of the word. "Tails."

At the door, Stephen looked back, one eyebrow quirked. "You were in the dragon all along."

"Yeah."

Stephen looked away and rolled his shoulders in a squirm. "I'm not going to think about that right now. And I've been watching for the girl all along. Give me a minute to check the hall." He opened the door and slipped out, shutting it behind himself.

"I'm with him on this one, Bobby. Thinking about how your mind got crammed into a little bitty dragon while your brain was here the whole time... Nope, don't want to go there. Crazy enough I can control other people's bodies and he drinks blood. You're just out and out off the scale."

Shutting his eyes and hoping the drugs would fade quickly, Bobby mumbled, "Thanks."

"No offense."

Bobby grunted. They heard crashing outside and a handful of gunshots. Dan pulled his gun again and pointed it at the door. Stephen's voice roared in rage through the muffled door. Bobby noticed Dan relaxing, the tension draining out of him. Either the vampire's anger or the prospect of doing more violence calmed him. Nothing like having a deranged psychopath on his team. Like Matthew, though, no one else could hope to control Dan. If this counted as 'control'.

"C'mon and try it," Dan breathed. Suit One threw the door open, gun up and ready to shoot. Dan took one beat to check him over, then he squeezed the trigger and put a bullet between the suit's eyes. "Too slow." He grinned as the body crumpled and kept the gun pointed at the open doorway. Someone flew past the door to crash into something loud and clattering.

Stephen stormed past, putting a hand up for their benefit. "I got this, get moving."

Dan smirked and saluted him with the gun. He shoved the corpse out of the doorway, then reached inside and yanked the wheeled bed through. Bobby turned his head to the side and watched Stephen bear down on Walker, aka Suit Three. The man had one arm in a cast, yet still held a gun after being tossed for distance.

Stephen grabbed the gun and flipped it aside, not bothering to use it. The two men scuffled, though Walker had no chance against Stephen in a 'fair' fight. Dan kept going, kicking debris aside and dragging the bed to the elevator at the other end of the hall.

"There's more." His mouth felt less stupid, so Bobby pushed out a few more words. "Another suit. Four, 'Nita killed one, hurt one. Boss left."

Dan grinned wide enough to seem manic. "Awesome, a boss fight. Time for the big guns."

As the elevator doors opened, Stephen caught up with them, swooping in and holding his side with a scowl. "That sonofabitch tased me."

"You kill him?" Dan asked, eyes alight with interest.

"Yes. I gather there's another suit. Five bucks says one of us will have to shield the pigtail girl from him shooting her."

"No bet," Bobby grunted. He rolled onto his side while the elevator carried them down two floors. It took a lot of effort, and his eyes went wide as he saw something unexpected in the corner. Unable to keep himself there, he slumped onto his back again. "Guys. Pigtails. Right here."

Both men turned to look. The little girl with the red dress and shoes, her blonde hair in pigtails, sat curled up in the corner. Maybe eight or nine years old, she clutched a teddy bear and stared up at them in terror with wide, icy blue eyes. Hers were otherwise normal, lacking the odd tilt all of theirs had. At a glance, though, she could be easily mistaken for one of them.

Stephen rubbed his forehead and mouthed a curse. He breathed deeply and crouched down to her level. "Don't worry, we'll protect you. I swear on my father's grave that I won't let anyone hurt you. We're not going to take you away from whoever you're here with, either."

"We ain't the bad guys, I swear." Bobby licked his lips and prayed for Dan to keep his mouth shut. "There's gonna be shooting, though, so stay small."

The girl nodded and hid her face, pushing herself closer to the corner.

Stephen stood and put himself in the middle of the doors. Dan braced himself between the back of the elevator and the bed. The doors opened. Four soldiers pointed guns at Stephen and fired. Stephen grunted as the bullets hit him. He reached over and pushed the button to shut the doors. Bullets clanged as they hit the metal and dimpled it inward.

He flipped the emergency switch so the doors would stay shut, making an annoying bell ring. "Dammit, I'm going to have to feed again soon."

"Maybe it wouldn't creep you out so much if'n you called it 'eating' 'stead of 'feeding'." Here he lay, taking all of this in stride. He could freak out instead, except that wouldn't help anything. Bobby took a deep breath and lifted a hand, flexing his fingers. "The drugs're wearing off."

"What are you?" The little girl's voice managed to reach him despite the bell.

Bobby smiled at her, hoping for the best. "Superheroes. Misunderstood superheroes."

"Like Wolverine?"

"Yes." Stephen reached over again to the elevator panel, meeting Bobby's eyes and asking without words if he was ready to try again. "Exactly like that."

Bobby offered the girl his hand and inwardly groaned at the words he intended to say to her. "Come with me if you want to live."

She blinked, sniffled, and nodded. Surging to her feet, she grabbed his hand and jumped to get onto the gurney with him. Ignoring how much he hurt he curled his body around her protectively. Nestled in his arms, she asked, "Is my Mom okay?"

"We made an effort not to hurt anyone too much," Dan reassured her. "Except the as—er, guys that want to lock us up and treat us like lab rats. Them, no mercy."

"Are we ready to do this?" At the affirmatives from Bobby and Dan, Stephen flipped the emergency switch off and let the doors open. He spat the bullets out, causing the eight soldiers now waiting for them to stare with varying degrees of disbelief. "Would you like to shoot me again?" He took a step forward and lifted his hoodie and shirt to show them his intact chest. "I can do this all day, really."

One man turned his gun on the one next to him and shot him in the leg. Another soldier decked the one with the gun and took a bullet in the shoulder for it. Dan's handiwork, no doubt. At the other end of the line, another soldier shot a different man in the leg.

Stephen reached the group of men and backhanded one of them so hard he spun around. "Shame to ruin my clothes, but hey." Grabbing two by the collars, he smacked their heads together and flung them in opposite directions. "The things we do for friends." He threw a punch that sent the last man standing to the floor.

"You're a goddamned showboater," Dan snorted. "It's fun to watch." He wheeled Bobby and the girl out while Stephen cleared a path for them.

Glancing back over his shoulder, Stephen grinned. "It's not like any of these guys can—"

A gunshot cut him off. Stephen jerked and twisted, a bullet punching out through his neck. He collapsed in front of the gurney. The second shot hit Dan in the shoulder, missing his head because he ducked. With no ability to regenerate or deflect anything, Dan dropped to the floor, wheezing in pain.

"Animals, every last one of you," Suit Two snarled. He stood between them and freedom, feet apart and gun held in both hands. "Rabid dogs that need to be put down." Stepping calmly over debris to reach them, he let go of the gun with his left hand to retrieve a syringe from his jacket.

Bobby's heart stopped. Unable to see Stephen and Dan anymore, he couldn't be sure if either of them would survive. "I got you," he whispered to the girl. Together, they turned and looked at the suit. She buried her face in his chest and he scowled. Inside, he could feel the rage building, and knew he'd been free of the drugs long enough. "I said I was gonna kill you for trying to rape my friend. I meant it."

Suit Two's eyes narrowed, focusing on the girl. She must have looked much younger to his eyes, terrified and huddling for safety. His gun twitched so it pointed more at her than him. "There aren't any children in the program anymore. Which one of you does she belong to?"

"What program? Where's Jasmine? Did you kill Mr. Peterson to set me up?"

Suit Two's nostrils flared and he sneered. "Never mind that. I won't bother trying to injure this time, Mitchell. There's a level of acceptable risk, and we're past it now. Hand over the girl and come quietly or die."

It seemed to Bobby that the suit figured he must still be harmless, since he still laid on the bed. In fairness, he did feel pretty useless right now. The swarm had so much rage, it took every drop of effort he had to hold it back. His dragons hated this man, so much. No matter what, Suit Two would not leave this building alive. Bobby would let them loose already, except Kaitlin said the girl needed to understand, and to see the whole picture. "I don't really like those choices. Is there a third option?"

Suit Two's mouth curled into a disdainful smirk and everything slowed down for Bobby. The gun fired and he saw the bullet spin out of the barrel. He burst into the swarm and let it have its way, so long as it protected the girl. The dragons noted three different innocent people watching him. Stephen got up on his hands and knees, gasping for breath. Dan, pale and bloody, clutched his shoulder.

Three dragons dove at the bullet, all willing to sacrifice themselves to keep the girl safe. One let it rip its wing off, the second bounced off it, and the third threw its body in the way. Their efforts knocked it far enough to the side to hit the bed instead of the terrified girl.

The rest of the swarm went for Suit Two. They pushed Bobby aside while they converged and destroyed him with claws and fangs and fire. Suit Two screamed and shrieked until they tore his throat out. His arms flailed for another half a minute, then he stopped and sagged, held in place by the swarm refusing to let him fall.

When he felt certain the suit had to be dead, Bobby mustered everything he had and forced the swarm to let the corpse go. They stopped and buzzed about for a few seconds, then swooped to the gurney and picked up the three damaged dragons. The corpse of Suit Two collapsed to the floor.

Bobby re-formed standing next to the bed in his jeans and boots, bandages gone. His hands and arms hurt all the way to his neck. He took a deep breath and averted his eyes from the gory pile his swarm made. The air carried the awful stench of fresh and burned meat. This little girl needed to get away from that.

Stephen breathed deeply and stood up. He looked at the girl, who watched his neck heal over with her mouth hanging open. "We're not full of sunshine and daises, but we aren't sadistic monsters, either."

Bobby saw her gulp and nod. He gritted his teeth and picked her up. He'd hefted appliances heavier than her on his own, though not when he felt this awful. "Don't you look at that thing on the floor. I'm gonna give you to one of these folks who works here. Soon as you can, you go find your Momma and tell her all about what you saw."

She clung to him, wrapping her legs around his waist. "He tried to shoot me," she breathed.

He grunted and stepped over debris to reach a side room with awe-struck people hiding inside it. "I think it was more about me, but yeah."

"You saved me." She kissed him on the cheek when he set her down and waved as he backed out. Both things taken together went a long way towards making him feel better about this whole episode.

"You have a fan," Dan croaked out from the floor.

"I thought I was supposed to save the girl. I'm the vampire, I should get the girl." Stephen smirked as he bent to help Dan.

Bobby rolled his eyes and returned the girl's wave. Part of him wanted to ask her name. The rest noticed people peering timidly out through doorways. Choosing one at random, he pointed to a man who stared up at him with his hands up in surrender. "More of these suit-wearing guys are going to show up here on our trail. You tell 'em something for me," he said, watching the man nod and gulp. "They mess with one of us, they mess with all of us. We're coming for the rest of ours, and we ain't playing around."

Stephen pulled Dan to his feet and supported him to he could walk. Bobby turned and strode out through the front door, holding it open for them. This part had no real plan. Everyone needed to get back to the van without getting caught, killed, or followed. Back in his body, with the pleasantly warm midday sun shining down on him and all three of those suits dead, he felt invincible. How hard could it really be to get out of a military base?

Surveying the chaos, he sighed. Lizzie had gone hog wild. The entire end of the base they came in through burned. She'd set a handful of vehicles on fire, and one hangar had gotten engulfed. Multiple types of trucks circled in that area, with more still heading that way. Lines of soldiers streamed that way, and Bobby thought maybe they ought to have had her set the distraction up on the other side of the base.

Jets firing up their engines momentarily drowned out the gunfire filling the air. That whoosh and boom sounded more likely to have come from a rocket launcher than Lizzie. She'd started a small war, one they needed to get out of before somebody got the bright idea to use satellites for spot-targeting them with smart bombs or space lasers, or whatever they had. "Stephen, you need to get Dan outta here. I'll see if I can get the others going."

"I suggest no one tells Lizzie I been shot so long as it can be avoided." Dan panted, dark circles forming under his eyes. Sweat beaded on his forehead, and his one arm dangled, useless.

Agreeing completely, Bobby nodded. Lizzie did all this just to have fun. He shuddered to imagine what she could do if she got angry. "Yeah, you just go straight for the van. Get it started up and ready to move." Because it would be faster and safer, he burst into the swarm and headed for the center of the mayhem. That's where Lizzie would be, and everyone else should be nearby.

Chapter 19

From his new vantage point, Bobby saw Stephen carrying Dan over the fence. Sunlight glinting on metal pointed him at Jayce. Several squads of soldiers hoofed it towards him. These Air Force folks probably never saw anything like this before, and he felt sorry for them. Screaming distracted him. Nowhere near Jayce, an exploding fireball threw three soldiers into the air. One might have been lucky enough to survive when he hit the ground.

The werewolf ran out and pounced on that soldier, ripping him in half. Bobby revised his opinion of the definition of 'lucky'. Another soldier on the run emptied his weapon at the werewolf. Although he failed to hit Matthew in the chaos, the soldier got his attention.

Jayce could take care of himself. Matthew needed to be lured out, now. The swarm dove with all the speed his dragons could muster. He watched in horror as Matthew, too quick for Bobby to prevent it, pounced on the shooter and tore his arms off. The swarm surged in and buzzed around his head, belching fire out to singe his fur and tugging on his ears. Matthew swatted at them, catching and crunching four.

Rage bubbled up in the swarm, pushing him away. The dragons wanted to deal with this, their way. Bobby held them off. Matthew needed help, not death. No matter what he did, no matter how low he sank, he still deserved a chance to figure out how to control this side of himself. Everyone else got that small favor. It looked like Matthew left the building when he sprouted fur. So did Bobby, when the swarm got angry. How could he look himself in the mirror if he judged Matthew for something he'd done himself?

He had to flee. The swarm flowed off the werewolf and towards the fence, taunting Matthew by staying just out of reach. Movement distracted him, so Bobby sent a handful into his face to goad him. Another dragon got crunched. The rest of that group hauled it out of reach with them, devouring it on the way.

At the chain-link fence, the dragons streamed through. Matthew stopped. Too many targets on his side of the fence gave him no incentive to try to climb out and chase the swarm down. Bobby re-formed and clenched his jaw against the pain. "C'mon, buddy, I ain't leaving you behind, no matter how many of my dragons you swat." God, he hurt worse than he had before. At this point, his arms hurt from one end to the other, and his feet ached up to his knees. If he kept going, he'd be a walking ball of agony in no time flat.

Matthew roared at him, grabbing the fence and shaking it violently. Right now, they needed Stephen or Jayce. Either of them could take what Matthew could dish out. Bobby wanted to be able to, but he couldn't, not even at his best. If he stayed here and kept trying to pull Matthew out, he'd only succeed in getting himself killed. Considering this operation was entirely about rescuing him, that would be pretty rude, not to mention counterproductive.

Getting away from Matthew became his top priority. He whisked out into the swarm again and, steering clear of the angry werewolf, poured back through the fence. Despite worries about what Matthew would manage to do in his absence, Bobby streamed away to find Jayce. Fortunately, that turned out to be easy. There he stood, glinting in the sunshine next to with Lizzie, Andrea, and Alice. Ice formed a high wall around them in a horseshoe shape with Jayce at the mouth. Alice had to be working hard to maintain it against all the incoming gunfire, and her skin had turned blue again.

Landing and re-forming in their midst he immediately punched Jayce good-naturedly in the arm. "Hey, you can retreat now. Somebody's gotta get Matthew, though. I tried, but my way ain't working."

"Good to know. Alice, you shield them out. Andrea, set up an obstacle course for anyone following you. Lizzie, time to stop and run for the van. I'll go get Matthew. If I'm not back before you see Stephen, send him to help." He took off in the direction Bobby pointed, running at full speed.

Bobby breathed a sigh of relief at his words. Jayce not only accepted responsibility for the werewolf problem without argument, he also chose not to punch him back with that big metal fist. Lizzie pouted, of course. Alice pushed a wall of ice out around them and forced Lizzie and Andrea to rush for the fence. Irregular craters blew out with a shower of dust in their wake, which he assumed to be Andrea's power at work. These women truly terrified him.

"I should mention I saw fighter planes taking off. Also, I'm going swarm." Pain went away for the swarm. He might have considered that weird, except everything else about his power fit that definition, too. One more thing hardly rated notice.

"Oh!" Lizzie squealed with glee. "I've never blown up a plane before."

"And you're not going to start now," Andrea said, her voice strained by concentration. "We're trying not to kill people, remember?"

Lizzie pouted. "It would just be one guy."

"That really doesn't make it okay."

"Spoilsport." Lizzie reminded him of a kid called in from the playground by her momma. "Maybe I should just go off on my own."

"Go ahead. Just keep in mind you're not immune to bullets and Dan is back at the van now."

Lizzie heaved a sigh Bobby considered meoldramatic. How in heckbiscuits had she managed to make it this long without getting herself killed or thrown in jail? She probably had one of those stories that winds up in a crime show, telling the woeful tale of how a rotten childhood can turn a body into a monster. Maybe someday, he'd be forced to listen to it.

Bobby flew along with the girls, staying low to avoid catching lead. The dragons noticed something coming from the side and he focused in that direction to see a missile streaking in ahead of a jet. Flabbergasted, he directed the dragons around Andrea to roar and point as a group. She could stop it. Right? After everything that happened so far, getting obliterated by a missile would be unfair.

Andrea flung her hand out and grimaced with effort. It closed in fast, then appeared to hit a wall that reduced it to find dust. "Christ on a cross," she breathed. "I can't do that too many times."

"Guys, I'm getting tired." Alice slurred words, and she panted and stumbled. "I can't keep this up forever."

"There's the fence!" Lizzie sprinted for it, sending a huge ball of fire out in front of her. Immune to its effect, she plunged in and out of sight.

"I really wish she'd stop doing that." Andrea blasted another hole in the ground behind them, then scanned the skies.

Bobby re-formed next to Alice and grabbed her arm. She radiated enough cold to make it a special form of torture. He still tossed her arm over his shoulders. "Lean on me, Alice, I got you." He grunted in both pain and surprise when she collapsed onto him. Scooping her up into his arms, he gritted his teeth and ran as fast as he could manage.

Andrea's eyes widened as she ran along with him. "I can't disintegrate everything coming at us. Just so you know." When a bullet whizzed between them, she glanced back and squeaked.

"Great." Adrenaline helped Bobby push past the pain to get this done. The flames had died down, so they plunged through the gap in the fence together.

Alice passed out in his arms and the ice stopped flowing. Her limp arm fell forward, and her body shifted. It knocked him off balance and he pitched forward. Curling around her protectively, he cried out at the agony of hitting the ground and rolling. More dust hit them, attesting to Andrea sticking close enough to help.

Part of him wanted to lie down and die rather than keep going. Glancing the way they'd come, he saw the soldiers hanging back. They stopped shooting, taking up defensive positions a few dozen feet inside the fence. Maybe they figured out their tactics didn't work. Took them long enough. "Help Alice," he grunted at Andrea.

"Not leaving you behind, dumbass, that's how we got into this mess in the first place." Andrea grabbed the waist of his jeans in back and hauled him to his feet.

"Jesus, woman," he growled.

She ignored him and took Alice by the wrists, dragging her across the grass to the street.

Her actions gave him what he needed to keep going, which meant he had nothing to complain about. He caught up and grabbed Alice's ankles to suspend her between them. Something about those soldiers staying back bugged him, niggling at the back of his mind. It could be they'd decided to defend against Matthew on his way out, he supposed.

Then again, they had the planes go past once already. He looked up and saw dots in the sky. With the missiles having failed already, possibly twice, they'd probably try something else. "Fighter jets have regular big guns, right?"

Andrea's mouth fell open, her eyes wide with panic. She gulped and nodded. "I don't think I can stop those. I have to target things specifically, that's why bullets are hard."

"How in heckbiscuits are we gonna get outta here? I mean, even once we reach the van." The dark blur of Stephen zoomed over the fence and into the base. That meant Lizzie had reached the van, which meant she knew about Dan. Would she fawn over him, or come for the group? Within a second of the thought crossing his mind, the van screamed around the corner and screeched to a stop in front of them. Lizzie at the wheel sounded pretty scary to him. He had no ability to drive right now, though, and maybe crazy would turn out to be the best way out of this.

At the end of the street, two puffs of dirt and debris plumed into the air. Bobby and Andrea dove for the van and threw Alice into the back seat. More pairs of plumes marched up the street to greet them. Lizzie slammed on the gas and launched the van sideways, out of the strafing line, then managed to get the vehicle turned around. She floored it towards the plane, which seemed crazy until they screamed down the next street without getting shot up.

Flanked by houses, Bobby thought they might be safe for the moment. If those planes were willing to strafe through the houses here, they had bigger problems than he thought. Peering out the back window, he saw no more plumes, and figured the planes must have diverted to go after Jayce, Stephen, and Matthew.

"We need radios," Bobby croaked, in fresh agony. When the van had turned, he, Andrea, and Alice had all tumbled around, and now both lay on top of him.

"Do you think any of them got a good look at the van?" Lizzie checked her mirrors and sent them hurtling through the neighborhood.

Andrea levered herself up and into the front passenger seat. She buckled herself in. "Probably not, but I bet they noticed the color."

"Stop someplace and I'll send a dragon to show the guys the way to us." He shoved Alice off himself, wishing he could protect her from whatever else Lizzie might do. At the moment, he could barely protect himself. The swarm could get him up into a seat. It couldn't help him get Alice into one. Besides, they refused to touch her skin when it went frosty blue. He didn't like that either, but could suck it up if he had to. Raising himself up on his arms made him whimper.

Lizzie slammed on the brakes, throwing him into the front seats and pulling a sharp, short scream out of him. He heard Dan hiss in pain from the cargo area in the back, too. "Don't do that again, baby, it really hurt." He sounded like heckbiscuits, and they had eight hours of driving ahead of them.

"Dan," Bobby groaned, "you get bandaged up yet?"

"Not really."

"Great." He gave up trying to move. "We're gonna have to stop someplace and get him some genuine medical attention. 'Less one of you ladies has some experience pulling bullets outta shoulders."

"I could try?" Andrea looked back and patted Bobby's arm, which made him wince. "I don't *think* I can disintegrate living matter."

The van had stopped moving. Bobby said he'd do something. It took him another second, then he popped off a dragon and sent it out the window Lizzie lowered. He sent it on a mission to find Stephen and lead him back to the van, wherever it wound up. "We can't go far, on account of Jayce. He'll have to run to catch up. Maybe drive around the neighborhood some? Park in a driveway?"

"No offense, Andrea, but I don't want to be your guinea pig only to have my shoulder disintegrated."

"None taken, and I don't want that, either."

"Is it still in there? You sure about that?"

"Yeah." Dan groaned as Lizzie hit the gas again. "It didn't come out the other side."

Bobby groaned, too. They drove around, both men making pained protest every time Lizzie turned a corner. As he lay there, trying to brace without hurting himself, something occurred to Bobby. He hated it, but a solution was a solution, and if he turned his nose up at weird, he'd be in a world of confusion. "You think it might be small enough for one of my dragons to crawl in?"

A few seconds of silence passed before Andrea finally said, "Ew."

"Maybe?" Dan sounded more hoarse and less clear.

"Nothing for it but to try." Deciding not to worry about the state of his body, Bobby popped ten dragons off and chose one to send his mind into. The small swarm zipped to where Dan, ashen and panting, lay on the floor of the van with one hand barely holding a wad of bloody cloth to his shoulder.

"This is gonna hurt, isn't it." His hand shook as he pulled the cloth away, revealing a ragged hole in his flesh. Blood glurped out in time with his heartbeat.

Bobby felt confident the answer would be 'yes'. The dragons converged on Dan's shoulder. Neither Bobby nor the dragons wanted to do this. What if he made things worse? He could cause more problems than he solved. He could kill Dan by accident. One dragon chirped, and he agreed they either had to do it or give up and figure something else out.

Five dragons gripped the sides of the wound and forced it open, eliciting a whimper from Dan. Two darted off elsewhere, and the last two grabbed a corner of the cloth and daubed at the blood. Bobby's dragon folded its wings down flat and crept into the injury. Warm and squishy, the hole felt gross. Bobby and the dragon both wanted to get this over with as fast as possible.

Dan's whimpers turned into screams. The dragons didn't like that at all, and Bobby pushed his to wriggle faster. He found the bullet lodged in a bone and had to grab and yank, yank, yank to pop it out, making Dan shriek. Worse, it had mushroomed enough to cause more damage on the way out.

If he had teeth, he'd have gritted them. Bobby maneuvered around the bullet, knowing it made things worse, and pushed the bullet as hard as he could. Another dragon reached in and grabbed from the other side. Together, they tore the bullet out. Dan had gone past the point of screaming, now shaking so hard his teeth rattled and his whimpers sounded like a tiny helicopter rotor. When Bobby pushed out of the wound, awash in fresh blood, he saw Matthew's face looming over him.

"That's freaky." Haggard and wiped out, Matthew reached down and put pressure on the wound, using the already sacrificed wad of cloth. "Anybody got a needle and thread? Some alcohol? I won't lie, Dan, whatever we do, it's going to hurt, at least as much as that did."

Bobby saw that Dan had a pen in his mouth, keeping his teeth apart. Those two dragons thought to get that. The ten of them lifted out of the way, his work there done. On their flight back to his body, they bathed each other with fire, burning the blood off. He left them to that, returning to his body now sitting upright in a seat. Jayce stretched the seat belt across him and clicked it. Stephen sat between the two front seats, murmuring to Lizzie, probably keeping her calm while Dan made all that noise.

"Welcome back." Jayce sat back and the metallic sheen faded from his skin.

"Yeah, you, too." Bobby lifted his missing fingers to rub his face. The dragons arrived and re-formed them.

"I have some dental floss in my purse," Andrea offered. She rifled through the glove compartment. "There's duct tape, and a wad of napkins."

"He really needs actual medical care," Matthew said, shaking his head. "I only have basic first aid training."

"Can't." Bobby winced as the van went over a bump. "What d'you need to do the best job you can?"

"The duct tape should work well enough, but I'll need something to clean the wound. If we can stop at a drugstore, we can get rubbing alcohol and gauze."

"Does anyone have any money?" Bobby's question got him a couple of head shakes.

Stephen shrugged. "I have money, but it's for gas."

"Well, heckbiscuits, we can push the van if we gotta. Lizzie, you see a drugstore, you stop. Hey, did anybody think to swap out the van's plates yet?"

"No, but it's a good idea, and we can do that when we stop." Stephen pointed to a place, then directed Lizzie to a place to park. It put them out of obvious sight so they could swap the plates and still not have to walk far to get into the store. The second she shut the engine off, Lizzie darted out with tear streaks down her cheeks and went to Dan. Stephen nodded for Andrea to drive while Jayce headed into the store. "Bobby, give me a hand."

Although he knew what Stephen meant, he let his hand fall into dragons and sent that group out with the vampire. More conventional assistance required him to be less chewed up and spit out.

Stephen snorted. "Smartass."

"Starving smartass," Bobby corrected.

Andrea grabbed the cooler and shoved it at Bobby. "Take whatever you want. Andrew packed plenty." She watched him wince and open it. Without paying much attention to the contents, he grabbed a sandwich and stuffed it into his face. "It's nice to meet you, Bobby. Don't take this wrong, but I hope you were worth it."

His mouth full already, he glanced around the car. Matthew and Lizzie both tended to Dan. Alice lay slumped on the other seat. These people had all gone to bat for him, and most of them almost died, himself included. "Yeah." He swallowed the bite and sighed. "Me, too. There any leads on Jasmine or the others?"

"Not yet, no. That name you and Stephen got, we can't find him, either. It's like he doesn't exist. His son, too. Both of them are ghosts."

The sandwich tasted like sawdust. Bobby still chewed mechanically, but they'd hit a dead end. "We'll figure something out." Inside, he fretted over what kind of torture Jasmine had to be enduring right now. With what he knew they'd done to him and Ai, it made his stomach churn.

"Eleven of us were taken, everyone else is accounted for. There was some talk of going back to the site you woke up in, but Sam found a news blurb saying it was burned to the ground, two days after you escaped."

Later, when he might care more, he'd ask who Sam was. "Not a big shock, that."

"Whoever 'they' are, they're pretty good at cleaning up after themselves."

Bobby nodded, forcing himself to take another bite. "We just weren't what they expected."

"Best guess is you have a higher metabolism than they could have predicted. Stephen says you eat like a horse, and the times you've been dosed, it didn't affect you very long."

His mouth full, Bobby grunted. He turned to stare out the window, not wanting to hear any more bad news. If he could sleep on the way home, that would be a small mercy. If the place could actually be 'home' for him, that'd be a greater one.

CHAPTER 20

Either they somehow missed the roadblocks or checkpoints, or none were set up. Bobby dozed off early in the ride. He woke in the dark, finding the van quiet and Stephen driving. He felt much better for having slept, with the pain in his arms and legs much more manageable. Hungry again, he rummaged through the cooler for more food and bolted it. Filling his belly improved his mood more and he unbuckled to roll forward and perch between the front seats.

"How much farther?"

"We're almost there, maybe fifteen minutes."

Bobby nodded and looked up through the front windshield at the stars. "Thanks. For coming after me. And bringing food."

Stephen glanced down at him, smirking. "It didn't seem possible they would be feeding you as much as you can pack away."

"Not even close," Bobby confirmed, a grin forming, then fading away. "However it works out, I'm going when we find out where Jasmine is."

Stephen nodded. "So am I, and I expect Jayce and Andrea will want to, also."

"Means while the brains are working on it, we ought to train together."

"Good idea. We'll start tomorrow. Most of us have barely discovered what we can really do."

Reaching up, Bobby scratched at his chin, reminding himself he had plenty of beard. The act hurt his fingers, so he stopped. "Man, I ain't had a shower in...I don't even know how long."

"There's hot water at the farm." Stephen grinned. "I'm sure Lily will be happy to help you shave."

Bobby coughed and looked away. He and Lily hadn't even talked much yet. "Shut up."

Stephen chuckled. It sounded like he suppressed a much louder belly laugh. "Would you like a lecture about safe sex?"

"From a vampire?" Bobby snorted. Part of him wanted to punch Stephen in the face for talking that way about Lily. He told it to shut up. "No, I think I got it covered, thanks."

Covering his mouth, Stephen shook with the need to laugh. A few minutes later, he pointed at a red reflector on the side of the road. "There's our turn."

The rest of the van woke up when they turned down the bumpy, tree-lined dirt road. Bobby had every intention of helping to carry Dan or Alice inside, but Stephen scooped Dan up effortlessly and Jayce had no trouble picking Alice up. Matthew gave Lizzie his shoulder to lean on, which she only took because she'd just woken up. Andrea didn't need or want help, either.

Someone must have heard the van, because the door opened when Jayce reached it. Ai held it open for everyone to troop through. When she saw Bobby, the last of the short parade, she gave him a conflicted, pained smile. "I'm glad you're okay," she whispered.

Well heckbiscuits, this had all kinds of awkward all over it. What was he supposed to say? 'Even though you left me behind, I still managed alright, except I had to be rescued on account I couldn't escape on my own. By the way, I got shot twice.' He had no reason to get into it right now. Unable to come up with anything else, Bobby shrugged. "Yeah, me too, for you."

She didn't meet his eyes and shut the door behind him. "Um, are you tired? Hungry?"

"I dunno." He shrugged again, watching the parade keep going deeper into the house. When he'd been here in the dragon, he hadn't paid much attention to the layout. Even if he had, no one showed him to whatever he'd use for a bed. "Guess I ought to try to get some sl—"

"Bobby!" Lily ran into him and wrapped her arms around him. "You're here, you're safe."

He grunted in surprise and pain. "Yeah." His arms slid around her to return the hug, and it felt damned good. He noticed Ai scuttle away and closed his eyes with a sigh. Lily's body pressed close to his bare chest, warm and soft, and wiped away all the pain and confusion and distraction. If he could stay like this for a while, he'd be a happy man.

The second she shifted, it broke the spell and he let her go. She stepped away and tucked some hair behind an ear, looking at the floor. "Sebastian will be really happy to see you in the morning. He keeps asking about you, and even more since your dragon showed up yesterday."

"Oh. I like him, too." It almost sounded like she meant the boy liked him and she didn't. That confused him, because her hug felt welcoming enough. "Uh, I kinda need to rest and heal up. If'n he's gonna expect me to wrassle with him, I mean. I ain't in no right shape for that just now."

"Okay, here, I'll show you to your room." She tossed a thumb over her shoulder and smiled at him, bright enough to melt him into a puddle.

"It's just down the hall from ours. They're small, but it's a bed and a roof."

Bobby nodded and followed her, watching her hips sway. He should've kissed her. She stood there, in his arms, and he let the moment slip by. All kinds of excuses welled up in his head. Only one of them mattered: he couldn't force himself to piss on her husband's memory. She'd be ready to move on when she decided to be ready to move on. He had no right to force it.

"This is it." She stopped and pointed into a tiny room. It had enough space for the twin bed already inside it, and not much else. Good thing he had almost no clothes. "I guess I'll make sure Sebastian doesn't run in and wake you up."

"I'd appreciate that, thanks." He stood in the doorway and stared at the bed. In his head, he turned, pulled her close again and kissed her.

She patted his arm, forcing him to bite back a tiny yelp and disrupting his ideas. "Good night, Bobby. Welcome home." She walked away.

"Yeah. Night." Stepping inside the room, he rubbed his arm and shut the door. In the van, he thought he still needed to sleep. Here, having fumbled that with Lily, he needed something else entirely. He couldn't get it by wandering around the house or out in the dark. Sitting on the edge of the bed, he unlaced his boots and considered running himself through a shower.

Soon, they'd find some kind of lead on Jasmine. He'd be the first one out the door. Not because he wanted to spend time away from Lily. Now that he had those experiences to reflect on, he thought he could do this stuff. Yes, he'd gotten captured. He'd been naïve. He knew better now.

He'd learned his lessons and itched to take the test. As soon as he knew where to find it, he would, and he'd finally get a grade worth showing his Momma.

Books by Lee French

The Maze Beset Trilogy

Dragons In Pieces

Dragons In Chains

Dragons In Flight

Fantasy in the Ilauris setting

Damsel In Distress

Shadow & Spice (short story)

The Greatest Sin series

(co-authored with Erik Kort)

The Fallen

Harbinger

ABOUT THE AUTHOR

Lee French lives in Olympia, WA with two kids, two bicycles, and too much stuff. She is an avid gamer and active member of the Myth-Weavers online RPG community, where she is known for her fondness for Angry Ninja Squirrels of Doom. In addition to spending much time there, she also trains year-round for the one-week of glorious madness that is RAGBRAI, has a nice flower garden with one dragon and absolutely no lawn gnomes, and tries in vain every year to grow vegetables that don't get devoured by neighborhood wildlife.

She is an active member of the Northwest Independent Writers Association, the Pacific Northwest Writers Association, and the Olympia Area Writers Coop, as well as being one of two Municipal Liaisons for the NaNoWriMo Olympia region.

Thanks for reading! If you enjoyed this book, please take a minute to review it on Goodreads and wherever you buy your books.

www.authorleefrench.com

20736265R00153

Made in the USA
Middletown, DE
06 June 2015